Sanctuaries of the Heart

Santuarios del Corazón

Sanctuaries

of the Heart
Santuarios del Corazón

A novella in English and Spanish
by Margarita Cota-Cárdenas

Translated from the original Spanish by
Barbara Riess and Trino Sandoval
in collaboration with the author

with an introduction by
Tey Diana Rebolledo

THE UNIVERSITY OF ARIZONA PRESS
Tucson

While this book is based on actual events, parts are
fictitious, including some of the characters, and with the
exception of public figures, the names of actual persons,
other than public figures, and most places have been
changed to protect the privacy of such persons.

The University of Arizona Press
© 2005 Margarita Cota-Cárdenas

⊗ This book is printed on acid-free, archival-quality paper.
Manufactured in the United States of America

10 09 08 07 06 05   6 5 4 3 2 1

Library of Congress Cataloging-in-Publication Data

Cota-Cárdenas, Margarita.
    [Santuarios del corazón. English & Spanish]
    Sanctuaries of the heart = Santuarios del corazón :
a novella in English and Spanish / by Margarita Cota-
Cárdenas ; translated from the original Spanish by
Barbara Riess and Trino Sandoval, in collaboration with
the author ; with an introduction by Tey Diana Rebolledo.
        p. cm.
    Includes bibliographical references.
    ISBN-13: 978-0-8165-2465-5 (pbk. : alk. paper)
    ISBN-10: 0-8165-2465-3 (pbk. : alk. paper)
    I. Title: Santuarios del corazón. II. Riess, Barbara.
III. Sandoval, Trino. IV. Title.
PQ7079.2.C69S26 2005
863'.64—dc22
                                2005005822

Publication of this book is made possible in part by the
proceeds of a permanent endowment created with the
assistance of a Challenge Grant from the National
Endowment for the Humanities, a federal agency.

For my late father, Jesús Cota, my dear friend, Tey Diana Rebolledo, and my husband, Tom Parrish, all of whom have provided me support and inspiration throughout my years of writing.

♥

Don't reject love
even though you no longer believe
though you no longer expect it
There awaits us
an embrace so wide, so wide
it knows no borders.

MARGARITA COTA-CÁRDENAS
translated by the author from
Marchitas de mayo, 1989

Contents

Creating Sanctuaries of the Heart: An Introduction

Tey Diana Rebolledo

The writings of Margarita Cota-Cárdenas lie at the heart of the Chicano/Chicana movement from the 1960s to the present. Her first book of poems, *Noches despertando inConciencias* (1976), spoke to the challenges of Chicanas, young and old; mothers; and single women who were struggling to survive within a culture that denied them full power. Were they to be feminist when their lives were still determined by their families and *queridos viejos?* Were they to "behave nicely" in a society that proscribed their actions? Were they to follow their dreams and desires only to find a yellow brick road that "never, never" led anywhere? During this period, the lyric voice of her poems counseled us to "look to ourselves," to determine who we are and how we will act. It is that same lyric voice that recognizes that, in our multiple roles, this was not easy to accomplish.

Her second book, *Puppet* (1985, bilingual edition 2000), dealt not only with society and culture at the early stage of the Chicano movement but also narrated the conflict that some Chicanos felt about the farmworkers' boycott of the 1960s and 1970s. It was a conflict about the desire and effort to come into an awakening of personal identity amid a backdrop of the social and economic struggles for self- and social sufficiency that were taking place on many levels during this chaotic and exhilarating epoch of change. This epoch also saw the protests against the Vietnam War, the Black civil rights movement, and the growth of feminism.

Puppet, a vanguard and experimental novel, challenges the reader. In many ways, its form mimics the historical times in which the narration takes place. As I wrote in the introduction to the 2000 edition,

> In addition to the fractured narrator, the multiplicity of voices that intermingle, the brutally honest yet funny colloquial language that rubs up against official language, the simultaneity of past and present, the political oppression of Chicanos by Anglos and by other Chicanos themselves, the different literary registers that are present in the novel combine to create a cacophony of narration that even Homi Bhabha would be proud of. All these elements are further complicated by a visual text that is punctuated by ellipses, fragmented through voices that wander eerily in and out of context, much like the voices from the cemetery in Juan Rulfo's *Pedro Páramo* (*Puppet*, xviii).

Puppet marked an important state in the development of the Chicano narrative. The level of sophistication of its narrative form as well as content contributed to its stature as a Chicano cult classic, taught in university literature classes and commented on in literary criticism. Its recent translation into English has accelerated the recognition of Margarita Cota-Cárdenas as one of the most important writers of Southwestern and Chicano literature. *Puppet* is more than a detective novel, a social novel, or an insightful historical narrative—it is a novel with its finger on the pulse of society. It is also political—building on an atmosphere of ambivalence, fear, paranoia, and oppression.

After *Puppet*, Cota-Cárdenas published her second book of poems, *Marchitas de mayo (Sones pa'l pueblo)* (1989). In this book she continued to question the rules society sets for Chicanas in particular and examined our own Mexicana/Chicana attitudes toward Chicanos and other women in society. She recognized that although the seed for change is awaiting its flowering, in reality we are still at the same place, socially and psychologically, as the Mexican nun Sor Juana Inés de la Cruz during the colonial period, who accused men of criticizing women for not giving in to them, but then criticized them when they did. While Cota-Cárdenas's ironic tone masks an uneasy relationship between the genders, it also masks one with both Mexican and American cultures. In her poem "Todavía es así, Sor Juana" (Things are Still the Same, Sor Juana), Cota-Cárdenas acknowledges that men perceive that the worst sin is for women not to pay attention to them at all. It is a powerful book of poems that forces the reader to examine her own perspective on these issues. Cota-Cárdenas also ponders the necessity of writing, calling her poems *malcriados* (badly behaved), and she acknowledges the difficulty of staying true to one's own ideals and words.

In all her books some of the characteristics of Cota-Cárdenas's writing that lighten the tone of the narration are her ability to capture colloquial language in all its nuances, bilingual facets, and ambiguities; and her utilization of this language to make us laugh (although at times it is painful laughter). This allows Cota-Cárdenas to tell us certain truths we would rather not acknowledge. And finally, her books are permeated with a sense of the ironies of this life that create ambiguities of culture and of knowledge.

In her more recent *Sanctuaries of the Heart: Memories in Fiction,* Cota-Cárdenas continues in a political and social vein, where she examines the concept of sanctuary in all its manifestations. The novella begins with her concerns about the sanctuary movement, most active in the 1980s with the brutal repression of civilians by right-wing military dictators in Central America. This is a subject articulated also by Demetria Martínez in her novel *Mother Tongue.* But the narrative quickly goes on to examine the idea of sanctuary in a broader sense, as in rest homes for the elderly, asylums for dementia/Alzheimer's patients, convent schools for little girls, home sanctuaries for dying AIDS patients, safe places for gays and lesbians, and the university for farmworkers and Chicanos—as well as the reasons that might initiate the need for sanctuary: political, social, and economic. The book is triggered by the fact that the narrator's father has, in a state of dementia and rage, set fire to his own home and been taken to a "rest home." The guilt the narrator feels about not being able to take care of him and to release him from that home is evoked from the beginning.

> The night that my father burned his house down, well, I was just beginning to gather newspaper clippings and notes for my novel, which was to be about the sanctuary movement. My name is Petra Leyva, I am named after my *Nana,* a strong-willed Mexicana from Sonora, and for my *Tía* Leyva who was known amongst the relatives for her sometime witty retorts and often sharp tongue. Talk, talk, talk. So many memories and secrets.
>
> Writing, working it out through writing, has occupied me irregularly, mostly in intense whirlwinds that can pick me up, whip me about for hours, even days on end, slam me down, and wham, I'm *face to face* with whatever I'd been running away from. And so with my novel, it turned out to be not about the sanctuary movement itself but about sanctuary, discovering loving as well as terrifying memories and secrets, and offering acceptance of the night that my dad, drunk and vengeful, struck a match and threw it on his living room floor, destroying the photographs kept there, perhaps our letters, and certainly his dead wife's doilied French provincial furniture. (3)

Thus begins part one, "Death Is Not My Business," where Petra's narration zigzags between past and present with ruminations about loss, the imminent death of loved ones, especially that of her father and her mother, and the many challenges Chicanas and their families encounter in their daily struggles. We have met Petra Leyva before, as the embattled heroine of *Puppet*. The bittersweet memories and family secrets that are revealed in *Sanctuaries* range from political repression to the sexual abuse of young girls by their own family members, cousins and uncles. Nonetheless, as explained in the paragraph just quoted, it is the telling of the secrets of the memories that enables the young women to survive, and that also, in the writing of the book, a sort of sanctuary is created. Thus sanctuaries are not only specific places that provide healing—rest homes, churches—but also can be internal, psychological spaces that heal, affective relationships that sustain.

Once again the cruelty of the political system to the subalterns (political prisoners or rebels, women, Chicanos); the scars experienced in school, at the hands of relatives, by dissolving relations are represented. Those are the challenges of life we all experience in some way or another: perhaps the key to survival and to being able to experience oneself to the fullest is if we are able to find some sort of sanctuary. Moreover, one of the ways to healing, beyond the telling of secrets and finding sanctuary, is in the ability to laugh, and to find humor in a situation.

Though *Sanctuaries* is a novella about many things, it focuses in particular on the narrator's relationship with her father, and to a lesser degree on her relationship with her mother. Her connection to her father is that tender, ambivalent tie to a man who is feared as well as idolized. The narrator wants to save her father from the nursing home—just as he saved her from the convent school her mother put her in when she was young. A sense of loss for the man who was "hilarious, clever, witty, sharp," but who was also feared "in his seriousness or his drinking," is also a reminder of the ambivalent relationships we maintain with our parents, especially after they are gone.

As stated, Cota-Cárdenas has an uncanny ability to replicate the oral, spoken language into the visual. Her capturing of the colloquial is often humorous, helping alleviate the burdens of oppression. In part two, "Memories and Secrets: The Taboo Stories," she writes,

I never knew how to cook well. When I was little they didn't make me help out in the kitchen, and so, what I learned about Mexican cooking was by watching and remembering, and later by making disappointing attempts until whatever it was came out well. Tortillas? They always came out crooked on me, although sometimes they came out really tasty. Tamales? I make them out of turkey now. Tacos? Chuppie (Chicano Yuppie) style with bought tortillas already fried, with turkey meat, ready-made salad, grated cheese, and everything *toditito* low calorie, non-fat. *Y* salsa? When I feel like it, I make it from scratch: I toast the chiles, etc. But generally, ready-made salsa, Don Juan's, El Pato, La Rosita, whatever brand, but everything ready to pour. And when we go to my mamá's house, well, what is it that we crave? Everything homemade, from tortillas to salsa, stew and beans. . . . Don't tell me that we aren't all fat and happy eating our traditional plates prepared as fast food and in a hurry! "This is it, the show, the one you're living. No refunds." (33–34)

Part two brings out in the open all the family secrets that are normally suppressed: budding sexuality, Uncle Toro's six wives (although one wife, Choli, was never "actually" his wife), Petra Leyva's father's infidelities and other peccadilloes and bigger sins. The distresses of families are revealed in trying to accept gay children, children with AIDS, and in trying to find other mechanisms to cope with a changing world.

Thus, working on the premise that everyone has secrets, part two names and remembers some of them, all the while struggling with the guilt about disclosing what perhaps should remain unsaid. As she tells us, "Yep, things are pretty strange in real life, even stranger than in tales. I guess I don't need to tell you that." (50)

As she discusses various family members, we see that they all have their silences. As Petra says, "Secrets, maybe we shouldn't remember them, nor tell them to anybody. . . . And, you ask yourself, is there any good that comes out of reviving secrets, offenses, bad memories?" (55) At the same time that she reconstructs all the elements of the past, good and bad, she remembers the funny and mischievous things that happened.

The many cultural myths that permeate Chicano/a writing also appear in Cota-Cárdenas's narrative, but changed. In *Puppet* La Malinche appears. She was the woman Hernán Cortés took as a mistress during the conquest of Mexico. But Cota-Cárdenas subverts the traditional image of Malinche as a traitor, instead representing her as a woman who not only questions traditional values that keep women in their place but also as a woman who achieves her own power by questioning the historical representation of her actions and imposing her own history. In *Sanctuaries* Cota-Cárdenas inverts the myth of La Llorona, the wailing woman of folklore who is reputed to have drowned her children and is crying from grief. The woman by the river is indeed heard wailing, but it is from the pleasure of experiencing an orgasm, not from grief. The substitution of pleasure for loss underscores the power contemporary Chicanas desire in the representation of their myths.

Petra continues the family narrative detailing her parents' divorce, the encroaching poverty of her family, the difficulties of her growing up, along with the antics of her mother and father and the gradual change in them as they grow old. In structuring the chronology of the narration and revealing family secrets, Petra takes control of her own space as a subject, her own destiny, and achieves a better understanding of the life of her parents and of her family, good and bad. These are the relationships that have influenced her and have made her the person she is.

In part three, "Sanctuary and Resolution," Petra finally understands that she has unearthed a kind of sanctuary in the writing of the memories. She defines sanctuary as "a safe place, where hope can bloom" and give birth to positive attitudes, that by participating in the concept of sanctuary, one can "deny" the negativity of the bad that happens. (79)

To conclude the stream of consciousness narration in the novel, Petra introduces the *cuentos personales* (personal stories) of some of her students who were farmworkers. These students have survived and even enrolled in the university, despite incredible obstacles: poverty, no support from parents and family, and, indeed, often resistance on the part of family. The survival of the students is connected to Petra's earlier own survival at the university. She acknowledges that it was her father who encouraged her to go to school, to get an education.

At the end of the narration, Petra's father dies. It is something she has feared, but it is, in actuality, a release, as he has spent the last years of his life as a dementia patient in "sanctuary." She comes to understand the importance of memory and of secrets: "Some good, some bad, but still some funny ones and all our own." (91)

Because she has finally articulated her family history in its totality, with the entire spectrum of participatory memories, claiming the good and the bad, Petra is able to appreciate her relationships with both her parents, as problematic as they were. She acknowledges that both gave their children "a will to live," a "stubborn zest" for life, and persistence. (93) Too, she recognizes that they lived *life* passionately and fully, just as she wants to live hers.

The novella ends with the words of her father, similar to the incident with which the novel begins: "Just look at this damn one-legged pigeon, how it jumps and flies and eats more than the rest of them! Just look, how great, how *alive*, ha, ha" (4). Finding sanctuary is finding a way to move forward. It is finding a way to fly, without a leg, handicapped by life and love—and to fly high. "Look how high! Ha, ha, ha." (94)

It is evident that Cota-Cárdenas, as well as other contemporary Chicana writers, sees the importance and power of the written word and the act of writing as a measure of personal, social, and cultural survival. Like the father's one-legged pigeon in *Sanctuaries*, they are able to fly more vividly and higher than others, they have created new and vital images of the women they want to be. It is a writing that has arrived at its most truthful, mature, and profound moment, a writing that is creative and original, one that has envisioned, as does the work of Margarita Cota-Cárdenas, a special, safe, and healing sanctuary for survival. It is a sanctuary of the heart as well as of the mind.

Bibliography

Cota-Cárdenas, Margarita. *Marchitas de mayo: Sones pa'l pueblo.* Austin, Tex.: Relámpago Books Press, 1989.

———. *Noches despertando inConciencias.* Tucson, Ariz.: Scorpion Press, 1976. Second printing 1977.

———. *Puppet.* Austin, Tex.: Relámpago Books Press, 1985.

———. *Puppet.* Bilingual edition, Albuquerque: University of New Mexico Press, 2000.

Sanctuaries of the Heart

part one

Death is Not My Business

The night that my father burned his house down, well, I was just beginning to gather newspaper clippings and notes for my novel, which was to be about the sanctuary movement. My name is Petra Leyva. I am named after my *Nana,* a strong-willed Mexicana from Sonora, and for my *Tía* Leyva, who was known amongst the relatives for her sometimes witty retorts and often sharp tongue. Talk, talk, talk, so many memories and secrets.

Writing, working it out through writing, has occupied me irregularly, mostly in intense whirlwinds that can pick me up, whip me about for hours, even days on end, slam me down, and wham, I'm *face to face* with whatever I'd been running away from. And so with my novel, it turned out to be not about the sanctuary movement itself but about sanctuary, discovering loving as well as terrifying memories and secrets, and offering acceptance of the night that my dad, drunk and vengeful, struck a match and threw it on his living room floor, destroying the photographs kept there, perhaps our letters, and certainly his dead wife's doilied French Provincial furniture.

Well, to begin with, my *papá* hasn't died yet, but it's as if he's gone already, like that, like that. We can see it, when we go to visit him. I can tell you that he is in a place of rest, that's what they call them, "rest homes." They're also called *asilos* or *santuarios,* like where you put crazy mad people, like asylums or sanctuaries. They're for old people, rest homes. He had never thought about it, or said to us, about whether they were to put him in one or not. I imagine that he would have told us, if he had thought about it before it happened, that he didn't much care for the idea. How it came to be that he got stuck in there, like it came about, well, let's see if I can get the nerve to tell you. He's been in there over eight years now, and it all seemed to start at once, in a series of weird, sad events. But really I think it started way back. I dream that I'll manage to snatch him out of there, out of that insane asylum, I mean that home for old people on their way out. . . . That's how he came and got me out that time from the Convent of the Good Shepherd when I was only seven or eight. How long ago was that, how long, let's see, some forty, fifty years back, over there in New Mexico, that's right, when we used to visit the aunts and uncles over around Las Cruces, Mesilla. I think that, back then, my daddy knew that I was waiting for them, that I couldn't stand it locked up in there with those industrious, single-minded nuns. Like that, just like that, that's what I wish I could do with him, like when he came for me. I felt like he had *saved* me, you know?

You're seeing that your father is happy this morning there at the wharf in Monterrey, a pretty day at the California beach, and the pigeons are flying and jumping even to your father's arm as he holds out a box of popcorn. Everybody laughs, your Dad enjoying the pigeons, the pigeons so accustomed to the tourists that they're not afraid of them, your sisters taking photos of their daddy giving food to the entertaining, lively pigeons, your mother hiding behind somebody so that your father can't talk to her.

"Just look at this damn one-legged pigeon, how it jumps and flies and eats more than the rest of them! Just look, how great, how *alive*, ha, ha," exults your father. Soon every one tires of the birds, you all walk along the dock with its tourist traps, and your sister Vinnie asks: "What time do we have to get Dad back to the rest home?"

"Not 'til tonight, but we have to leave him off on the way to take Pat back to the airport in San Jose," says Ben, your sister Belita's husband. Your father interrupts, exclaiming: "Don't go so early, you trying to get rid of the old man, ha, ha?"

Walking towards the parking lot, you all are laughing, even your mother, who is still trying to keep away from your papá. They got divorced more than thirty years ago, you're remembering, and you walk along thinking, we've all come so far since. It wasn't all this complicated and sad and full of rest homes for old and confused fathers and chock-full of divorces and sweet bitter memories.

That afternoon, as you're all eating roast beef tacos and refried frijoles, your father has told the group about how his family had come from Mexico to Arizona and then to California. He told it in an orderly manner, his thoughts well detailed and telling jokes and laughing about how innocent they had all been back then. You, the eldest, have heard his *cuentos* before, but every time your father would tell his stories, he managed to remember something new and funny, like what he was just saying:

"Pos sí, when we would go up north, from Brole to Bakersfield, we would go up the Grapevine, the old Highway 99 through the mountains. Once we went when there was snow, and the road got slippery. Damn, what a job we had with the jalopy! We would go forward a while, then the car wouldn't climb any further, and we had to get out and push, yeah, pushing that way we made a little headway, and then we would get in again when we were able to. Damn, what a pain it was sometimes when we made those crossings! And all of it so we could eat, live, a few *centavos* more, ha, ha, what a pain it was!"

A granddaughter has just asked her grandfather, your dad, "Grandpa, when did your family come to the United States?" Your father answers, "I was naturalized when I went into the Navy!" and then, his confused gaze trying to fix on your Mom's furtive eyes, "During the Second World War? When was that, eh?"

"It was like in 1936, '37, something like that," said your mother. "I was eleven years old and we lived in New Mexico in the *ranchito* that belonged to the boss, Colonel Nelson, and his wife. I had been dancing in the bedroom, where I was supposed to be cleaning, but they had a very fine mirror in there, one of those long ones that stood on little animal feet, the mirror frame was made of wood. Somewhere in the house, a radio was on; I started to jump and lifted my legs, and I was doing a real good high kick, my skirts flapping and lifting when I see that I have stains on my panties! Well, I got scared, and ran to wash myself in the tin tub behind the house. I thought that for doing such strong kicks, I had hurt myself! Well, there I go again to the bedroom to finish my work, but since the music was still playing, well what do you think? Well right away I found myself jumping about again to the *ranchera* music, well there you go again with the stained panties! This time, my Tía Sara, who was working in the kitchen, asked me why I was running through the hall acting so scared and sneaky. Embarrassed, crying, I answered: 'I have blood on my pants, I think I hurt myself dancing!' And your auntie, my auntie, laughed loudly, saying, 'Ah, silly little one, I forgot to tell you about something. Don't be scared, it happens to all girls!' I was so timid that I didn't believe her until after when it also happened to Yoli, the neighbor girl who played house with me."

Your *mamá* always had said that she wasn't even of legal age when they were married, but none of you could get her to say exactly how old she had been. Her ancestors, she would tell all of you, had been not only Spanish too, *but French too,* but the details had been varying through the years, and none of you knew what she had remembered well and what she had composed. You yourself were scolded one day because Aunt Rosalía Leyva had called laughing and gossiping that "Pat told her other cousins that her mother is Apache and her papá is Yaqui! That you told her that! Oh, what a barbarian you are, ha, ha!" Your father just about gives you a whipping but you escape because Tía Rosalía, Tía Leyva, was supposed to be one of the most storyteller, gossipy aunts in the family, and although they feared her sharp storytelling tongue, your father let you get away with it, for often the more outrageous you'd be, the more he'd spoil you. Your mother would say, frustrated, "Just like your father!"

Shortly after his second wife died your father barely found his way to your home, north of Southwest City. Depressed and fighting sorrow, seesawing between needing the bottle and needing to connect, he would respond to your questions with his own memories: "We lived for some years in Arizona, mostly we worked at what there was, in the fields, whatever, but your Tía Herminia also worked there as a cook in the house of that *ex-Presidente de México,* what was his name? Well, he lived in exile over here, I mean, there in Arizona, yeah, in the same little town where our family came from, and your Tía Minia remembers that they had her make tortillas every morning, for the *gran hombre.* I was only three years old or so when your grandparents brought us. It was around the time of *la Revolución* when they came, because things were bad there. I was very little, but your aunts still remember those years about Sonora, about those other *pueblitos.* Once, sí, sí, I returned as an adult many years later, we went clear to Empalme, Ciudad Obregón, over there, and we saw the house where they said the oldest of us had been born. How dirty, how a little ol' place like this, only made of adobe. Have you seen the photograph of your Grandfather? Your *Tío* Pelón looks a lot like him, black hair, like that, very Indian-looking and with a big moustache. What? *Ay, Mija,* how could it even occur to you that he looked like Pancho Villa! Ha, ha, if your tías heard you, you'd really get it!"

"These people have fled here because they fear for their lives, they are not only seeking economic solutions; when they state before you that they flee from death squads and repression in their homelands, they are appealing to you for their very lives. Call it political amnesty, call it sanctuary, but be assured that they . . ." Thus goes the argument of the red-haired woman attorney from New York who is defending the group seated at the defense table. You recognize them on the television, from the newspapers and the magazines. They are a group of three who have worked with refugees from several Latin American countries. Now they are accused of helping some of those refugees to illegally cross the border. Even though they crossed in order to live and not die, you mumble to yourself, even though they had to leave, even though over there, they lived with death, *even though . . .* "Pat! Pat! Hey wake up, what are you thinking about? Oh yeah, those people, well, why don't you go interview them, you know, start that book you've been threatening me you were going to start. What? Really, there's already about ten books being written about them, the Movement? Oh, I don't know, what you said about the one woman, that really grabs you, I think," your *compañero* Bob says to you, shaking his own legal drafts, brought home to edit on the computer, in your face. *In your face.*

Your friend Lulu Espinoza, who works with you at the magazine *Southwest Cities and Deserts,* brings you another glass of iced tea with *limón.* You recall, as Lulu goes to her desk, another young journalist from New Mexico. You start thinking about other people that began investigating and defending, and you know what they got for doing that. You think on your mother's words, repeated all those other times, "Why do you butt in where it's none of your business? Why go looking for trouble? They're not your concerns, and who do you think you are, Mija, you always were exactly like your papá!"

"This time it's different, Ma. Besides, why do I have to be like you or like Dad? This is something else now, Mamá, don't you think that if you were one of those women, you would want to get out of there too, and can't you imagine what they must have been living through to have had to." The *campesino* and student movements will never die, you tell Lulu, but the *movimiento del santuario* will perhaps be the next most important event affecting Chicano/Chicana life in the Southwest in the

'80s and on. "These women," you say to Lulu, "these women, the ones coming over and the ones helping them, well I think they really have *ovaries*, you know, *balls, ovaries!*"

"I look like my Nana," you wistfully say to your Tía Elsa one summer when you were looking at family photos on her wall. Tía Elsa, younger than your father, blurts out, "You, Pat? Don't think so! I don't see . . ." as she tries to recover, she offers, "No, no, you look more like *your* mother, don't you think?"

"I shouldn't even have compared myself," you muse dejectedly, and recall when your Nana, a very hardworking woman who had managed and raised her large family alone, despite being almost blind, died in an explosion in the basement of her family restaurant. You were in first or second grade in Betaville, eight miles north of the Mexican border in California. You console yourself: You too have Nana's memories, and you remember being loved. And of Nana's sons and daughters, all loved, some coddled, your father was, of all of them, the favorite. As Nana went down into the basement with Humberto, the teenage kitchen helper, to check out why the hot water wasn't running, as Humberto struck the *fósforo,* the match igniting the gas that was leaking, as she and he were slammed into the basement ceiling, did she think of death, did she think that soon she would be outside, sitting and leaning against the back wall of the Nogales Café, telling her children there to look after the youngest one, did she?

"My dearest daughter: don't be surprised that I'm answering your last letter so quickly; I'm very occupied. I'm looking out that these buddies don't escape from this insane asylum. Not more than a couple minutes ago I caught one guy in his 'moto—his wheelchair. He was going out the hatch. You can imagine what shape the others are in, that I should be the one to have caught one. I'm not as far gone as they say, it's only a put-on of mine."

You respond to your father's note, five, six years ago: "Pop! *Cómo estás?* We just got your little note. Oh, you don't remember, did somebody write it for you, or what? Well it looks like it's your handwriting, but since it's been years since you've written me much, well, I was only sure of the signature. Yeah, my husband is fine, the kids, too. Where do I live? Well, same as last time I saw you, close to Southwest City. Oh, they brought your pills and you have to hang up. *Bueno,* okay, I'll call you in a few. . . . Cool?"

You tell Papá that you love him, he says "me too, same here." You remember that he never said that, that you could remember, "I love you," or *"Te quiero."* It was never what he said. You wonder if it's really so, what the psychologists say these days, that you really had to tell each other at every turn. How did we know it then, that we feared him in his seriousness or his drinking, thought he was hilarious, clever, witty, sharp, so very sharp, but did we think about it then? Were love and fear close, but death and dying distant? Loss, we still breathe it. When your mother and father were in the same room, you remember that they addressed each other formally, using *"usted"* instead of *"tú"* with each other. Was this only a play, we wondered. "I wonder if they did that in bed?" you once asked your sister Belita.

"I couldn't stand him sometimes," your mother is saying. "He was a big womanizer. I didn't love him then." You laugh, remembering your parents, when you were all young, and hugging her hard, you tell her softly and close, "Oh sure, Mom, you had us kids, let's see, how many of us are there? And you were, you were jealous, boy were you jealous. *Ya,* I know you were right, time and again, well isn't that how they all were? Boy did you love him, oh sure tell me about it. Ha, ha, Ma, you yourself are hard to take. You're so stubborn and proud, man oh man, oh woman. God you're cute, give me another smoocherino! In recent years, she's told you that he hit her, not only when he had been drinking, and several times over some other woman. *God you're cute; give me another little kiss.*

"He was the Singing Rage of Brole," you remember that your mom used to tell you when you all would ask, How did you meet? "I'd heard him sing before I ever met him. I will say that for him, he was a good provider for his family, sí, I can say that much for him, that's so. . . ."

Your compañero comes into the kitchen. You chirp "Hi, Honey! I talked to Dad just now. Sort of okay, I guess. He couldn't remember again, where we live. No, he didn't remember that either. I can't tell if he wrote it all or what. Yeah, I know, I know, but it's hard!" Honey eats, remotes on the TV, and instead of the news he starts watching a program on the Drug Wars. There's some guy that they're interviewing that says that "No, I don't think the Drug Wars are being won. The American public is being lied to. Well, by their leaders, the 'suits', in the highest government offices, that's right. By what authority do I? Well, I say it all in my book here, that the leaders of this country have their own agenda with these foreign governments in Latin America, those raids by the military to supposedly burn fields of all those drugs, cocaine, heroin, why for every one of *Borriega* there's dozens of other guys that our government has made deals with. Well, because they have bigger things to wheel-and-deal with those governments about, like these bank loans to these countries. Those places can't make payment on those huge loans if we really busted their drug crops. I was a DEA undercover agent for over twenty years, and I'm telling you all right now, you're being lied to. Yes, I recognize this guy beside me from when I worked the Southwest cities region, he's right, the DEA did what they could. And Immigration tried to cooperate along the border areas, he's right. But back to the main point of my book, the 'suits' have the power, and you're all being lied to."

You have read that one of the women seated there in the courtroom, accused of violating immigration laws and who knows what else, had been hoodwinked by an American government agent, a Chicano who works with Immigration or the secret police or something like that. He made love to that woman, courting her in front of and including her entire family, over several months. He'd take the woman out, sometimes with her children or relatives along. He deceived her, making love to her, so that she would confide about *whom, when,* and *if* she was in fact helping those people or not. Like an *ingenue,* like a *fool,* the poor woman fell in the trap, falling in love smoochereening, a slimy lying AGENT TESTIFIES IN COURT THAT HE TRICKED PARAMOUR INTO REVEALING *cabrón, cabrones* damn you, you sleazeballs "And you're all being lied to."

"People are basically good in this world," Lulu is saying to you. "You have to learn to trust people," your compañero tells you.

You write to your son, Ricardo, an evangelist who is moving to Mexico to work for a year there and help start new, non-Catholic churches: "Do you really think God loves everyone, forgives everyone?"

"Yes, I do think people can change and gain salvation."

You ask your son if he's heard of *"carnalismo,"* meaning the symbolic spirit of the Chicano movement. "I don't know about their brotherhood, Mom, but I've heard about some secret society to overthrow the government."

"Mijo, it's not what I was asking. Anyway, if you all know about it, it can't be such a threateningly secret society now can it? No, César Chávez took, like Martin Luther King, Gandhi's nonviolent model of activism. No, I don't believe they were *just words.* Well, that's true, I wasn't marching with them, yeah. Yeah, I know they had strikes, *huelgas,* when Grandpa was in the strawberries. Mijo! I just wanted to know if you believe in forgiveness, *in change!"*

And how you treated your own child and weren't really there when your own often needed you whole, together—not in love and not screwed up by slimy, lying guys, and you a fool, a struggling fool, yet needy, romantically wounded, too needy nonetheless, so was it ever way too late. What were you thinking? Did you think when you were young?

My little brother Samuel was very well behaved as a young child. As an adult he played out the macho women-drinking cycle for a time but has struggled, educating himself, his children. As I have had my *secretos,* so he has also, secretos waiting, lurking. Still, when we were young, we loved each other though not as much as now, when I know that someday he will need me. Anyhow, as little kids, we used to go often to market in Mexicali, on the other side of the border, as we did this one time, with our mother and our Nana. This one time that I'm talking about, my Nana and Mamá left us in the car with the windows down. That's right, it was long ago, in those days when you could leave little children in a car without worrying. Well, when my mother and Nana returned towards the car, they saw that several people were standing around one side of the car, some pointing, some laughing too.

When they reached us, we were a very quiet pair sitting still, inside in the back seat of the car. On the crowd's side, where some of the hombres were pointing, was a dark streak down the outside of the back car door. When we spied our *mami*, my little brother screamed, "Look Mami! That hombre over there, going away, him, he shit on the door!"

Well, the people walking by and that were standing around near the car, really started to snort and laugh. My mother, very embarrassed, got in the car, and after traveling a little while towards our small town, which lay eight miles or so to the north, she stopped the car, pulling over. Carefully, both women examined our clothing and panties. No signs of anything, they didn't know what to think, so we started up again towards Betaville.

After a short time and due most likely to a tiresome mood after the long morning, my brother and I crankily started to pick on each other in the back seat. Soon, my brother says to me in a low voice: "Pati, if you don't behave I'm gonna tell *mi'amá* who shit on the door!"

Why naturally, when the two señoras in front heard the threat, it made one of them ask, "Let me see, Samuelito, who shit the door?"

"Nobody, Nana, nobody . . . eh, that man that ran away did it."

A couple of miles down the road, after a few more pinches and scuffling in the back seat, the story came out.

When we finally got home, mi'amá pulled me to the bathroom to give me my good whipping without my Nana knowing about it, but here comes my *'apá* since my Nana wasted no time letting him in on it, and well, what do you think, well that was another time that I escaped getting a really good one! My dad thought it was really hilarious, and still I never know when the family gets together and starts to swap the old family stories, but that some mischievous stoolie will bring up our trips to Mexicali and here comes the shitty door story. Sure, then as now, we still had our *secretos*, and our underwear was clean as clean could be.

"Well, as grown-ups, Mija, 'cause if you 'shit the stick,' well, one way or another, they'll get to you," Mom still will say, sometimes adding, "As your Grandpa would say, 'Goodbye, kid, the boat just sank!'"

You reply this time to your mother that Give me a break, you gotta have hope, you gotta believe in the goodness of people, you know, brother/sisterhood and charity and so forth, and she answers back another of her *gente's* sayings about the more you stoop the more you show, and you ask her if she also believes that when the monkey climbs the tree his ass is there for all to see. "What does that have to do with anything?" she asks, and you laugh, oh, how we women have yet to learn. *In your face.*

Haven't you been here before? you ask yourself, when Lulu suggests that you ought to go interview some of the Sanctuary workers. Didn't you have to jump off, asking for leave from the university with its intrigues, the politics, overwhelmed by the lack of people, good people to trust and the bitterness of seeing that not even the Movimiento, that even the promise of brother/sisterhood, not even. What then?

"Remember when you met me, how all that other was, so we decided for then to let it go? I just wanted some peace." Your compañero reminds you, "You also said you wanted what your *campesina* lawyer friend, Venus, offered, *another way.* Remember? *Peace. Love. Justice.* Well then, what?"

JUDGE SENTENCES NUN IN SANCTUARY TRIAL . . . strikes, protests, headlines, violence, DÉJÀ VU, you tell me.

"Tell me about when you wanted to be a nun, Mom," says your son, hoping to entertain his children/your grandchildren.

"Dear Mami, please come to get me, *pronto*. Love, Patty." Finally, it was your father who came to get you, arriving determined, stern faced but looking so welcome to you, to fish you out of the Convent of the Good Shepherd outside Las Cruces. Years later, you all have a good laugh over the many undelivered begging notes you had written, given to the nuns so that they would forward them to your mother's New Mexican relatives close by.

"Your Dad was ready to explode," said your Tía Sara, "because what the Devil had your mother *done?* Taking you to the Convent and you only seven years old. Well, you spent a good month and a half there before your father got here from California and he snatched you out, swearing at the nuns for telling him over and over breathlessly that you still weren't *'ready'!"*

Your mother still remembers it, "Well you wanted to be a nun 'cause you'd seen a Mexican movie with María Félix, and you got over it, didn't you? Why sure, you were cured!" YOU HAD WANTED TO BE A...

On the road to Clarkston, the pueblito where you wanted to take some boxes of good, used clothing to the Protestant church, you begin again thinking about the Anglo couple that run the *centro* there. They receive and help out refugees, campesinos/campesinas, the undocumented, the poor, the desperate. The people, you have read in the newspaper article some months back, come from Mexico, Central and South America. Refugees, farmworkers, sometimes whole families appear at the church. They seek not only a *better* life, but often just to *have life.* Oh, here's the woman. She's come out from the church to greet you as you park. You recognize her from the newspaper photo. "When the reporter came to do the story on what my husband and I have been doing here, he brought a photographer that kept taking pictures of everything. I had to tell them that they could take pictures of me, of my husband, the *Reverendo* Loyd, as much as they wanted, but they weren't to take any photos of la gente. The people who come here, well, many are in danger, well, you know how things are with us here."

Those people have named her "Sister Lizabet from 'Glareston'," and they have arrived at her church, sometimes families, sometimes one or two or three alone, fleeing from that distant place, from that place of Terror Death over there we have come they told us that if we got here you would help us. Sister Lizabet and the Reverendo Loyd give assistance of such a *subversive nature* that the government considers their work *dangerous:* they find the people that need shelter, help obtain medicines and medical aid, give clothing, even track down furniture, dishes, pots, and pans, they translate documents, help fill out forms and official applications or documents requesting, for instance, amnesty. Yes, of course, amnesty or immigration, public assistance. Besides these *dangerous acts,* they often transport, in their own old van, these desperate people when they can, or ask for help from some volunteer nuns in the Catholic churches in the surrounding communities. "We have to be careful, you understand, who we let help us. You never know."

JOURNALIST INDICTED FOR TRANSPORTING ILLEGAL ALIENS

It also happened in New Mexico, in Arizona, in . . . YOU NEVER KNOW. "This writer Guillermina that we met last year at that poetry reading, just made the papers today," Bob looks up to tell you. "Seems like the government got some women that testified your acquaintance drove them across the border."

"They said they needed help, and they told me about their children, their babies. Their stories touched and interested me, and I never suspected . . . I never thought that it would come to this."

"All this is very ugly," you write to Aurora, a mutual friend of yours and Guillermina's in New Mexico, "but at least they didn't further humiliate her sending her a big hombre macho handsome with a moustache too, solely to make love to her while all along they'd been spying on her through him. No open warfare, they find your weaknesses, and how and where you're vulnerable, and that's the way they get in, get you, to open you up. Sorry to be *gross*, but that's how they can 'mount the horse', or get inside, whatever. She really has *huevarios!* It takes a lot of guts, and you sure are some gutsy women!"

"And how naïve I was," your college confidante and fellow *crítica/ writer*, Aurora Bustamante, had told you some years before. "It was during my undergraduate years at that elite women's college, back there in Connecticut, and the shit that happened, happened to me because I believed them. Sí, it was also in the sixties. It was in a psychology class. If sometimes you think you're going mad, well, let me tell you, I really *got crazy.*" Then you begin to imagine that. . . .

Aurora, one of the scholarship students, goes into the classroom, where at midsemester they had been told that they were to do an exam-type of exercise, and that all of them, all Anglo except for one Cubana, Hilda, and the lone Chicana, Aurora, were to wait until they were called into the examination room. They were to go in, explained the male Anglo professor, through one door here and they would exit through a door that led directly outside. In this manner, those students already interviewed couldn't reveal any details to the young women still waiting to be interviewed. "We want this to be a *clinical, scientific* kind of test," the professor had told them all.

Myra Greenfield sat down beside Aurora, gossiping chattily, and Aurora listened amused because Myra was so honest, so direct. "You're the most forthright, outspoken person I know, aren't you ever afraid of offending somebody?" Aurora had said this to Myra once after one of her long political arguments in the cafeteria. Hilda and Aurora, the two lone *Hispanas,* had become close and would smile knowingly as Myra would discuss, argue, contradict, and respond on whatever issue or topic whenever. Aurora loved Hilda, but openly admired Myra for her lack of fear: Myra would confront and get into it in class with every professor they had. "Myra, I felt, was a great bitchy argumentative *sharp cookie.*"

You reconstruct again that Aurora, once inside the examination room, sat down where they indicated, and a projector began to run. A voice instructs, "Watch closely, and tell me which door the little cartoon figure ends up choosing and going through." You see the little figure bob around and tumble finally towards and through the door on the left side of the screen. You say, *"Left!* Is that it? Is that the test?"

At that moment, the projector stops and in come Aurora's classmates, through the real doors of the real class/examination room where Aurora is seated, and Myra as usual sits down next to her, Hilda on the other side. All the girls take seats surrounding you/her, and the Voice now asks, *clinically,* "Which door did the figure choose, let's run that by once more quickly, and then each of you answer one by one." The projector repeats the scenes where you see the little cartoon figure bob and tumble towards and through the cartoon door to the left. Then, one by one, your classmates say, "The figure chose the door *to the right!"* And each time that, to your/to Aurora's shock and horror, they say the opposite of what you/Aurora have seen, they pause and ask you/Aurora, *"Are you sure?* Aren't you mistaken?" and then, *"Don't you want to change your mind?"*

"When it came to Myra's turn," Aurora recalled, "well, I knew that finally the truth, what I had really seen, would finally come out, only by this time I couldn't understand what madness, craziness they were all up to."

"*'To the right,'* Myra said, 'The figure turned to the right, went through the right. I mean the door on the right!'

"Myra had lied too! Then, over some five minutes, what horror was this, the entire class tried to convince me, to make me see that I had been mistaken, had not seen the picture right. Well, since by then I was horrified at I didn't know what, and since I *had so much faith* in Myra, my unshakeable friend, *my ally,* I doubted myself, and finally I couldn't stand it, going against such an opinion, so unanimous, so Myra. 'I guess it was the *right,* I mean the door to the right. I thought, I guess not, but I had thought. . . .'

"My father, a university professor himself who had long ago come from South America to live in the Southwest, asked me, "How could you let the school get away with it?" After what that incident did to *me*, after that, well, it was the beginning of *my rage,* that's when I stopped being so naïve. Can you imagine, it was purely a psychological experiment, that's all, *all set up,* I was the only student there that didn't know until afterwards that I had been the Chicana guinea pig. They told me later, that it was probably a *cultural,* not an intellectual *weakness.* I went *crazy full of rage* mad. Like I was telling you, a rage that still, sometimes, still. . . ."

One of these days, your father will not recognize any of you, not even your voice. What will he be thinking? How? Will he think about death? Will it seem really near? There are two of them who are recuperating from cancer. Surely they must, or they must try not to. And Tío Pelón, he already went on, last year, even after chemotherapy, also, colon cancer. The oldest, Esteban, died of cirrhosis of the liver a while ago, and his wife, Tía Lita, went last year. She went out kicking and screaming, funny as hell, she was a riot, cussing right up till the end. The youngest, she and her husband, they almost went too, but, there you have 'em, still livin' lively. Their generation still with representation, hangin' in, getting together for baptisms, weddings, anniversaries, *la familia* more or less seeing each other at wakes and burials. Not gone, not dead, not yet. At every wake and burial, there have been wails, tears, but always later at the gatherings, sons, daughters, cousins, brothers, sisters, eat, drink, remember, catch up on family and gossip. So-and-so died, did you know? *Did you know* those two cousins over there have HIV? Sí. They're *gay,* probably *die.* Sad, huh? Get sad, some remembering, then somebody tells a joke, laugh. Man, those *velorios* are something else! Papá, do you think of dying? What are you feeling? I want to take you from there and I don't know how."

"Grandpa's safer there than out," says your eldest daughter, María. Safety, *sanctuary,* feeling secure, not wanting the chaos, the violence, looking for something better, so your grandparents had brought them here, that's what once he had recalled. *Not gone, not dead yet.*

YOU HAD WANTED. . . .

You had wanted, had started out, to write a novel on the sanctuary movement, and *el camino* led to family memories, SECRETOS, losses, loved ones, *Self.* Aurora, now also in her late fifties, says to you last year, "It's weird, really weird, strange, but I know nine, no eleven, no, more people who have died within the last few months. I asked mi compañero Miguel Angel that what was this, a hex or something? Anyway, I mean, couldn't it *just stop* right here? What's going on with my life? Geez!" We almost lost her, Aurora, a couple years back, but *qué bueno* she's still here. "Did I tell you about the crazy homeless lady on the Llorona bridge in Las Vegas, who pulled at my skirt, wanting to talk? It was before all those deaths started, maybe it was *an omen.* What do you think, ha, ha?" Still fighting, bouncy, creative, funny, ALIVE, still telling people when to fuck you, fuck off! *In your face.*

The same year your father got put into the home/the sanctuary, they also put your daughter Marisa's beloved little old French nanny, your friend, frail and failing, in a rest home, a nice little place near Hannibal, Missouri, very nice (for an asylum). And one of these days she'll leave us too. *La muerte,* should I think about death?

A friend's daughter calls her up sobbing: "Ma, my stepmother was found dead in a motel room, she OD'd. They found out. Yeah, she was an addict. Oh, pills, heroin; I don't know, she did everything. But then, so does her husband, my *real* father. Boy, some family we are, huh!" So, should you, could you think of death now? "Ma, I have something to tell you." This too, eight years ago, these past eight years ago set you thinking about, thinking about . . . What should I remember? What shall I, can I tell? "Ma, I'm sorry, but I have something to tell you. It's about Dad." Sobbing, her/your child, her/your beautiful child that he/they held once as a baby, not his own, yet still his daughter from four months on until, UNTIL . . . . "About Dad and me, we, I. . . . When I was eighteen. . . . *We,* I'm so sorry, Ma, I'm so sorry, I don't want to hurt you, but yesterday, when I was driving him back to those friends he was visiting, he tried to. . . . And it brought it all back, all of it. I thought it was over with, but he won't stop. He keeps trying to. . . . Now I can't forget."

"Would it be simplistic to think," you ask Laurel, an artist friend of yours in Southwest City, "that I simply don't have the energy to always be mourning, waiting to die?"

"That's what I told you years ago, when you were struggling with your demons and your pain. Today is our only business, death is not. It is not our business."

Life, death, DRUGS, SEX, ALCOHOL, INCEST, *and now I can't forget.*

part two

Memories and Secrets: The Taboo Stories

CHAPTER ONE

It was being said around the labor camp that day that they had reported the Menchacas. They had left the littlest one in the room, locked up all day. "Those barbarians," the Mexican mamás were saying. "What bad people," mi mamá said, "how dare they." Papá said, "So they caught them." I heard my uncles say that it was very ugly what they had done to that little boy, leaving him alone inside a big cardboard box. That *chamaquito* was barely crawling, I remember, and later, as a grown-up, I would ask myself if his parents had done it because they didn't have anyone to take care of their little baby while they worked, or if they had done it because they were mean, like it was being said around the camp the day the authorities caught them.

The tomatoes grew thick, they looked heavy and fat, green, orange, and red. I used to pick them and smell them first, they were so meaty and juicy, I thought they were going to burst. Now and then, we would find a great big worm, and one had to be careful where one stepped so as not to smash the rotten or accidentally fallen tomatoes on the ground. Those tomatoes I ate tasted really good. Even though I had been eating the fruit for lunch, I was able to harvest a whole box before my father caught me. "I told you that I didn't want them out working in the field with us, woman, why didn't you do as I said?" I thought that they were really going to give it to me, but they didn't, my dad just scolded me with "I want you to go to school, so that you don't have to go through what we did. You better all do as I say. I don't want my kids in the fields, tomato or strawberry. I want them to go to school."

"We lived in tents once," I told my children. "No you didn't, Mom!" Although they didn't believe me, it's one of my oddest memories from *el campo*. I couldn't understand why people would make such a fuss about living in tents, because of some emergency or difficulty, and well, people in the campo did it, and somewhere, I assure you, they still do. And many times, they live in worse places. Well, no, since my father was one of the camp associates at that time, "the one who had the hardest job," as my mom still says, they made us a tent with a wood floor. I remember my mom had the tent spotlessly clean, well swept, and the tent even had screens, so the flies could not invite themselves in. Others, *pues,* not all of the families or single men had tents with screen sides, although every tent I saw had wooden floors. My father's partner lived in the big building by the camp entrance, where there was a dining room, kitchen, and bathrooms, and also an extension where Tommy and his family had their rooms. When they started, the partners were all excited. They had met each other as *chavalos,* as young men in Brole, in Imperial Valley. Then they broke up, Mamá said, because "we were working like mules, and they were bragging it up that they owned the place." Later, I remember the fight father and Tommy had.

For entertainment we used to talk, fight amongst each other, and listen to the radio. There was a movie theater in town, and they took us to see Mexican movies. It was customary for the Mexicans to sit in the back of the theater. That was the custom, that's what they told me to do, and that's where we sat. Now, they can't say shit about where to sit, not in California nor Arizona. Who knows whether they still make you go through that in Texas, but that was the way it was back then.

The type of construction of the camps where we kids used to live was very similar to others I saw when I was a child. The Rosas family lived in a more established camp. They had central buildings, but they had small houses for families, and some even had fences and *yardas* where las mamás had planted roses and other beautiful plants. There was always a mint plant where the water dripped from the hose or the outside faucet in the garden. "Walnut Labor Camp," they used to call it, because it was on Walnut Street, I think, a couple of miles from the little town of Masterton. Around that little town I remember no less than three labor camps. And there were a lot of *mexicanitos* that lived around there, and through the years, we used to run into each other around the small towns of the San Joaquin Valley.

My father's other woman at that time, the *vieja*, caused the quarrel between my parents, back then in the camp with Tommy. The other woman would call him at Tommy's house and one time, after we had moved from the tent to a very old wooden house in the middle of the dirt fields a couple of miles from Tommy's camp, the biggy broke out between my parents.

We had all gone off together in the car, because my father had to talk to Tommy about some workers. Mamá waited with us in the car in the darkness, and my father went inside to call. "What the hell is he doing, taking so long, and here we are in the dark! Stay here, *chamacos*, I'll be right back." Soon she was back, crying and screaming, and we couldn't understand her. Papá came out like a shot, he hit my mamá, who was crying and was telling him things about that shameless bitch, and take me home, and I, working like a mule, and you, you . . . She was mad for many days after that, and my dad didn't get over his bad mood until my mom's operation. It happened that they had to take my mom's appendix out, in an emergency, a few weeks after the fight, and soon, they were talking to each other in that soft and tender way.

My mamá told me years later, "Even though it was already known your father and Esmeralda had married, that same woman was still hanging around in Gilroy, older, you know, and married to a rich old man." Through some aunts of mine I learned that when my folks were young and married, that woman was with a famous boxer from the Valley and that neither young nor many years later with wrinkles could she control her hormones. "How did they meet? In the fields, in the cantina, I can't remember anymore."

"She's just like her dad," some men are saying at a party. You remember that party when your sister got married, the sister they brought from Mexico many years earlier. Your parents took her as their own; they brought her to the United States, and now she was getting married in your father's and stepmother's house. "They say that she has married many times, and that she has kids all over the place. Look at her; there she is!" You take in, shocked, what you're hearing about you, in front of you and one of your brothers, who is trying to talk to you. And you think how was it that you had forgotten how people, bigger assholes than you, than I, you say to yourself, while your brother is wanting to tell you, "We didn't think you could make it to the wedding, Sis. Why were you so late?" Charlie and I got lost, you tell him. We had to come all the way into Gilroy, and then to the chapel here in Monterey. Carmel-by-the-Sea, whatever. Yeah, we got lost. We didn't even go into the chapel, instead of coming in late we waited outside for them to come out. How embarrassing! "Let's see if the marriage works out," you tell yourself. Well, we don't have "a good track record" in this family. Who knows? "Let's go eat some tamales or something," you tell your brother and his girlfriend. "I don't like it here," you say in a louder voice. As you watch your father's two supposed friends, drunk, still talking and looking at you now and then with that lascivious look, fucking old men they hurt me and they don't even know me, mustachioed old men, surely very Catholic or very horny in their own time.

"At first, we used to make tortillas every day, for each meal," your mother is telling you. "Later we would start to make sandwiches and other kinds of food for them. Instead of making the tortillas by hand, later on we bought a tortilla maker and we would make them daily, but not by hand. They came out fluffy, anyway, and nice and warm."

When I was about fourteen, they had me helping out in the little store at the last camp my parents had. I would help take care of the clients, taking money for candy, sodas, paper, soap, cigarettes, whatever was available at our little store next to the camp office. The men that came in varied in age, by that time they were almost all *braceros,* hired hands in that camp. They always came in and greeted me and ordered directly and politely. Their different personalities showed, because some of them made jokes, others didn't. One day, a young, very polite but quiet man came in, bought what he wanted and I told him, "Thirteen cents is your change." He looked at me with surprise, and quietly said, "No, it should be thirty." Well, I kept stubbornly saying that it was thirteen and that I had given him the correct change. The poor guy looked at me, annoyed, turned around, and later returned with another bracero, an older man that I knew, who said, "Look, Miss Petrita, for the soda and the comb that Lalo bought here, he should have gotten thirty cents change for his dollar." And, now a bit scared, but still insisting that I had said the right thing, I said again, "No, it is only thirteen cents." The two men looked at each other, shrugged their shoulders, and left, talking softly and then laughing. And, now breathing a sigh of relief, really happy that I had done my job well, I began recounting what I had in my head: "One dollar minus seventy cents are thirty cents change, thirty, not thir . . . teen!" Well, they had already left, cheated, and I was so embarrassed that, that I had thought it out correctly, but it came out of my mouth wrong, the change for Lalo the bracero. Well, it was just a little detail, but I haven't forgotten it. I was really relieved when Guayabera, another worker that helped my mom in the dining room and in the store came back. I never told my parents because I didn't know how to confess that I had mixed up "thirty" with "thirteen."

Another bracero, Gallareta, knew how to make bread—*pan dulce*—sweet bread and cake. He knew about French pastries. I never tasted

"French pastry" until I met Gallareta. For a while, he helped my mamá in the camp kitchen, at Tommy's camp in Masterton, and later he went with us to work at the camp in Newdale. Before they built the second camp in Newdale, when the buildings were still under construction over in the fields far away from the town, they put up a bakery for Gallareta. They made it in the garage, in the small house my parents had rented. It was an old garage that had its own brief story in the life of my family. Well, for a while, Gallareta lived there. And they put in a big stove for him with enormous griddles and two ovens. There, "Galla" made his little cakes and breads and with the help of my mamá and her friend and helper Marieta he would make tortillas for the boarders and the braceros who worked with my father and my uncles. In the camp, there were already tents with floors and separate showers and bathrooms, but still, back then, neither the dining room nor the kitchen nor the office had been built, nor the little houses where some of my uncles later lived, and where my parents would stay overnight if they had to.

And Marieta? Marieta was the most loved of the señoras that came to live with us and to help Mamá with the household chores. She was also my mom's confidante, and she would take me to the movies when, once in a while, they would show Mexican films. Later, she would even go to the English ones, like we used to. They had raffles and contests some weekends at the movie theater, and we really enjoyed getting together and seeing the other folks from the little town. Sí, I remember it as having been a nice little town. And there, our lives changed forever, in many ways.

One time in Galla's garage, a drunk carpenter, one of my dad's drinking buddies, molested my little sister, Vinnie. I say that he molested her, because he didn't actually rape her, but he did something to her that he shouldn't have. It was in Newdale, that little agricultural town, and like always, my father had many friends, among them the carpenter that every once in a while worked for my father and other people in town. "Ted" was the carpenter's name, and every once in a while he had to come by to talk to my dad. Mamá never liked him, because as she said later, "That smelly man, he's more of a drinker than your father." One day, when my parents were not home, when it was just me and my little sisters and Marieta, Ted came to the door and asked for Papá. He had come in his old pickup. Well, upon seeing Ted, my little sister ran up to greet him, as she was and still is the most open and affectionate of all of us. I don't know how it could have happened, because the man walked away from the door, and we got busy doing other things.

Suddenly, we heard a little girl's screaming from the backyard, and I ran through the kitchen door and I saw, through the garage window, Ted standing with my little sister in his arms, and she was crying. And when I went into the garage I said, "Vinnie! What happened?" My little sister, who was about three years old, sobbed to me, "He took off my panties." I yanked Vinnie from the liquor-smelling viejo, and I don't even remember what I said to him, something stupid like, "Get outta here," or who knows what I said. I went inside with her, and I told Marieta, in front of my other little brothers and sisters, that the viejo had done something to Vinnie and to call my mom who was working in the camp kitchen far from town. I went to the front door and saw Ted swagger over to his pickup where his oldest daughter and grandson waited for him without the least idea of what had happened! It all seemed crazy to me and I, angry, scared, and feeling terror, went to the phone that Marieta handed to me to tell my mom that yes, my father's carpenter friend, the famous Ted, had taken off Vinnie's panties.

Papá was up around Modesto in the fields, but Mamá soon arrived to take Vinnie to a doctor, "To see if that stinkin' drunk had hurt her." Later, my mom took me to the district attorney to say what I had seen. They arrested the viejo, and soon after that he was free, because Papá did not want to press charges. Besides, nothing happened to Vinnie, that maybe I had imagined everything, "You know how Petra is always exaggerating things. I don't want any gossip around town. It's best that Pat doesn't say a thing, nor Vinnie." Well, the truth is that Mamá almost killed ol' Ted; she and my father fought and fought about what she wanted to do to the viejo, and about what Papá didn't want people to know. My mom kept a grudge against dad, again, and still, even today, at seventy years old, it is best not to bring up that dad's drunk friend, Ted the carpenter, had done something bad to the *gordita.* She has said things like, "Those drunk men, you know how they cover each other's asses." Sometimes, in spite of all of her years of Christian-ness, she has even said, "They are always covering each other's shit," or things of that nature.

The years we lived in those camps in Masterton were when the family had those long dogs or "wienie-dogs." Because they were so short and long, my father called them *los Chapos.* El Chapo and la Chapa had many *Chapitos* that my folks gave away to people we knew. But Belita was the Chapos's favorite. She was such a little cowgirl always wearing blue jeans and T-shirts and boots, that's how she liked to dress for many years when she lived at home. Because of that, they called Belita *marimachita* or tomboy, and that always made my mom mad. My father adored Belita, she was always with him. Sometimes he used to take her to work with him in the pickup or in the car. Out of all of us, the fair-skinned, wily Belita was Daddy's little girl. Oh, yeah, I was telling you about Belita and the Chapos. She loved those little dogs but sometimes because she paid too much attention to them, she would get over-imaginative in the games she would invent with those little dogs. I've already told you somewhere that she wanted to take one of the Chapos's teeth out with some mechanic's pliers, right? But that little *güerita* really made those Chapos suffer.

One day my dad was telling my uncles a story, and she was playing doctor with another one of the Chapos. But that day my parents spied the dog dragging himself across the dirt. Well, when they went to see what was wrong with him, they saw the stick that was up the dog's rear. It was another one of Belita's "experiments." Her curiosity caused her to take apart watches and toys, because "I wanted to see what was inside them." They also called her "that skinny, fearless little rascal" things like that, courageous, terrible, and amusing—that was my little sister, la güerita Beli. Later after having lived a couple years as a Christian wife and mother, she managed to behave herself. And now, according to some of the family, well, she doesn't behave.

Forbidden love, those things that one should not talk about, that is something else about our culture. That's really taboo, that's even more taboo than it is in the Anglo world.

CHAPTER TWO

Lulu has called to tell you something about her daughter and her daughter's father/stepfather, the one that was your friend's husband before. When Lulu went into Stacy's apartment her daughter told her. "I have to tell you this. I'm sorry, Mom, I'm sorry, but Dad and I, when I was in college, He, we, he said that he wasn't really my father anyway and that he had desired me—had feelings, sexual feelings since I was five or six. And he gave me marijuana to smoke, when I was eleven. It was our secret, and I began to believe we had a secret special relationship. I got mixed up about what I felt for my dad. He was the only dad I'd known. You know?" I'll tell you the worst part later. *And they told her that she shouldn't tell anybody.*

You have told Aurora long ago about your first sexual relationships: "I got pregnant the night before my high school graduation, on a canal bank, in the rural neighboring community. Lewis wasn't my first boyfriend and by the end of the next year, I had had my first child out of wedlock, had settled a paternity suit with Lewis, the baby's father, had started college full-time as a drama major, had promptly met my first husband-to-be at the semester's first dance and had gotten pregnant with my second child. But what I really need, want to talk about now, are the things that *they* told me not to talk about. Yeah, what someone or somebody told me, "Don't tell anybody. Don't say anything, because if you do, something will happen to you, to somebody. Don't tell your mom, your dad—nobody."

"Don't tell anybody," the neighbor's fifteen-year-old son was telling me under the bushes beside their house wall. Don't say anything, as he fondled me in the dark, crouching besides me. Shivering from fright and excitement at once, I whispered "Yes," as he kept asking, "Don't you like it?" Serge, the neighbor's son, was our frequent babysitter, a good-looking, curly-headed, friendly young man, was very trusted by my mother, probably owing to his phony polite manners. He helped his divorced mother out by earning extra money at various odd jobs after school and on weekends. I loved going to get pomegranates from their yard. I was five or six, and he liked babysitting me. "Get on top of me," he said, and when I asked, "Why are you so wet here, what's this stuff?"

"You'll find out later," he told me. I got a crush on him, and he began to avoid me after a while. And I never told.

My cousin Huesos was only fourteen or fifteen when he came to visit us in El Centro, but then I was about seven or eight, and thought he was very handsome. Under my bed once, he had my panties off, and then he got off, pushing himself against me. He was my mamá's favorite nephew, from New Mexico too. Years later, outside an uncle's house during a family party, Huesos came up to me while I was sitting in my papá's car. "Do you remember, Pat? Have you done it yet? You'll get hot all over." I told him that that had been a long time ago, and turned my head away from his hot beer breath. Yeah, I remembered. *Don't tell anybody.*

Your mother is explaining to eleven-year-old you, "This is what it's like inside you down there. It's a thin film like this nylon. And when you get married, the man breaks it. Yes, you'll bleed."

Your father, drunk again, is making his midnight raids on you, and you wake up to his raspy voice. "I have to tell you something. Your mother wasn't a virgin when we got married." Trying to avoid turning into his whiskey smells, you turn away, wondering, "What do you mean? Dad she's not a saint, I know." Your absent, sinning, errant mother not the Virgin Mary? It didn't any of it make sense for a long time.

"Stay away from boys, they only want one thing. Just remember, it's a doggy-dog world, Mija, a doggy-dog world. And men, boys, they want only one thing." You had forgotten some of your dad's boozy warnings, but your sister Vinnie is now telling you, "Dad used to wake me up sometimes during the night, and tell me strange stuff. How old was I? About six, eight. I don't remember. It was stuff about boys and sex. I was so scared, and I didn't know what he was talking about for the longest time."

"Is there something you want to tell me, baby?" you ask, and Vinnie answers, "There's some things I can't remember full-out, but there's like pictures or feelings that flash across. . . . I get glimpses of some things. What? Yes, cousin Gonzalo did, he sat me across his knee and took off my panties, and, yes, I remember it hurt. But I don't remember Ted, that old drunk man. Oh? You *do* remember? How old was I? Three? Lord, I don't believe it! And then I think I remember, one time we stayed with Dad, at his bachelor apartment, and I was about twelve or so, and we all had to sleep in one bed—two of us and Dad, I think. But I can't remember exactly what. There's just like a blackout of whatever that scene is. When I try to remember, but I have a feeling, like a faint, bad memory. But I try to forgive him now, I mean, I do forgive him now. And he might have been drinking, yeah." Don't say a word.

These are some of the things that they didn't want us to talk about. I needed to tell them, in this conversation, like about what they told me, they used to tell us, "Don't tell anyone, it's our secret."

One learns by doing, they used to tell me at home. I never knew how to cook well. When I was little they didn't make me help out in the kitchen, and so, what I learned about Mexican cooking was by watching and remembering, and later by making disappointing attempts until whatever it was came out well. Tortillas? They always came out crooked on me, although sometimes they came out really tasty. Tamales? I make them out of turkey now. Tacos? Chuppie (Chicano Yuppie) style with bought tortillas already fried, with turkey meat, ready-made salad, grated cheese, and everything *toditito* low calorie, non-fat. *Y* salsa? When I feel like it, I make it from scratch: I toast the chiles, etc. But generally, ready-made salsa, Don Juan's, El Pato, La Rosita, whatever brand, but everything ready to pour. And when we go to my mamá's house, well, what is it that we crave? Everything homemade, from tortillas to salsa, stew and beans. But we are an inventive people, I think, and for that reason, if our taste buds are satisfied, well, why not, and that way you don't spend too much time in the kitchen. What good did it do our mothers, aunts, and grandmothers after all, stuck in the kitchen, over the hot griddle and grill. Meanwhile they're so tranquilly waiting to be served. Tradition, passed on values, are still important to us, I think, but, give me a break. Anyway, I laugh at myself, I know that my, ahem, my cooking, it's all gringo style, but I also know the reality in which I live and I tell myself, why not? Don't tell me that we aren't all fat and happy eating our traditional plates prepared as fast food and in a hurry! "This is it, the show, the one you're living. No refunds."

And them? Ay, how I love them, but let's take a good look; according to them all they needed to know was: how to drink, expertly, how to go around with women, expertly, how to get home at whatever time, whenever they felt like it, expertly as well. Cook? In general, nope; wash clothes, clean floors, help with the dishes? No way. Now there are exceptions, but, in general, according to them, it is not their responsibility, but it *is* ours. Bathe the baby, change the diapers? Well, what do you think? No way, too bad, and what could one do?

In your classes, a couple of times, two guys murmur "Llorona," and the others laugh. You notice it, it hurts, but you also have learned to like them as well. "Forgive them, they just don't know." Nope, they know that one all right, and they love it, they sure do. Without a heart, without a heart, we're. . . . Someone is producing, churning them out that way.

In Masterton, while you were living at that labor camp, your cousin Tere made love to you. How old were you? You were about eight or nine, and she made you, she made you do something erotic. That's true, it wasn't "love," rather a sensual episode, as far as you shamefully and resentfully remember forty years later. They had left Tere to take care of you and your little brothers and sisters while your mother ran errands in town. Your cousin was from New Mexico, and they had left her "in charge" of you all. She was your cousin Huesos's little sister, and you knew nothing at your young age, about "abuse" or "incest." They were your cousins, your mom's relatives, and they were there to take care of you. It was a custom to have family members take care of the children. "Come and lay down on the cot with me, take off your clothes." And she kissed you, and you liked it, and you rubbed up against one another and kissed each other with clumsy kisses, you were warm all over, like you were on fire. And your cousin told you, at the end of that long, arousing, and—you knew it—forbidden episode, "Don't tell anybody."

The refried bean sandwich? It was something I invented one day when, alone with my brothers and sisters, a poor man, dressed in rags and begging for food, came to the house: "I'm hungry," he said simply in Spanish. "Would you give me something to eat?" And I, being an adolescent who just wanted to help, went to the kitchen where I found some cold and hard refried beans, and a dry loaf of bread. The only thing it occurred to me to give the man, 'cause I didn't know how to cook a thing, was a bean sandwich. And that's what I gave him. He took the small package and simply said, *Gracias,* and went on his way towards Main Street. I looked through the bedroom window and saw that the man suffering from hunger, of course, that's what he had told me, sat to eat what my inexperienced hands had made as a gift to him. The poor guy, he took a bite and spit it out, and then he threw the sandwich on the ground. The man got up and went to the house across the street from where he was sitting and asked for alms, charity for the poor, something good to eat. I still remember that, and I remember that later Trudi González told me, "We had some cooked meat and vegetables, so we gave the man some *taquitos*." He must have loved eating those taquitos, that poor man who just wanted something good to eat. The refried bean sandwich? Among all of my confections, that's one I don't recommend.

At the camps, they used to make the workers tacos with tortillas, beans, and stewed meat, or chorizo with potatoes or something of the sort. They also gave out fruit. That's how it was until some of the boarders and braceros started asking for American food, just for a bit of a change, and so, the sandwiches, the American lunch began. So, the cooks would clean up after breakfast, and would begin to prepare *el lonche* for the workers, assembly-line style. Everything in order, that's how my mom used to organize the kitchen help. In Masterton and Newdale, El Galla was her main helper. Later, they brought Marieta in once in a while, when something special was going on, or when my mom was sick, but, in general, Galla and two or three other braceros worked in the kitchen. Sometimes I would hear my mom say, "Now they're complaining about always eating tacos, later, that they get American food."

For some years later, my father had a bail-bond business. That was how he came to deal with the UFW Union representatives, because once in a while they called on him to get one of the Chavez's syndicate members out of jail. Years before that, they had thrown a brick through my father's window, in the house where he was living with my stepmother. At that time my dad worked as a labor recruiter for the Strawberry Growers' Association, and of course that didn't sit well with the Union strikers, but, later, they called him to get their people out of jail.

"My, how the world turns," said Esmeralda. "Your friend Chávez's people threw a rock through a window during the strike, and now your father's getting them out of jail." Esmeralda, she was such a *pícara*, such a sly woman, she knew I had my secrets about not being a friend of the strike, rather, I showed my "good contractor's daughter" face. Not to be confused ever, not in the least, with just the "good daughter" face.

CHAPTER THREE

My Uncle Toro was my favorite. He managed to get married six times, and he never ended up with the woman he really loved. Even in his old man's memory he thought of Chelita, the girl from New Mexico, whom he first truly loved. Still years later, when he'd go to Mesilla, he'd tell me, "I'm goin' to see Chelita; she's still got real nice skin." Every time he went there he said he was going to leave the wife he had, but he didn't. He's been married more than twenty-five years to this last wife, a graceful, strong, and patient Portuguese woman.

Tío Toro was as mischievous as he was attractive. One day, as they were going to the *fil*, my Uncle Toro got Gallareta all into going to look for honey. They were on their way to the strawberry field to drop off the lonches. They had seen, up around Modesto, on the edges of the strawberry fields that there were, underneath some enormous walnut trees, some columns of honeybee houses. Some ranchero was raising them, and my uncle and Gallareta got such a craving for fresh honey. Some way or another, Galla got elected to go and open one of the houses/boxes, the hive that was closest to the *troque* they had that day. And the whole seething mass of angry bees attacked him. They managed to get out of there, but some of the guys from the fil had to come and help them because Galla was really stung, and began almost instantly to swell up while screaming, "Ay, ay help! Ay, it really hurts, ay!" or something like that, according to my Uncle Toro, who told me later, laughing mischievously, "Gallareta was so swollen, he looked like a tomato ready to 'splode." That's how my tío *travieso* Toro told it. He was really good with us nieces and nephews, but I know that he had suffered from love.

One of Uncle Toro's "wives" never actually got to be his wife. She was going to be the third, I think, or the fourth. Back then, no one paid attention to that series, but I really felt bad for him, because he really lost sleep over that young woman. She was from Mexicali, from a "decent" family, as my mamá would say. I'd seen my Uncle get all gussied up, pack his suitcases, and get into his convertible to go, from San Joaquin Valley where we lived in Newdale, to Mexicali. He had been sending money to this girl for some months. He'd met her in Mexicali, when he still lived down that way in El Centro or in Betaville, and he had come up to earn some money to be able to go back for her. Meanwhile, the girlfriend was saving the money for the wedding, her dress, and the honeymoon. Two days later, Uncle Toro returned, all quiet, he didn't want to talk to us kids, not even to my dad. He came back without a bride or a wife. "They didn't get married," said my mom, who had gone out to the convertible to see what had happened to my uncle. "She stood him up," she told Marieta and us. "She spent all the money, some of her father's debts, or something like that." She also told us that Choli, the girl, told Tío that she had never loved him. He didn't want to see us for a while, we just knew that he went to live in a little hotel in town, and that he was on a binge for a couple of weeks.

I wasn't a bit sad that my uncle didn't marry Choli. I had met her when they took me down there for a visit, a very short visit I remember, before the catastrophe. The only thing my adolescent eyes saw in the girl were her great big eyes with long eyelashes, and a beauty mark, big and black, right in the middle of her forehead. Many years later, I was getting onto a bus from Modesto to Stockton with my kids, right there in the San Joaquin Valley, and I saw a solid and serious woman sitting with a little girl with the same straight hair and big eyes. It was Choli, older, more serious, with that same big black beauty mark right in the middle of her forehead. I remember that my mamá, back then, many years earlier, had said when my uncle came back all frustrated, "You'll see, if I ever get to see her again I'll grab her by her bun!"

My father doesn't remember a thing. They say he has Alzheimer's, but you and your sisters suspect it was the alcohol. As a young man, he was terrible. One thing your mother cannot forget was the woman with the dirty neck. She was from "the other side," from Mexicali, about eight miles from the little town where we all used to live. "We saw your old man at the bullfight on Sunday. He was with a girl. They looked *so in love.*" That was what your Aunt Rosalba told my mamá. She said that some nights he would come home very late and drunk, especially on the weekends. And one time, when he had gone to Mexicali with some friends, he didn't come home until the next day. "He wasn't even ashamed at all. His underwear had the vieja's blood on them. She was such a pig, and he couldn't control himself." "Why did you stay married to him, Mamá? Did you love him?" "I don't know; no one got divorced." "But, did you love him?" "Well, yeah, when we got married, but I don't know. . . ."

Your father and your uncles, that whole family were partiers, they got together a lot when they were young. For many years all of the children lived together at first, then in the same neighborhood, even though they already had a husband or wife. They were all good-looking and had personality; the most handsome had been our father. And they liked to fool around, to tell jokes, and they used to play practical jokes on each other. At my Uncle Mingo's camp they had a party one time that lasted through the afternoon and all night. I don't remember the occasion really well, if it was a wedding, a baptism, or just a get-together to eat and drink. My uncles got so drunk with my dad, and there were little kids dancing and running around the dining room full of people. They were playing records, guitars, singing, and my papá and one of my uncles came out in drag, as one of my other uncles said, "Those two crazy guys, with a bra and Hawaiian skirts and underneath, barely any underwear."

In Salmas, a bus carrying a ton of braceros was destroyed by a train when it crossed the tracks. Many died, others were seriously injured. And even the federal government got involved in the investigation to find out how it had happened. My father had to go to the site, minutes after it happened, to see what could be done. "It was really ugly," he said. "They died for nothing. They don't know why the troque, with all those people in it, tried to cross. Someone's going to pay." They let other officials come from Mexico to be part of the investigation after complaints were filed and official formalities were followed.

"Hello, Mija. I'm in Puerto Rico," reads the postcard that your father sent from Puerto Rico, where they had sent him from Salmas, as part of the Ranchers' Association, and sponsored by the government, to see if they could come to an agreement about importing migrant workers. Yes, they wanted to bring agricultural workers to the United States from Puerto Rico. "It's beautiful here. Love, Your Old Man." Later he left the Ranchers' Association, because they brought "some young punk with a degree in Agriculture or something, trying to tell me what to do. Fucking owners, ungrateful gringos."

Mi papá? My father really liked green eyes. My mother ended up spying on "the bitch with the dirty neck," the one from Mexicali. My Tía Rosalba took Mom. She was a daring woman, even though my mom was a bit shy back then. They went to the bullfight unannounced one Sunday. There, they saw my handsome father, always out cavorting, really cozy "with that vieja. She was really dark with curly, greasy hair, and green eyes. Her collar was really dirty, and her neck looked stained, as if she never washed it. And whenever he went to see her, there I was, stuck in the restaurant working. You guys were all little, didn't know anything. *And what we knew, we didn't tell anybody.*"

The last camp they had, the one in Newdale, where they started using those machines to make tortillas, my parents lost it because "your father was a womanizer and a flirt, because he liked those green eyes from that *güera* from Juárez," your mamá is telling you. "That's where we lost it all, and later they fixed it so that they could get all of my earnings from me, to take them for themselves." Because my father was absent, my mother ran the Newdale camp, as always, getting up early and returning late, sometimes she couldn't even come home to spend the night with us. Marieta still lived with us, and Mamá from time to time had to stay in the little house they had built in the camp. And that's how my mom took charge of that camp that they had, and my father moved to a place near Visalia, to run a camp at a place that had been a government base, with a dining room, barracks with beds, all in an arid place. The base had been abandoned for some years and my father, uncles, and other partners had had the idea of being able to employ more workers from that part of the San Joaquin Valley. It was quite a distance from Fresno, at the very center of the Valley.

"Esmeralda was a barmaid. She used to work near where they had the camp at the abandoned base. He met her there. And she started to send me postcards from the hotels they would stay in. Later, I found out she had green eyes and was fair-skinned, and she colored her hair almost red." Your mother, who for years colored her own hair orange, is telling you again her version about how "your father got involved with Esmeralda."

CHAPTER FOUR

"Is this the great Mr. Leyva? Do you know who I am?" "Hello, Pat. Sure, it's Petra. *Aló,* Mija." And you start forcing yourself to be funny, to tell jokes. They have become a game to you, these calls to your father, and starting off the same way each time, you confirm that he still recognizes your voice. For how much longer?

You remember the last time you went to see your papá, it was six months ago, now he's in San Mingo, in a place with a strange name like the House of *La Casa.* The first time they tell you "now he's at . . ." you disagree on the name, thinking that they may have been mistaken, but later you concede, "Another dumb translation of Spanish, so what's new?" On the wharf in Santa Cruz that afternoon, Beli and Bob, your husband, walk ahead of you. Behind them, in front of you, your father and Vinnie walk arm in arm. As you walk past a boat rental place, loud rock and roll music blasts out at you. You watch as your father suddenly jumps a couple of times to the beat, does a dance step, this way, that way, and then continues walking, with Vinnie laughing and hugging him. He's still good for making funny faces and joking around. And he still knows what's going on. He's losing it quite a bit, and soon he may not even know where he is. On the phone? He still recognizes your voice, okay, except for one time, up till now. But in person, when you see him and when we go out, that's another story. Our old ones are slipping away, and our lives with them, you ponder.

The old Frenchwoman you met, the one who helped you raise Marisa in Southwest City, is also in a place like a sanctuary. It's a rest home, which is actually an antique home remodeled and done up beautifully, up there in Hannibal, Missouri. She lives really far from the desert, but her life is deserted now. In her case, which is not the same as your father's, she doesn't walk anymore, nor can she write letters because her vision and her hands are going. She still ascertains and complains, both perfectly well, that is, almost. "I have not hear' from you in long time. I tink you lost or somezing. Wher' you bin, Pat, wher' my Marisa?" *la viejita* asks you in her thick French accent, and she says that no one comes to see her, that no one ever writes her, that you all've forgotten about her, just like her own grandchildren.

Of her more than ten grandchildren and many great-grandchildren, only one granddaughter comes to see her in the rest home. The son she still has there comes by to see her one or two times a week—to ask for money. René is the son that never made much of himself, the other just retired from the Air Force. They had lived in Southwest City for many years, because he was stationed at the big base near there. Up until about five years ago, the viejita still lived independently, and then she fell. That is when they found the sickness that would end up affecting her just as it does now, not being able to walk, not even with a walker. Years ago, in Southwest City when all of you guys were younger, this viejita grumbled, and she would chew out anyone who offended her. In any case she was quite a lady all the way, in spite of her strong character. She used to tell me about how she had met her two husbands over there in France. And how she ended up in Illinois.

Santuario. The Convent of the Good Shepherd, in Las Cruces, New Mexico, it was like this, full of saints, but it never ended up being my sanctuary. The nuns taught us how to embroider. I learned how to draw, with a needle and thread, little flowers, little snails, fine leaves or big fluffy ones, little birds, little hearts, or little ribbons, you name it. That was the end of my teachings there. I don't remember that, that summer I spent there, I might have learned other, more practical things. It was to help in the nuns' assembly line. All the work the interned girls would produce, and I was only seven years old, was to be sold at the *kermeses.* As a little girl, I understood those to be a type of bazaar that was put on at some of the parishes. The money was for the convent or for the church, who knows. In addition, in the part of the convent where the older girls and the novices were, there was a laundry room and candy shop. Well, the part of the candy shop I might have imagined but there was a large laundry room. What did they used to do? Well, I really don't know. I do know I thought they had a big "industry" there, and it had something to do with keeping some Catholic linens and accessories clean, or as Sabine Ulibarri, a humorist from those parts, would say: *"de católicos y apostólicos"* . . . belonging to full-out Catholics.

They made us sooo Catholic, like I have told you somewhere else, that they made us thank God for the coffee they gave us. Yes, to put on our cereal instead of milk.

You write yourself a note: "Ask my dad what the sanctuary movement means." You ask your mother, "Do you know if your church has ever given sanctuary to any refugees or undocumented people? No, they're not the same thing, but I mean they're both worthy causes. Has your church ever been involved with that?" And your son, the evangelist, who is going on a mission to Mexico, what will he do? "Stay out of their politics," you admonish your son. Your tall, brown-haired son with brown eyes that have green flecks in them, answers you that he will, they're only going to "spread the word of God," to tell them, the Mexicans, the word of God. This seems so absurd, sad, and funny to you at the same time. To tell them about the word of God. Aha, haaaaaa!

Oh yeah, that's what the Mexicans—the Latinos—need, that someone come and explain to them, the true word of God. We're ending up where we started, you say to yourself, round and round, what historical life circles we go in.

"How long will you be there Mijo?" you ask your apostolic Pentecostal minister son. And you know, in spite of your mother's words that come out of your mouth: I love that kid, I really love him. "God bless you, and take care." Everything your son says could have been said by your mother or any of your other brothers that were raised Pentecostal. But they have good intentions, just some opinions that are either conservative or extremist. That's the way their world is: "Listen to the all-powerful God's word," they say, and then they make jokes about black people. "And Rastus said you got big-lips, black boy. Ha, ha." You ask yourself how one can be a good Christian on the one hand, and a racist/misogynist/elitist, etc., etc., on the other?

In His message, I've seen someone say something like, "Or let me save you or I'll kill, or you let yourself be saved (and for me, that means us) or I'll break your teeth. Either you do what I say (want, recommend, preach), or I'll fuck you over. I'll kick you in the balls (your tits, the ass). Just convert (by force not even to your own cause). Just like that, right?" But no, not just like that.

"Tía Marta's kids, two of them, the 'weird' ones, well, you remember that people said they were HIV positive. In other words, if you had doubted if they were or they were not, well now you know for sure. What will our uncles, their parents, do? God help them." That's what your cousin who was visiting from Los Angeles said. Those diseased cousins, and their parents, all of them were always nice to us. Your aunt, ever since your parents' divorce, didn't want to be disloyal to your father, so she didn't want to have anything to do with your mom. Your mom had left your father years ago, and they still held a grudge against her until recently, they wouldn't have anything to do with her. I don't know what they were thinking, but it was like your mother was at fault, for leaving him, even though all of your father's brothers knew about his "crazy youth and his even crazier old age"; if you asked them, they pretended not to know. Well, all that aside, your uncles were about to go through the most horrible thing that a parent can go through, to see one of your children, let alone two of them die, and from AIDS.

"And your cousin Chayo's son also tested HIV positive. What do you think of that? How ugly, huh? No, not him, what's happening to him, but it's really ugly, huh? Isn't it awful? I pray to God that it will not happen to our sons." To us either, you answer. But to see one's child die, slowly and in agony at the end, I hope that will not happen to our own sons or daughters.

Your friend Mercedes is telling you something, something very serious. "What, what were you saying, Meche. Who's a homosexual? What? Bisexual—your daughter?" Amidst sobs and tears, your friend keeps on telling you. "She told me she always knew she was different, and in spite of having fallen in love a couple of times, she was even going to get married that time, remember? Still and all, the bomb she dropped on me, well. She confessed to me that the first time she had been under the influence, drunk and drugged, and they cornered her. Finally, she admitted to me, for the first time, that they seduced her, a woman friend from the university, with whom she studied. Women's Studies of la Raza, something like that." So, your friend's daughter is gay. And your cousins are gay. So, Chicanos and *Chicanitas,* can also be one of them—gay.

"You can't be gay and be Chicano!" insists a very nervous older man one time you went to talk about Chicanas in literature and stuff about books in Albuquerque. A couple of quiet but attentive Chicanitas walk behind him, and then they ask you, the professors, "Is that guy for real, or what? What an idiot!" That's right, they are your blood, your people, your family. "Homosexuals are an abomination. That's why God has sent AIDS." That's what your mom and your son have said to you. "That's why all those weirdos are going to die. God is punishing them by sending them AIDS!"

"Mijo, that sickness, AIDS, affects the entire population, not just homosexuals. Yeah, by mistake, but not from committing a sin." These are the prohibited topics in our family discussions, which you and your son have talked about while you were alone one afternoon. It seems to you that what everybody recommends, "Just say NO," is not very effective. How can you stop young people from feeling passion? How can you get them to take care of themselves, protect themselves from so, so much danger? Only by saying NO, and you are saved?

You already know what your mom will say. "We are near the end, these are the last days, that's why."

"I'm tired of hearing that, Mamá," you think to yourself.

CHAPTER FIVE

Just say NO. That is the way, the solution to so many problems. Then how come your friend Lulu's sister-in-law, the woman who died of alcoholism before fifty, didn't say NO? Your oldest uncle, the one who also suffered from the same illness, the two of them, some called them winos because wine was their favorite alcohol. Why did they have to drink themselves to death having so much talent and promise? And your father, who doesn't recognize his children's faces, doesn't recognize, yet still remembers your voices? Oh, how people lie with propaganda. Lacking spiritual motivation, you "just say NO!"

"He met the Simón sisters in the field," your mamá tells you. "He would find some of his women at the job site, the Simón sisters, over there in fields of Fresno in the camp that your father ran along with your uncles. Your father had a grand old time, two sisters and an old vieja with red hair and green eyes." Later you remember that your father tried to convince your mother not to leave him. He was a pilot, he asked to borrow the plane from the strawberry grower, his friend Hakagachi, and along with your father's oldest sister, they take you to Reno to get that idea out of Lorenza's head. In Reno, the oldest sister, your aunt, tells the woman at the residence where your mother is living while the divorce is finalized, "Tell Lorenza that her youngest child has been in an accident with her husband, and they need her at home." Later you realize that among families, they act like that, they help each other as it should be, including the men in all their coarseness. Yet, when it comes to the daughters'/cousins'/sisters-in-law's stupid moves or mistakes, well it depends, and I would hate to be you.

"Your sister Lupe is a loose woman," your mamá is telling you. They brought her from Mexico. Yes, she's the only Mexican of all of your father and Lorenza's kids, from the real Mexico. And she's the one who while growing up didn't want to be Mexican. Not a word of Spanish, she would say she didn't want to. A few years ago Lupe writes you: "I want to go find my real mother. I want you to go and interpret for me." You tell her that it would be impossible, you don't want to go in search of another mother for your sister, that her natural mother, according to the conditions in which she lived, was probably no longer alive. Your sister Lupe, she was a twin. She'd had a little twin brother. It was the town doctor close to Truenos in the mountains of Sonora, that's the one who told your mother about an Indian woman who had just given birth to twins. "She lived around there in a shack in the outskirts of town. I went into the shack and saw the two little lumps on the floor. The little girl was sick, and the mother, well, we gave her some money and we took the baby girl." "Take her, Señora. Maybe she'll survive with you." And the indigenous woman cried, "She cried when she gave me *la niñita,* and she cried when I gave her the hundred dollars. 'I know this won't pay you for your daughter, but I will take care of her.' That woman was the mistress of a rich guy from the town; he had light skin, and she, well, she was Indian."

"Your sister Lupe hates me. You should see how she talks to me." "Mamá, you used to hit her with a broom, as if you didn't love her because you already had my other brothers and sisters with your second husband. She does love you, but maybe she can't forget."

"No, no, your sister goes to bed with men from all over, she brings them home while her kids are in the house. She yelled at me the other day: 'You weren't such a saint!' Can you imagine? Imagine her telling me I hadn't been such a saint. She's a wild one, that one!"

My parents found out years after having brought Lupe from Truenos that a pig had entered into the shack and bitten the face of Lupe's little twin brother. "That woman had other children, of all ages, older than the twins." The Sosa family, who worked in the fields with our father, had told my dad about the little boy and the pig. The Sosa family was the same family from the story about the huge wedding in Truenos, when the wedding party got run over by chickens and dogs on the way to the church.

One time, when we were coming back south to Imperial Valley from the San Joaquin Valley, my little brother Sammy and I were the only ones in the back of the big truck. We had boxes, furniture, and sacks of food like beans, potatoes, onions, and we also had a cooler, water, and there were a lot of mattresses in the most closed and protected rear part of the truck. Well, my little brother and I started fighting. Our parents were up front with the baby, Belita, and they didn't see us fighting. Well, in combat, I drew blood from my little brother, giving him a punch, ZAS! in the nose. I wanted to hit him in the face, but we were so mad, about what, I don't know, that I connected with his nose.

Some days later, when we were at the house in El Centro, my mamá called me in to where she was doing laundry. There, she had my dress, the one I used to stop my little brother's nose from bleeding. I thought she knew about the whole thing and that I was in for a spanking, when my mamá just asked: "Petrita, do you know what menstruation is?" I told her that I had no idea what that word meant. "Well, you're still young, but this blood on your dress, what can it be from, Mija, do you remember?" I answered her, in a very confessional tone, that I had hurt myself in the truck, and much later I confessed about giving my brother a bloody nose in a moment of rage. He, of course, never said anything either. Of course he wouldn't, he was really macho and did not want anyone to know that a girl had made his nose bleed. As brother and sister, we had our little innocent secrets too.

Fight with my brothers? No, not really. There were only two fights between my brother and me, that I can remember. The last was in what ended up being the final days of my parents' marriage. They were separated, one at the camp in the town where we lived, and the other at the abandoned air force base camp near Visalia. Well, the phone calls at home began, either I or my brother would answer. We were the oldest. La Marieta still lived with us, but my father fired her when my mother left him. "That old lady's a conniver," he would say. Well, after a few days of phone calls, where women's voices would say stuff like, "Your mother is going out with another man," or "Your father is sleeping with a green-eyed woman," or "Your parents are cheating on each other," we began to understand what was going on and were very worried. We were only fourteen and fifteen. And for some unknown reason we began hitting and slapping each other. I had long nails, that was during a time that I didn't bite them mercilessly. Well, to make a long story short, my brother won that one by giving me a few good punches in the stomach.

As always, I cannot remember for the life of me over what. . . . I only remember that I had broken my longest and most favorite nail. And, although my brother had my nail scars on him for days, we never told my parents that the ideal brother and sister had exchanged blows. And the strangest thing is, is that when I try to remember that last argument, that last time we would fight, we, who had always gotten along so well, I will never forget the force, the violence with which we fought that last time. We were propelled by a hate, an overwhelming emotion, cruel and furious.

CHAPTER SIX

Your mother had her secrets, too, you tell yourself. "Your mother wasn't a *virgen* when we got married," and you remember her telling you, "I should've married another man, Felipe from New Mexico. But he left for the army. I married your papá later, and Felipe never came back. He was killed in the war, the one guy I should've married." In some other state, you have a half-brother you don't know. Well, Vinnie has seen him, as has your mamá. . . . One of your mother's cousins had him from that time when the cousin went to visit your mother when your parents were just married. And same old story, Dad, a handsome and smooth-talkin' horny young man, made it with that cousin, and, *adiós, Nena*, wham, bam, thank you ma'am, and the rabbit died! What a sad story, and you've stopped trying to figure these things out. A half-brother? Well, I don't think he knows. I think they told him that his father had died in the war. Yep, things are pretty strange in real life, even stranger than in tales. I guess I don't need to tell you that.

Well, I promised taboo stories, secrets. I'm picking and choosing, it's my choice, and as they say, if you don't like it, go to . . . well, there's the door, and all that.

After doing bail-bonds for a few years, your father returns to working in agriculture. He convinces a partner of his to manage some land outside of the city, on the way to Santa Cruz, where there was a share-cropping system. All of the campesinos who worked there would share in the strawberry earnings. "It's a better deal for them," your papá says. He was working there when you all notice that your father doesn't joke around the way he used to, that he looks insecure and fragile when you go to visit. This time, you've gone to visit so he could meet your husband. Vinnie, her husband, Tom, and Belita have gone with you. You had called the day before and worked it out so that he would come down to your hotel in Monterey to see you, but that day, he never arrived. Then, you all went up to look for him at work, up there by Gilroy, where you found him in the strawberry field office. *"Qué pasó,* Papá?" "Nothing, why?" You're puzzled somewhat, still, you all invite him out to eat. There, in a restaurant on the bay, you notice a big change in your father. You can tell, he looks at you nervously. Within a couple of years, your father is a different man, inhibited, introspective, not remembering details, not recognizing.

You suspect one of your sisters to be "one of those," those that like other women. Yes, maybe bisexual. You remember having read a few of your sister's poems a couple of years back, out of her diary, she wrote, "And I kiss you there, my secret love." She managed to stay married some fifteen years. "Your sister and her fat friend, they say that they spend their mornings together. Your sister is spending all of her days off with that gringa friend of hers, *la gorda.*" You said, "It can't be. Her friend, Ginger, works at the Bible College. And my sister and her husband, well, they're married, aren't they? They have kids, right? It can't be, don't pay any attention to the sisters-in-law's gossip. They're jealous because my sister is so clever, and so kind to everyone." And a really strong personality just like her father, you remember, she went everywhere with him. "You were Dad's favorite," you tell your sister. "You're Mom's favorite." And so you would joke back and forth. And if they knew the secret, and if they really knew who loved who, and how and where, in detail? Would they still love you the same?

When they divorced, her husband accused her of unnatural love. Your mom and your brothers and sisters think this is absurd. Later, they begin to tie things together, remembering details, little things they hadn't noticed. And that's the way that "perfect children," just as "perfect parents," lose their saintly appearance. That's what happens when you idealize, you scold yourself for wanting everything to fit the mold. "Look at yourself first, instead of judging." To each his own, and it's not true that something will happen to those who do their own.

Some of your friends are really against gays and bisexuals. "He's a fag. This guy came out at one of those literary conferences; he pronounced himself as one of those, not straight." "Do you know so-and-so? He's one of those strange ones. Haven't you seen how he speaks (dresses, walks), his gestures? Don't they seem effeminate to you?" And, "She is such a butch." "So manly." "She is, you know, one of those lesbians. Look!" And her parents didn't even know. Secrets. Emancipated, you tell someone, "You can't tell by looking!" Really emancipated.

On another occasion, you read that some nuns in a hospital in Chiapas are in danger because they take in whoever comes to their hospital and offer them relief, a place to stay. They give sanctuary to those that arrive, and some *rancheros* have taken to accusing them of being accomplices in the Indian rebellion. There, according to the rancheros, they hide the "bad" campesinos, the so-called Zapatistas. According to the nuns, they tend to the wounded and the sick. Los Zapatistas maintain that the big ranches have robbed them of their land, acre by acre. The ranchers accuse the Zapatistas of having taken their privately owned land. Both sides accuse each other of expropriations, etc., etc. Among the ranchers there are PRI officials, so the PRI takes the ranchers' side. According to the Mexican nurse-nuns, "We don't get involved in politics; we just give sanctuary to those wounded or in need." To do charity, to try to do a good thing, to help one's brother, so that's sticking your nose into politics? So you ask yourself, turning the newspaper page to find where the article continues describing the Zapatista revolt, the new movement that has returned in Mexico. Wow, there are really some courageous people, some really valiant women.

"I feel sorry for Chicano politicians," a Chicana student is telling you when you are still living in Southwest City. "Most of the time, they simply cannot accomplish what they need to or want to for their people, because that is precisely what they are, our people, part of the minority. And they can't get anywhere, sometimes even after long sessions and discussion, they can't vote in mass because they are the minority."

That's how that young woman who wanted to be a lawyer after graduating from the university saw things. She had seen a program with Chicano politicians and ended up getting very sad. "In the end, a Chicano politician is a voice in the desert, and most of them are frustrated. They've even elected a Chicano governor? That's just lip service, and on top of that, there's even a Chicano politician from our state in Washington, but this state is tough," she says.

"Should I go into Spanish in graduate school? Somebody told me that I couldn't get a job later, if I had a degree in Spanish because I'm not a minority female," a student in his last year of Spanish asks you. He thinks only minority women, Hispanic, get jobs at schools and universities because of the famous affirmative action, the so-called legislation to rid society of religious, racial, age, and sexual discrimination. You tell the student that really, it doesn't matter, men still get jobs and to continue with his goal, his dream. And you well know, that to be Chicana doesn't protect you from half of the injustices that one, as a woman and Chicana, can suffer. You are the lowest on the totem pole. On top of you, the Latinas and the *españolas* or the administrators' lovers, especially at the university. Just ask the Chicanas who are trying to survive there; ask them about their frustrations and bad encounters. "Maybe there are some solutions," your Chicana linguist colleague tells you. "Maybe we should continue with the Chicana caucus. Join us." You, not very fond of joining associations, resist, and they stop inviting you. "How's it going?" you ask and add, "Tell them to find themselves someone to guide them as a mentor, but ask them not to let the so-called mentor lie to them, and not to let anyone fuck them over."

CHAPTER SEVEN

When you were thirteen and still in the San Joaquin Valley, your cousin Cheno died on a highway near Fresno, outside Firebaugh, on the way to Masterton. He and your other cousin were coming back from where they had gone to see *unas güisas,* some girl friends. They were from your mom's side of the family, originally from New Mexico. Well, cousin Chenito, tall, dark, with thick hair and a little mustache, was always such a good kid, he ended up on the side of that highway. It had been at night, and that night he died. They also used to work in the camp, in the fields with my father's people, and they lived with my grandmother Lencha, my mother's grandmother. Marieta woke you up saying, "Petra, come here, something's wrong with your mom. She's crying and your father can't console her. What? Something about your cousin, one of your cousins."

"Aaaaayyyy! AAAAAAYYYY, NOOOOO!" That's how your mamá screamed for your cousin Chenito, as if it were her own son, as if it were her own brother.

"Lorenza, if you don't calm down I'll have to call Dr. Garrison. What do you want me to do?" After a while the phone rang, and after your father talks a while, he says that he has to go out for some bottles of blood for the cousin, Huesos, who had survived, because without more blood, he wasn't gonna make it. He was gravely injured, grave condition.

"I want Petrita to come with me. That way I have someone to talk to and I won't fall asleep." We spent the trip to the biggest hospital in Modesto talking about my mother, cousin Chenito, and of those simple things, like how we couldn't see very well at that hour. It was two or three o'clock in the morning already, but at least there wasn't any fog, like in the winter. I don't remember much about the trip we made that night, my father and I, going for blood for cousin Huesos. On the way back, we had to go to the small hospital in the little town where we all used to live, to deliver the containers of blood for Huesos, the same cousin who had "played" with me under the bed when I was a little girl. And I never said anything about this, not even the night when I went with my father to talk to him so he wouldn't fall asleep during that trip in the night.

Later, we had the funeral for Chenito, and a lot of neighbors came, like the Portuguese and American women that knew my mother. It was the first time I learned about that custom, where people bring cakes and food to the house where they mourn the death of a family member. My Tía Lita did it a different way. For many days, she accompanied my mother to church, where they prayed for cousin Cheno. They took me a couple of times, and my mother gave me a black veil to put on. My aunt had brought them, and she also said that we had to go to the restaurant they ran for a short time, and that my mom should not cook for so many people during those days. So, along with my memories of death, the trip for blood and Chenito's wake and funeral, I also have memories of my aunt and uncle's restaurant, where we ate fiesta-style meals for many days in a row. We had menudo, tamales, tacos, enchiladas, chiles rellenos, chorizo con huevo, papas con chorizo.

"Eat whatever you want, Lorenza, eat, you need to get your strength back, come on, eat up, anything you want." It was all prepared with love and care by Tía Lita, who loved my mom so much. "I felt sorry for your mamá," she later told me, "with all that she went through, working like a mule, while he . . . and still your mamá, a very, very hardworking woman, you should have seen what she was like when we all used to live together, when we were younger, over there in Betaville, that little ranchito."

Secrets, maybe we shouldn't remember them, nor tell them to anybody. Maybe, that's the way most people want it. Most feel that you, that no one, should say anything. And, you ask yourself, is there any good that comes out of reviving secrets, offenses, bad memories? "They were part of what happened, part of what together makes up, with the good and warm memories, with what happened, with what you did, with what they did." You also remember, among all this, funny and mischievous events, as they happened. "Let's see, Grandma, how's that story go about the guy that shit on the door of the car that one time in Mexicali. How's it go? Oh, yeah, 'Once upon a time there were two little kids. . . .'"

"Your father went away to Mexico with that woman with the green eyes. She was from Juárez, the one he met over there by Visalia," your mother tells you. You knew your parents were not going to last together when she, returning from Reno, comes back to live with you. "You're not gonna stay Mom, are you?" She answered you with, "Well, how did you know? You're so smart." And you told her that you simply felt that they were not getting along, and that things were not the same. Neither of your parents, you saw, were like before, laughing or telling simple jokes. You noticed details, things like that. Later, your father's lawyer came, talked to your mom, and she asked you to sit with her to talk to the lawyer. Neither your mother nor you, at fifteen, understood why your father's business, the camp, had to be sold, and that they can only pay as much as they determine, the lawyer is telling you. "You won't get any money, though, because the sale price will just pay off the debts on the business." The house will also have to be sold. Your father has gone to Mexico with the woman with green eyes, and your mother was "left behind with all the debt and no other choice," she told me. She, teary eyed, looks at me and asks, "What do you think?" And I am the one who, at that moment so impressed by the fact that I was the one they invited to observe these proceedings and, as always, a bit confused by the business dealings of the grown-up world, answer in English, something like, "The amount being offered for the labor camp is quite COM-parable to. . . . " And I answered my stupid answers to impress the lawyer/accountant with my English pronunciation of "comparable." And that's how I, being the oldest at fifteen, helped them to steal my mother's business.

CHAPTER EIGHT

Our new life without a father started with inevitable changes. My mother had sold the camp, and she herself had to worry about selling the house, dealing with the bills, and with supporting us. They had already sent Marieta back to Mexico when my mother went to Reno. That was when my father told her that "Marieta, she's a troublemaker." And he sent my mother's friend, Marieta, straight back to . . .

Christmas arrived, and my mother didn't have money to give us "gifts, as it should be." One morning, my mother opened the front door, and on the porch there was a box full of gifts, jars of jams and preserves, some sweet breads, like those made with pumpkins, bananas, or nuts, fruitcake, those bars of bread wrapped in pretty paper with ribbons, oranges, apples, and a sack of nuts. Mi mamá still remembers that they had put a ready-to-cook turkey in the box. I don't remember the part about the turkey, but I do remember the little gifts, the candy, and as always the other sweets to eat. We never knew who our benefactors were. My mother tried to thank our neighbor whom we loved a lot and who always talked to us. Her daughter was one of my best friends, and she always denied that it was they who had played Santa Claus. A few weeks later, my mother and my little brothers and sisters went to Modesto to live, and that started our welfare era.

My brother and I, the oldest, stayed in the little town to finish our high school years. It was my last year, and he, very active in school as well, didn't want to lose the opportunity to continue with sports. Like me, he was in the band and the orchestra, and he was class president, and involved in other things as well. The following year my brother stayed with the family that had taken him in. My mom had given the woman, the mother of these family friends from school, our freezer, that big freezer box that we had, that before was always full of meats and fruits and vegetables and that now was most always empty. "It's not much, but I'm grateful," your mother told the woman who took your brother in, so that he could finish high school. Finally, halfway through the school year your brother's girlfriend, a petite, cute Portuguese girl, who, according to some big mouth friends, "swears like a sailor," ended up pregnant. They got married with a sweet, simple wedding, and he left high school. He didn't finish then. But my brother, as stubborn as my father when he had it in his head to do something, started school again and graduated from the university. He works as a coach, a director and advisor for some sports in a community college in the San Joaquin Valley. They say my brother keeps accomplishing all that he does due to the good woman he has now, but I think it is because of his spirit and perseverance. Just like our parents, my brother, like my mother especially, tended to have a reserved personality, but after many hard knocks and falls, he got up. That's what being stubborn and persistent is good for.

My father was the one who would take me to the spelling bees, those competitions they had at our schools where you had to spell out loud. I was very "advanced," and had won the spelling bee at my elementary school in eighth grade, and my father brought me to the district spelling bee in Modesto. There I went, with flying colors, until they gave me the word *squirrel,* and I said "SQEE-R-R-E-L." And they threw me out of the contest for wanting to pronounce the word instead of spell it letter by letter. I did that so many times, got myself into things without thinking, and they would throw me out. Sometimes, yes, sometimes by sheer luck or for being stubborn and hardheaded, and sometimes not.

My father was there the day I graduated from eighth grade. At that time my mom wasn't interested in my school things. She was up to her eyeballs with the life she had, but my dad, like I said, he had it in his head that we, his children, needed to go to school and fight the good fight with the books. For that reason, I always tried to do well in my classes. At first, in order to get good grades, as my father had insinuated that he wanted us to do, but later, just for my own pleasure. I became the privileged child at home due to my report cards and my prizes and my good reputation with the teachers. And my parents left me free, at home, to study and continue with what some of my aunts called my "high-falutin' things."

I had many happy days thanks to my high school years, and I went from wanting to be a doctor to wanting to be an actress. From an early age I played parts in shows and acting programs; I even sang a couple of times on the radio. I also learned to imitate characters like Jayne Mansfield, Marilyn Monroe, Elvis, Tallulah. I used to sing, act, and I was invited to be Master of Ceremony for some events. I used to paint murals in the gym for the dances. They elected me here and there, and I, so happy, didn't care that not everybody liked me because a lot of people did. And during the Homecoming parade, the night of the football game, I was, in the last year of my successes in high school, the happiest Homecoming Queen. That night, even my father came to see me for an instant when I got on the convertible. I saw him standing among the spectators with a serious face and proud look in his eyes while they fixed the skirt on my white lacey cambric dress around me. "You came, Papá," I thought, and I smiled at him but we didn't say a word.

Of all my relatives, only my mother, my Tío Toro, my brother and my other tío, my father's younger brother, came to my high school graduation. According to my tío, my father didn't come so as not to see my mother. According to my mother, the woman with the green eyes didn't want my parents to see each other. All those events—bad days, happy days, prizes, everything—have remained with me as if they happened yesterday. Like the night of my graduation, the night that my years as a "lost woman" really began. That's what my father ended up calling me for listening to the boys, to young men. The night before I graduated from high school I got pregnant with my first child in a old Oldsmobile on the banks of a canal.

"I'll marry you, but I don't love you, Pat," the young blond man with blue eyes explained to me, saying that his mother didn't want him to marry me. That how come I hadn't married my first boyfriend, the one that was of my "same race"? "Why doesn't she marry that Mexican boy? How do I even know it's your baby? Maybe she's a whore; nice girls don't sleep with boys when they're not married!" Those were the things his mother had said according to some of our friends. I, hurt but proud, answered, "I don't want to marry you if you don't love me. You don't have to." And in spite of the threats from my stepfather, who was at the time a deputy sheriff from the adjacent county, we didn't get married. Later, the young man acknowledged his daughter when my mother made me take him to court, because we had to make the "fucking, runny-nosed gringo contribute to the raising of the baby." That little güerita ended up being the most loved of all of my mother's grandchildren. "For all that we had gone through with that snotty gringo and his mother, the bitch. They had their doubts! The little creature is his spitting image. . . . It doesn't matter, they'll pay later. You'll see." Was my mother bitter? No. Now I say she was just quite loyal and determined.

On television, on a talk show, one of those programs where the interviewed talk about a variety of topics, some serious like AIDS, abortion, marriage, and divorce, etc., and some that are really silly, simple, or comic. Today they are interviewing women of various ages, asking them about topics of primordial importance: "When was the first time you had sex? What about your first orgasm?" Later, the questions break down into others like if they had their first orgasm the first time they "did it." If they always have an orgasm with each sexual encounter? If multiple orgasms are more pleasureful than one strong one? Questions like that, and you began to remember that you didn't have your first orgasm your first time, nor with your first boyfriend.

"We didn't know what had happened," said your friend, the girl from the other couple that was with you and your boyfriend, the blue-eyed *güero*. The four of you had gone to "the boonies," the woods that were among the places people could go to make out. Back then, they called it "necking." The same place where young men would lose control and the young girls "would let themselves go, would lose their virtue, etc., the men took advantage of them, etc." The *güerito* and I had separated from the other couple that was also a Chicanita from my town and a *gringuito* from another. And we walked in the dark between the stand of trees that was there, far from our two towns. We laid down on a blanket that the very well-prepared young man had brought. No, it wasn't my "first time," but we hadn't "done it" more than a couple of times before then. Well, kiss led to kiss, and squeeze to squeeze, and I began to feel all hot, my face, my legs, even my nails burned. And suddenly it came to me, like a lightening bolt, the pleasure. "YAAAAAAAAYYYYYY!" And then, still dizzy from the thrill, I asked the guy, "What was that?" What had just happened to me? Because the two of us were so naïve and inexperienced even though we weren't virgins, he could only say, "I guess it felt good?" When we came out of the woods, my friend Dora, taking me by the arm, said to me. "Qué pasó? I thought for a moment that you had run into La Llorona!" I, still very stupefied, whispered to her, "He said I came!" And the four of us went back to town really quiet. I think that it scared more than embarrassed the two young men. Dora and I, stifling our giggles and our embarrassment. Wayward girls. *And I liked it.*

In our little town, when I was in high school and I started my life as a "loose woman," the young couples that we knew had other places as options when they wanted to be alone with their boyfriend or girlfriend, or when they would run into a girl who "did it" or "would do it." Those places were the boonies or "the trees" or "the chickens" or "the canal." During that time, I had been in all of those places, I think the most isolated one was the chickens, an abandoned ranch where they had raised chickens and hens. There we would see parked other horny young couples like us. One girl or another would turn out "preggy," knocked up like me, and would have to get married. This is what one did at that time, and I was, of the girls that scandalized the town, the one who didn't get married first. And, as it turned out, I didn't get married until much later.

CHAPTER NINE

Your mother, at seventy-two years old, is taking violin lessons. Yes, to learn to play. "I found a secondhand violin when I used to go junkin. And I found the violin, really new, for twenty-five pesos, I mean dollars." A few weeks later, she is telling you during your weekly phone call, "Mija, can I call you later? They are giving me my first violin lesson. Aha, later, or you can call me." You hang up and laugh, it seems funny to you, surprising, that your mother wanted to learn to play the violin. What a mother I have. Just when you've pinned her down, ZAS! She turns around and surprises you again!

Your father used to sing and play the guitar, and very well in fact. For a while, as a young man, he played and sang on the radio over in Imperial Valley in Brole. Your younger brother, the one who followed you in age, played the cornet and the trumpet, and he was also good at sports, even though he was neither very tall nor well built. When they were young, your sisters had piano lessons, and your brothers learned on their own to play the guitar and the drums. They did a good job playing these instruments during the services at their Pentecostal church. And now, there are grandchildren that enjoy playing the guitar or the piano, and soon, one of them wants to learn, by her own choice, how to play the saxophone. But up until now, no one, neither on your mother's or father's side of the family, that you know of, ever wanted to play the violin. You have to look into it to know for sure. It's true, it's a big, big, family, there may be someone with a violin somewhere. "It's possible, it's possible, that my grandfather played the violin, among other things. He was a flirt and a womanizer, but I think that I heard through the grapevine that he had played lots of instruments." That's what you decide, and you promise yourself to ask Tío Toro to see who remembers.

"We have ministers in Chiapas, too," your son, just back from "checking out" Mexico, tells you while he's commenting about the indigenous and landowner issue in the southern part of the country. They have killed ministers in Peru, he tells you, that group that's fighting against the government called the "Shining Path." "They kill anybody who opposes them, or helps the soldiers. Even when our ministers only gave food. They give sanctuary, according to their conscience." Wanting to play the Good Samaritans cost two ministers in Peru their lives. You remember that your old professor in California, the one who had studied the history of Latin America, always said this about revolutions, "In Latin America, one *chingón*, or big shot, replaces another big shot." In Mexico, your son tells you, they're hungry for the word of God, especially in the big cities, where there is so much poverty. You think that in the outskirts of the cities, "what's true is that they're hungry." For what, you ask your committed son, for what reason do you want to go to such a Catholic country with your new ideas, for what? "One thing, Mom, I won't attack the Virgen de Guadalupe, that's for sure!" "At least he knows a little bit about strategy," you tell yourself about your Alleluia minister son, and you say good bye to him for now, "Let me know where you're going after you leave Texas," because from Texas, family and all, he will go to Guadalajara for the year. "My mission is, now I know for sure, to go to Mexico to evangelize and to convince them of the Word."

Your mom tells you, "He died of cirrhosis of the liver, or something like that," about one of your uncles. He worked all his life, and all his life he drank. He hit the bottle pretty hard the last few years, even though the doctors told him he shouldn't drink. They checked him into a hospital to cure him a couple of times, but he still hit it hard. That's your understanding of how your uncle died. In spite of the alcoholism, you have good memories of that one of your father's brothers. You got to know his wife better, Tía Lita. Yes, the one who defended your mom against them all during the divorce. Now, Tía Lita is in a rest home, the second one their exhausted children are trying out to try to please their mamá. Always of a strong personality and character, Tía Lita skillfully ran her house, the family, and her husband, and according to her children, "We stopped her from controlling us, and Mamá didn't like that. Now she's where she is because we couldn't please her. Pat, we couldn't find a way. We really tried." She was always an independent woman, but ended up crippled after the stroke she suffered a few years ago. Later, I think she suffered a few more. "They didn't want me with them, Pat. I don't have a place to live!" "It's not true! We didn't want her to be alone after the stroke, so we brought her to live with us. And she ran off the housekeeper-nurse that we hired to come and look after her during the day!"

"They leave me alone all day. I don't have anybody, Pat."

"We didn't know what to do, after we gave her an apartment because she insisted she wanted to live alone again, over there near her sisters. We gave her an apartment. And she didn't take care of herself. She didn't eat well; I think she drank a bit or something. Because of that, we couldn't let her live unattended anymore. I tell you, Pat, we tried, we really tried everything. And she's always complaining." You remember the strong woman who invited you to live with her and her children when you were fifteen years old. Your aunt, at that time, was around the same age as you are now.

You remember chatting, in Betaville in your aunt and uncle's house, making cookies and other goodies, and watching Mexican movies. How you laughed at the characters, how you cried at the old Mexican films' melodramatic stories. You jokingly began talking like the Indian women from the movies. "I wann you favor me." "You favor do yourself." Later, when you went back to your house up north your father tells you, "How fat you got, Pat. What were you doing down there with your aunt?" With Tía Lita I felt the warmth of a home where I was given love and support, all balanced by my aunt's company, humor, and strong character.

"My teacher said I know how to hold the violin very well. That I'm an excellent student," your mother has called to tell you about her first lesson on the new instrument, an old violin that is, according to her, in "very good condition, it's like new." "God knows where she found that violin," you tell your husband and María. "She's really happy these days, as if she was a sixteen-year-old again." Your girl-mother has not complained about her husband recently, your second stepfather, that's how happy she is. Later she tells you during another conversation about the violin and what she does with her fingers to play it, "I have a puppy! I forgot to tell you, and wait! Sorry about that. The puppy stayed outside and didn't see me and started to bark like the devil. *Quieto!* Ok, I've brought him in, and he's, I mean she's content. Yes, it's a girl. What? Oh, it's one of those dachsund, wienie-dogs. Yes, I got myself another Chapa, Chapita. You're right, I'd forgotten. Ha, ha. Now I have some-one to take care of me when he's working at night. Yes, she barks, boy does she bark." Well, there you have her, your mother, talking about her overeating, oversleeping lazy husband, her wienie-dog and a violin.

Aurora, a friend since your days in Southwest City, has just told you that she has to have emergency brain surgery. "I have fluid on my brain. They don't know from what!" Within a few days, your most valiant friend is at home, recuperating. This is the friend who has fought demons and injustice, ever since they did a "psychological experiment" on her in the sixties, the one who struggles, as you do with your writing, against mind control. Now, she's in danger of not being able to preserve her being, her intelligence. In the weeks that follow, you realize how much you counted on your friend's moral and professional support. You miss her, her special sense of humor, the long conversations, usually about your stuff, your worries, not hers. You very infrequently had occasion to listen to her problems, her frustrations, her cursing. Once in a while she would tell you about a good conversation she had, or some personal or professional success. You're jealous of the friends she has that live close to her. Your most intimate friends are, all of them, long distance. She always knows about your projects. "You should manage my career," you have told her, half jokingly, and she, always available, would answer, "Oh, sure, as if I have nothing else to do, ha, ha." "As if I had 'a career,' ha, ha," you answer. Her mother died of something related to alcoholism, just like your uncle. "I like to drink," you tell her, and she says, "I guess if a couple of glasses of wine with dinner makes you an alcoholic, I'm one too!" On one occasion you decided that all of your relatives and friends, almost all of them, could be considered alcoholics. "Is it cultural?" you ask Aurora.

A Chicana friend of yours from Texas, Chavela, has told you that when the great Chicano author, XX, finally came to speak at Yale, the first thing he said upon entering the room where all the Chicano students were, was, "Where's the booze?" Well, having arrived talking like that, he was very heartily received by the Chicano students. It was just like being at home, wasn't it?

Your son tells you that there isn't any alcohol at Pentecostal parties. "You don't need alcohol, Mom, when you have the Lord!" Not drugs, pills, sex. Just say NO! "Let's say no," you tell Lulu one time when you were talking about people's simpleton solutions, and you get up, run to the door, and yell, "Noooooooooo!" Later, laughing like crazy, you both go back in the room to have another glass of wine.

In your city, they have just arrested more than a hundred undocumented immigrants at the airport at different boarding gates. The federal agents of the INS, immigration and naturalization, said that they had seen a lot of traffic of people looking like refugees or without papers at the boarding gates, that on many flights there wasn't enough space for such traffic—the flights going, for example, to Chicago, Los Angeles, New York. And later, according to the papers, they apprehended a few of the "coyotes." The majority of the undocumented or refugees were from Mexico, according to the authorities, the rest, from Central and South America who say they're from Mexico and who also say, to confirm this fact with a cultural detail, *"chingar, chingazo, chingado,"* or whatever variant of "to fuck" or "to screw," that expletive verb so "typically Mexican." You laugh, despite the seriousness of what you're reading and hearing. "They really pretended they were Mexican? Did they say something like *'Tú chíngate,'* or worse, *'Chinga a tu madre'* to be convincing?" Maybe they preferred to return to Mexico than to their own country, maybe they thought it'd be better for them. "Maybe they'll be back *mañana* or the day after that."

CHAPTER TEN

Secrets. What one shouldn't tell, ever. You have begun to have bad dreams. They are not just nightmares, rather, you feel, while dreaming or having awakened with a start, that they are somehow evil. These dreams, they scare you, they overcome you. You and your father, in front of an altar, at a mission, something like San Juan Bautista or the Alamo, something like that. You with your father kissing, making what you and your father know that you shouldn't, but you are hypnotized, drugged, controlled by others. These others are there, watching, laughing, taking photos, shooting photos or video. And they control you, making you and your father, AAAAAAAAAYYYYY, Mamaaaaá!

You wake up and try to breathe normally, as you tell yourself, "It's just a bad dream." You only confess your dream to your husband. "That time we went to San Juan Bautista, I felt like I had been there before with Dad. Remember? And I got so anxious." Your husband tells you that they are just "anxiety-pill dreams. You sure have some whoppers!" Lies, all lies, that's what you dream, but in any case they bother you because you know that somewhere in your head there are bad dreams, secrets. It can't be, you try to convince yourself, it can't be, not this time.

Other times, your dreams are simple, just creations of your deepest desires, your truncated fantasies about things that never came to be. You dream, one morning at about three, a bit before waking to use the bathroom, about Vittorio. You are with Vittorio, his perfect little girl all grown up, beautiful and intelligent, just like the two of you. You are with Vittorio and he rips open your blouse or your camisole. And your breasts jump out, warm and pointy. And you take off, also with one pull, his silk embroidered shirt or his silk striped pajama. And you embrace with desire, and you ignite with passion, with . . . And then you wake up. You are making little noises, cooing into the pillow, and your husband picks his head up and says, "Petra, what are you doing? It looks like you're humping the bed!" "Oh, hi, Honey. I was just having one of those weird erotic dreams. What? Oh, I uh, I don't really remember now." Ay, Chihuahua, you think, what "hot" dreams I have! My mother would say I was a loose woman.

"That Petra, she's really wild, watch out. She would even get it on with her own cousins." That's what some of your girl cousins thought about you, I imagine, through a little coaching from their mothers. You remember that one time, at a big family reunion about twenty years ago, when one of your cousins came up to you to say hello with a hug, his sister pulled him back so that he wouldn't get led astray by you. It's not like I was that much of a slut or a whore, like they thought. I never felt up my brothers or my cousins, except for the ones who did it to me when I was really little, when they had the power over us because we were little. But no, I am not talking about those sexual abuse times when they did stuff to us. I'm saying that, in my family, they had given me this fame for being so loose that I'd even seduce my own first cousins. "I can't believe they did that," you tell your mother. "How can they believe that, because of a few mistakes, bad judgment or relationships, that I could. . . . I thought I had 'a dirty mind'!" Anyway, I don't deny that since I was a little girl, I began to fall in love. I wasn't as "wild" as those relatives said I was. Yep, for a few years even my own father called me that. It is true that since I was little I dreamed I was wild, but wild like a bird, a bird of the wild and free.

My "wild" flights varied, as did the dreams, the good dreams and the bad. Sometimes, and this is my favorite version, I am really happy about something and I jump up, and suddenly I go flying wildly above everything and everyone. Everyone is amazed, and I, well, I am really impressed with myself. Other times, I am in danger. They are coming to get me, they are going to kill me, arrest me, beat me up, spit on me, hit me, strip me, and I jump up PIIINNGG! And just like that, I escape whatever danger I was in. Sometimes I bring someone with me, the flight always works so effortlessly, so cool, whatever the situation. Ah, and there's another flight version: many times when I am having a bad dream and I need to get away quickly, all I do is wish it, and I do something like lift my eyebrows, or some other magical face, and my own volition saves me. PIIINNGG! Saved, free! And the bad dream is over, I'm in a safe place, and sometimes, even awake, saved and free, yes sirree.

When I fall in love in my dreams, they have a detail that annoys me, when I wake up. Almost always I am thin, really attractive, more so than any of the other women in the scene. Young? No, I'm not always young, but almost, yes, almost every time, I look fabulous, and no one can resist me. Once awake, I remind myself, "Don't believe in dreams. They're just that, and nothing else. Products of your consciousness, your sub-un-consciousness, nothing else." Mi compañero is convincing me, little by little, that my dreams are my own stupid inventions. I try to collect the good dreams anyway, to pick up the thread, to re-create, for whatever it's worth; I practice "mind control" on myself. "By studying dreams, one sets him or herself free," said one of your therapists. That blond psychiatrist with the tight jeans, from Southwest City. You prefer not to pay attention, but you do take inventory.

What you've learned about the border troubles you in your memories. Once in a while, an image comes into your head, like in scattered and disconnected instant photos. The doctor with the gold tooth, the one who is scraping your womb, telling you between your legs that it would only hurt a little bit. Later, he, that gold-toothed doctor from Nogales, tells you, "You're all right now, you'll just bleed for a couple of days. We're all family, you know, on that side or on this one. We need to be discreet," and, snapping his lips shut he makes a motion of locking it and throwing away the key. They called him to the door, he went out for a second, and from the other side you hear another masculine voice. You suppose right away that it's his son, the dentist. You hear him ask, "Who is she?" And your Mexican doctor, one of the bright lights of the border town responds, "No one. Just one of those girls that doesn't keep herself clean." You take out the thirty silver coins, no, no, you take the three hundred dollars out of your purse, the price you agreed to in your phone call from Southwest City last week. And that's how you learned that even doctors "of your own *raza*" could also lie to you, because by the next afternoon . . .

CHAPTER ELEVEN

This visit, your father can barely walk straight, he's walking curved over to one side, like he's had a stroke. He doesn't recognize you or your sister, but he does recognize your voices when you say, "Papá, it's Pat. Vinnie and Tom are here. We're going to take you out for a few hours. We'll go to Santa Cruz, to the wharf. Okay?" Vinnie takes him on one side, and you on the other, and you walk with him through the hallways in the "home." You've had to sign the file, the list where your father's visitors write who they are, when they take him out, when they bring him back.

At the restaurant on the wharf, where your father has enjoyed clam chowder and fish and chips, you ask him, "Dad, do you know who César Chávez is? Your father pauses, and repeats "César Cháv . . . yes." "Do you know who he is . . . was?" you ask again, and your father, with much difficulty, tries to finish the sentence and tell you what he's thinking. Yes, yes, he remembers the name, he tells you, but he doesn't know who he is—he doesn't remember who he is. "You worked with him, the bail-bonds, remember?" You remind him that that's what he told you. But your father, eyes vacant, just says, yes, yes, I remember the name. Later, after you've all finished eating, you tell Vinnie, I want to ask him something else, I'll explain later why. It's something I'm working on. And you ask your father, before the four of you get up from the table, "Dad, do you know what the sanctuary movement is?" He looks at the three of you, a little confused, and answers you with some effort, "No, I don't know, what is it? It isn't coming to me. What?" "Don't worry, I just wanted to ask you now. Don't worry about it."

Within twenty-four hours of your second abortion, the pains in your abdomen, the contractions, are so strong that Vittorio had to take you to the emergency room. The American doctor who examines you says, "Who did this to you? You've still got parts of the fetus in you, and it looks like whoever did this, did it halfway on purpose, so someone else could clean it up! Who did this half-assed job?" You, staying loyal to "your people," don't say the name of the Mexican doctor who had left, now you know, half of the aborted fetus in your womb. The quack doctor knew you'd have to go to a doctor on this side, so he could finish the "operation," knowing that you, all scared and vulnerable, wouldn't want to say the name. Didn't you promise you would not repeat his name, would be discreet? Discreet or not, in the end you don't tell the American doctor, who, furious, calls Vittorio in to watch the operation, having asked him the name of the villain, and Vittorio, wanting to avoid any legal problems or any others, for that matter, didn't say anything either, and they did the operation more hygienically and completely. The American doctor was mad and scolded both of you for helping out this business of illegal abortions. You had responded, "Well, we couldn't get a legal abortion here!"

One of the times your father, a renegade macho, wanted to get rid of your mother, he put her on a bus to Gilroy. He put the three of you, you just two, your brother just months old, and your mother, on a bus. One of your mother's friends had given her some relatives' phone numbers, and so your mother arrives up north to stay for a couple of weeks with that family.

"It was one of those times that he was in love, and he did it because he was drunk. I knew that was when he was with that other woman, the dark one with the green eyes from 'the other side,' the one he used to show off to all of his friends in the cantina. Sometimes, I worked in the cantina restaurant. No, not the Nogales, the restaurant your Nana had, but the 'Aguila,' the cantina. But I guess when he knew I wasn't going to be there, well, then he would bring in those women. One day, they had called the house a couple of times, and he wouldn't let me answer the phone. All of a sudden, he decided he was going to open the cantina, and he told me that I should stay home that day, that one of the uncles would cook. It seemed really strange, the way he was talking to me without looking at me, and, about noon, I was about to explode. Well, I got dressed and went over to the cantina, and I left you all with my sister-in-law who lived down the street. When I entered the bar, like a hurricane, your uncle who was bartending and a couple three *compadres* who were also there, looked at me all scared. And I, furious, saw that your father wasn't there, but knowing he had to be somewhere around, said, 'And he? Where is he?' And, when nobody said anything, I asked my *comadre* that was serving food, 'You're not going to tell me either?'

"Well, your aunt, Tiá Lita, who would never be made the fool, and wasn't about to cover their asses, pointed towards the back of the room, where the pool tables were. I went straight back, I hadn't seen him yet, but when I got to the back of the room I heard laughter and low voices from the little enclosure that was above the enormous fridge they had back there. I went up the stairs, and there they were, your father and the woman, embracing. I can still see your father's scared face, that woman's, laughing mockingly, the two seemed drunk or something, looking at me, the two of them, idiots.

"Finally, your father gets up and comes toward me saying, 'And you, what are you doing here? Go home.' And he grabbed me by the arm, dragging me out of the cantina, while I was yelling things at him. In a bit, he got to the house, and told me he was gonna fix me, by hook or by crook, that he didn't want me any more, that I was becoming a busybody, that I wouldn't leave him alone, and that's when he sent me, with you two little kids, to Gilroy. He later came back for us, saying it had all been because of the alcohol. What? Why did I stand him? Oh Mija, I was a naïve girl, I didn't know what else to do, and that's why I went back to him. What? No, he wasn't always with those other women. Because when he wasn't drunk, he was a hard worker, very intelligent. He had a good head to do many things. Yes, maybe, maybe I did love him like you say. But when we would hang around those jerks, his womanizing compadres and those women, well he was another person."

CHAPTER TWELVE

The first time I saw a nude couple, I was nine years old. We had gone from the San Joaquin Valley in the north to the Imperial Valley in the south, where some uncles lived. We had gone there to stay for a few days with my uncles Martínez, who had a camp about five miles outside of Betaville, by the fields and ranches. My parents had gone to Mexicali to party with some doctor friends from the other side whom they had met through my Tiá Tacha Martínez. They left us there with my uncles in the camp. It was me, my brother, and Belita, who was still a baby. I didn't want to stay, I wanted to go with them, and I was a little afraid to stay there, with my uncles. She talked a lot and we liked her except that, like my father, she liked to play a lot of jokes on people. I didn't know how to take them nor could I understand half of what she said that made everybody laugh. But my uncle was very quiet with all of us, that's why I didn't feel comfortable about staying behind with them. Well, I was gripped by nostalgia and I started crying when my parents left and

I really cried until my tía got tired of trying to console me, and then she really got upset with me.

Later, quietly but not happily, I slept with my little brother and sister. At night, I woke up to go to the bathroom and I went to the living room where my uncles also slept, and I saw they had the light on, and that they, mi Tía Tacha and her husband, were naked. I thought, "They're *bichis!*" Because I didn't know that word *nude* at the time, so I thought, "They're naked!" And I walked, fascinated, to the big can they had as a bedpan. No, they still hadn't installed a toilet, sink, shower, and all that stuff. They didn't even have their own kitchen. At the time, they only had a few rooms attached to the barracks where they had the big dining room and the kitchen for the braceros. That's where my tía ran the kitchen for the braceros and her own family. In general, everyone ate the same thing. As I was saying, the night I saw my aunt and uncle naked, I sat on the bedpan and I stared and stared at them. And I started to feel ashamed but I didn't know why. Her skin color was really pretty, it was all even, she lay face up, her big *chichis* (that's how I knew them at the time) fell to the sides, her swollen womb, long legs with a dark area in between that I didn't know was there. My uncle, face down, looked big and muscular, tan and dark, except a little lighter on his back, his robust buttocks barely tanned, and his hairy, hairy legs . . . you could see where his shirt left a tan line, because his arms were two colors, lighter on top, and darker, below. Fascinated, but feeling that I shouldn't be seeing this, and at the same time I wanted to and I didn't want to look, so I got up quietly and went to my bed with my brother and sister.

That night I also wet the bed, and for many days I couldn't even look my aunt in the face. I didn't understand how she could go around just the same as before, telling jokes, smiling and making fun and flirting with her enormous breasts, and treating us good-heartedly, like always, "Come here, Mija, eat this rice. Take this tortilla, you'll see how good they came out." All the while I knew what I had seen, that, without clothes, surely they had done something weird to fall asleep like that, all naked, so far beyond my understanding. There, the feeling that they had done something bad to have fallen asleep like that began to grow in my childish heart, and left me, for many days afterward, feeling ashamed, confused, and in some way betrayed. I'm not sure, but I have imagined that if I were to tell Tía Tacha now, so many years later, what I had done that night, that I had spied on them, she'd probably crack up, laugh, and make fun of my infantile thoughts.

You start making plans to interview women from the camp, farmworkers, just as you had planned to do about the sanctuary movement, to ask them what they were doing now, where and how they had lived during the harvest, if they had changed due to their experiences back then, how and off of what they lived now. You would begin by asking questions like that. "When I find one, I'll ask whatever questions come to me, to see what I learn."

One of your friends' moms has called you, "They left me alone, and I got tired, and I said, 'Who can I call?' And, well, I said, Pat, even though I don't know her well, I wanted to talk to somebody. Is this a local call, d'you know?" You assure her that she can talk all she wants, since the call is not long distance, and your friend Laurel's mom says to you, "You know how Laurel likes to be alone. She doesn't even have a phone anymore, it's better that way, so people won't bother her." So, we talked for a long time about what Laurel was doing now, about her pets, etc., and how dedicated Laurel was to her painting, her art. Her mom mentions, while you listen to her, still surprised that she had called you, that she was from that ranching area where Laurel was. You like listening to the pleasant cadence of her voice, at first more English than Spanish. You tell her you're gathering stories about farmworker life and try to get her to talk to you in Spanish, curious about what she would have to say. And she, the mother, explains to you, in a slow and deliberate Spanish that "we were from there, where Laurel is now." Where? "Near where my father had a little ranch."

"Farmworkers? Yes, we picked cotton, sugar beets, tomatoes, corn. The cotton? Oh, my father used to sell it. Yes, he would pay us. He had a lot of brothers and sisters. They would gather the cotton in packs, and from the money I earned, I would make myself dresses, long dresses, for going to dances. I used to like the dances a lot. Later, as a grown-up, when my sisters got married, they would take me to the 'grown-up dances.' What? Oh, that's how they called those dances for older people, where the married people used to go. And they would take me there. And later, as a married woman, I would also go with my husband, even though he doesn't dance anymore, or hardly ever. Oh, yeah, I liked to dance the 'in' steps. We don't know how to do them anymore, but at the time, I knew the jitterbug and things like that. He? No, he was never much of a dancer, and he doesn't know how to cook. He can't even boil water. Well, when I get sick, he might make me a couple of eggs, but he doesn't cook for himself, he goes out. Oh, yeah, at a party he might dance a couple of songs with me, but he doesn't like anything like that, and cooking, not at all."

One night you dream that you are going to take part in a focus group, a meeting with those committed Chicanos interested in bettering the situation of the Chicano community. Your dream turns surreal, how funny, a very dreamy dream, how redundant. You are taking part in your first focus group when they start playing a ball game, softball or hardball, you don't remember which the next day upon waking and thinking about what you dreamed. But, in your dream, you do remember this, that they were going to play a baseball game, and you see that others get up to bat, and hit real hard, to hit some home runs for your team. You imagine yourself hitting the ball hard with the bat, really hard, a fabulous success, really big, and everyone would admire you. Your turn comes, and you are afraid of not hitting the ball hard, good enough, and you are afraid, like when someone says to you, "Do it; you'll feel better." And your turn comes, when, when the call comes from the left of the field, I mean left field, for everyone to come together for your first meeting. Your first focus group, when you have to go pee. Yes, you have to urinate, when at the same time you have to attend your first focus group. At the same time. Pee. You wake up. From your dream, I mean, and you have to go pee. Good-bye dream, good-bye focus group. Gotta go piss.

part three

Sanctuary and Resolution

"Who are you all? Are you Communists? What do you want anyway?"

Thus evoking your own guilt and memories of the Huelga of the sixties, when Chávez passed through, with the March of Delano and his farmworkers, you realize then that there is still one last step for you to take. You have already been gathering conversations and memories of friends and students who were farmworkers during these more recent years working at the university. Many times, the case was that he or she was from the valleys in California also, or had come from over there by Yuma or some other small agricultural town. "This is it, time to come through," you say to yourself, now you've got to pay your debts, give them a voice, let it be known through your recollection of those voices what it takes to fulfill a dream, reach a goal that so often is denied to them, starting in their own home.

Sanctuary, a safe place, where hope can bloom, gives birth to positive attitudes, where is that, where was it found, keeps on being discovered, by others like you. You, Petra, who now must absolutely participate, not stay behind asleep, must finally spit at hopelessness, deny the negativity of death, and of the bad that happened to all of you. With a set purpose, you begin the final piece of this search and journey.

My father lived for several years in those asylums, in a manner of speaking. His humor, his old real self coming in and out as we slowly lost him. The night that my father burned his house down, he had been drinking. His second wife, that beautiful redhead mexicana with green eyes he loved, had died too, the year before, and their home had been signed over to another family member. We suspected, we wondered: When? Who did the signing? Was Dad drunk? What couldn't he remember? Papá, prideful, grieving, drunken vengeful, bereft, was caught later on the day of the fire, sitting in front of the smoldering place, open whiskey bottle beside him on the seat. "Pat?" your stepsister Cecilia calls, "Dad, my . . . your dad is in jail. Well, it's a hospital lockup facility. He was drinking, there was an argument, he tried to burn their house down. I think you better come. . . ."

Inexorably, death does strike us. After more than a decade of fearing the effects of my father's illness, we lost him to a death that ultimately was yearned for as a release.

Years ago, when your father burned his house down, you were barely starting to write a book which was to be about the sanctuary movement, but it had led to this journey. Years later, on the road to your father's funeral in Salmas, you're overcome by the memories of your parents, happy moments as well, healing memories now that the final hour had come. You recalled the many times that he, still healthy, robust, would invite you for Chinese food, or to go to Monterey Bay to eat seafood at the wharf. When you were youngsters way back in Betaville, it would be, "Let's go to Mexicali for Chinese dinner at the Shangri-La," or "Let's go for *caguama* tacos 'to the other side.'" This last meal was greasy tortoise meat, the tortoises being imported inland from Ensenada or a closer bay. You didn't like caguama, but just as with menudo for their hangovers, your father and uncles loved to go for caguama to Mexicali every so often, on a Sunday. Mexicali was close by on the Mexican side of the border, "the other side" they called it. And these short trips and festive family outings, your parents together, sometimes accompanied by uncles or cousins, was something you later recalled occasionally. You also recalled always, the puns, jokes or funny stories that Papá had or invented in his humorous, ever-changing repertoire.

You remember also that your father loved boxing, and every so often he would take your mother along, if not also one or more of your uncles or amigos. Once, your mother recounted a particular boxing match, upon their return. "One of the boxers seemed to have a cold or something, I don't know what, but mucous started to come out his nose. The onlookers were getting rowdy, frustrated, and stupid, and they were shouting all kinds of stuff. Well, the boxer seemed to be trying to sniff the mucous back up his nose, while he moved and shifted from there to here, back and forth, but he really couldn't control the snot. Finally, someone out in the arena yelled out, 'Giv'im a punch, you yo-yo snot dummy!' or something like that." Mamá made us laugh with this one, even though boxing wasn't her favorite thing, and we're sure she did it just to go out with Dad. Still, even now, amongst Mother and our brothers and sisters, someone might say, "Come on now, punch'im out, yo-yo boogers!" or "Wipe your nose, yo-yo snot!," something like that, or even simply, "Hey, you yo-yo booger!" etc.

One of the students you later interview for a book on farmworker students who make it to the university, Jesús, tells you that Cesar Chavez (they called him by his English pronunciation, not "César Chávez," as in Spanish) was also a boxing aficionado. It's an interesting detail, you told Jesús, that a practicing pacifist, believer in the philosophies of Martin Luther King and Mahatma Gandhi, would enjoy such a bloody sport as boxing. But then, you reminded yourself that many a Mexican or Chicano found boxing to be highly enjoyable, and certainly in your family, there were many aficionados. "So Dad and César Chávez had something in common, besides farmworking and bail-bonds," you say to yourself.

Your friend, Ana G., had worked twenty-five years for an electric company and was among the first of those you interview. She tells you that for many years they were campesinos. "Went up there around Fresno, California, to pick raspberries." You ask her, not knowing where they found raspberries in California, how she knew they were raspberries, and she says, "Our hands were stained, that's how I 'member. I was the youngest, but I 'member. What? Oh, yeah, my father was a miner before, but he went to Coolidge, and it was there we stayed, working for a long time, in the cotton fields. Whad I do? Well, when I was very little, I used to, like, they would let me go in front of my dad, making little balls of the cotton that had fallen to the ground in the rows. How? Like this, look. I would pick up the little pieces and I would make them into bigger balls and I would give 'em to my father for his bag. They, the older ones, would pick from the plants. They told me to make balls from the stuff on the ground. For many years in Coolidge, my father worked with my uncles, doing stuff at the ranch. He drove tractors, I think.

"It was in Coolidge that I learned to drive by myself, when my father would get drunk. That was fun! My pa', you know, was a drinker, would get drunk all the time, and I was alone once, when I was 'bout eleven. I don't know why my ma' or nobody was there. Musta been visitin' neighbor buddies, but I was alone with my pa' and he wuz drunk 'n asleep. I went in quietly and took the keys outta his pants because he was always 'round the house in just his underwear. I don't know why. And there was the car, and I got in and left, jumpin,' jerkin' and stoppin', trying to do as I had seen my ma' and pa' do with the gear shift. Up meant forward, to the side meant faster. The first time I cun't go backwards, and I thought 'How my gunna do it?' And so, I just went in circles and then back home. Nobody found out, and they din't know later that I wuz watchin' them o'er their shoulders to see what they did to drive. That's how I saw 'em go backwards. I learned by rememberin' stuff in my head, how they moved the gear shift.

"That's how I went for the, what do they call her, the birth'n woman? She was American. My sister that lived with us wasn't married, and she started to—yes, have the baby, and my pa', I don' know, I don' remember if he was drunk, or 'cause nobody was home, only me, my ma', and my brother. And when my ma' said, 'I can't leave her alone. Who's gonna go for the doctor?' And I jumped, reeeeel excited, 'cause I knew howta drive. 'I know, I know, I'll go for the birth'n woman!' And I went, barely eleven years ol'. What? Oh, I knew where to find the birth'n woman. Coolidge was real small back then. The birth'n woman—oh, the word is *midwife?* Whatever! What's funny, wuz that my brothers or cousins or whoever came and they made us watch TV, they din' even answer our questions, about what was gonna happen to my sister Berta. It wuz funny 'cause it was a small three-bedroom house, really small. Well, we were poor, I guess, but we didn't think about it. Well, now that I remember, I don't see how they thought we weren't gonna fin' out what was happenin', 'cause there were noises, no, not screams, *pero* sounds, you know, so anyhow, we found out, because later we heard the baby, and they came out with this package of newspapers and ma' said, 'Don't look.' But we were just little kids and later, we went over t' snoop where the package wuz buried. We dug it up, but we saw there were bloody things inside and we din't want to see no more. We covered it up 'gain with dirt. Weren't they funny? They thought we weren't gonna find out, an' there we were, on the other side of the curtain, pretendin' to watch TV! Later, we came to Guadalupe, and since then the family's bin here."

Ana was abused by the only husband she ever had, for ten or eleven years. She divorced him, and later, with all of her hard times, with her drunken father, who made them pour the booze down his throat when he was sick, and her being so young then, and with the years she spent with her womanizing, alcoholic, and moody husband, she ended up like a lot of people with the same story. And it's not because of genetics, no sir, I don't believe in those cases, I know it didn't happen to all of them. It hurts me, I know that deep down, many suffer. Ana turned out to be bisexual or lesbian, in the end. And I love her a lot, she's become a member of my family. *Don't tell anyone.* Oh, yeah, in her own family there were those who would gossip, and her mother came to find out.

So, finally, Ana had to tell her mom something like, "Have you heard something, Ma'? Okay, tell me what you heard. Well, yeah, I'm one of them. It's true, Ma', don't cry!" Ana told me that both of them cried for a while, they hugged, and a little later, relieved by the tears, the weekly routine of driving her to the supermarket, they started to talk, to gossip about the people they saw on the street in the town, and that on the way back to her house, she says to Ana in a tempting, soft, and sweet voice, "Aren't you staying to eat with me? I made tortillas yesterday, doncha want any, mijita?" And that's how, without any more explanation, the whole controversy ended about what Ana, the youngest, most responsible, hardworking of all the sons and daughters was or wasn't.

Ana said that as far as going further than high school studies, her father was vehemently against it. "What for? Just to get yourselves pregnant? What do you need college for? Go to work!"

Mari L., another very intelligent Chicanita, chubby like you, studies with you during her second year at the university, and tells you something else. A bit reserved in class, both she and her brother have told you that their father, to the contrary, wanted them to educate themselves, to prepare themselves, to come here. "Yep, we worked in the field, it was hard. And my father said that we should get ahead, go to school." You ask her, "And your mom? Did your mom want you to go to school? Didn't she want you to stay with them, help out with all the work, you know, like in most families?"

Several students have told you that during vacation they still go to the field to earn money for school expenses, for the rent. "Well you know...."

"So what's new?" you ask another tall, dark Chicanita student from Parker, a small agricultural town next to the Colorado River. "How are your other classes going? You can ask your parents about Spanish, about what we study. Why did you come to the university?" etc., etc.

Estela D. answers, "No way! My father never wanted to help at all! And he has a business over there; he has land and fields and sells his harvests. Look, here's his business card, you see, 'A & Z Farms,' that's us. Yep, no way! He doesn't give a single penny to my mom, can you believe it? He keeps it all, I can't believe him; that's how he is with her. And I fight with him. Yes, I don't know why my mom doesn't leave him, really. I don't know why." Estela's brother was also in my classes before and after her, and he talked to me about his farmworking origins without scorn or anger. Of the two of them, the older sister and younger brother, motivated in class when they wanted to be, he was the one to babble and horse around. "Listen to this," Estela told you. "Just listen, my dad keeps my mom in a trailer with a rotting floor, and he won't give her any money to fix it. He's so tight, he just says, 'Bring me the meals. Where's my ironed shirt? I have to go out.' Just like that. No way! Who knows where he keeps the money, Teacher? I don't know! But any for me or my mom? No way!"

Estela and her brother, both activists and gutsy as hell, supported Cesar's Farm Worker's Union, the UFW, as do others. "But what a bum deal, *Maestra*, just imagine!"

A few years back, Emilia C. comes to do her graduate studies in Chicano culture and literature, and you invite her to your house, you meet her for soda and French fries, and that's how you become friends. A tall woman, in her thirties, and of a brusque and simple personality, she was from New Mexico, but had lived and worked for the Union in California. "I was an organizer," she told me. "I met César and others that lived at the headquarters. Why don't I say good things about them? Well, the truth is, that I didn't get along with Pasionara, the leader. And some of them started to play mind games, as a hobby, in some of the meetings at the headquarters. And, well, I didn't keep quiet, and I got in a fight with some of them. Well, I know about a lot of things that didn't seem right to me. And I left, yes, yeah, sure I met them firsthand, I met them, César, Pasionara, the head honchos. Well, disgusted, I went back to my home—to New Mexico. I came here, like I've told you, because they told me y'all were here, and they recommended you to me. The thesis, the work I have to write, the exams, well, that's why I came to talk to you."

After her comprehensive exams she fights with her director, and she stops by to ask you to help her finish her degree, that she wants to change her topic to *los corridos.* And, after lots of pushing and pulling, and a few knocks upside her head, she finished her degree. I've heard tell she's still a community activist, fighting and kicking ass.

Nikka L., a small, determined young girl with short curly hair, calls you when she's in her last year at Wellesley College on the East Coast of the United States. She tells me that she's originally from California in the San Joaquin Valley like me, and she says, "I'm doing my senior thesis on your novel, and I'd like to interview you." In our first talk, she tells you, "My family was also against the strikes in the Valley. Yeah, I remember they called us 'scabs'; it was like a really bad word—'strike-breakers,'" she said, but in her last classes at Wellesley, she read a lot, and now with your novel, she has changed her mind about the UFW and wanted to talk to you as a Chicana writer who had come from the same background, etc.

Later, after graduation, she updates you: "Now I teach in the same school the farmworkers' children went to in *The Grapes of Wrath,*" your new little friend tells you. She tells you that that modern school is right next to the labor camp. Yes, the one where those from *The Grapes of Wrath* had lived. In those long-ago years of the Depression, during the Dust Bowl, farmworkers from that place that Nikka is telling you about were not Chicanos or Mexicans, but "Okies." These impoverished peo-ple had also emigrated, but from Arkansas, Oklahoma, from way over there. "I like teaching there, but it's hard because my family needs my help, my salary. I just got them a little house. At least it's their own. But it's hard to get along with my dad and my mom. She doesn't help me much either. Yeah, they're proud of my education, but I think the rela-tives are jealous. I don't know what to do now. Like . . . I would like to do my master's, but, well maybe we can talk sometime?" Then, "Sometimes, those little kids, they really make me feel good when they learn, and they look up to you, you know?"

You answer, "Yes, I know."

"If you have any other question, *Maistra*, well you know how to reach us."

You, fifty-something, fat, wrinkled and tired, know that, yes, you still have a lot of questions, and that everything is not possible, that everything cannot be done or at least not at the very moment you wish it so badly. But besides that, ha, ha, ha, ha, I have made mistakes and some big, big ones, and I know well that not everything can be done. Why not give it a try? And not do drugs, abuse, and violent acts, like many of us learned in our neighborhood, in our school, or in our own home.

Pablito, your father's youngest brother, is recovering from cancer surgery. Weak himself from the chemotherapy, he began again to visit your father regularly, and reported recently, "Your Dad looks real bad. He may not last much longer." Your father, they tell the family, does not have Alzheimer's but still some form of dementia—loss of memory— signs of madness, flashes, pin drops of lucidity, sudden violence, weak limbs, vacant stares, then suddenly, "All the way from Southwest City, huh?"

"Dad, you know who this is?"

"Why sure!"

"You know who's calling?" Then, often, silence, and one of your aunts says, "Last week, your dad didn't even talk, he just stared ahead." Dementia, demented, loss of speech. It all started a long time ago. One of your daughters utters your own flickering fear, "Can it happen to me?" Years ago . . .

Aurora? Aurora is now one of the most vocal activist Chicanas *mujeres fuertes* in the Southwest University region. She told you recently, reminded about what she had told you and what you had written, that the psychological experiment had been as she had told you except for one detail, a terrible detail: it had not been her friend, Myra Greenfield, the Jewish girl, whom she had just seen in Paris this past summer, who had betrayed her with the rest of the class that one time. It had been her Cuban girlfriend, Hilda, daughter of an aristocratic family. Remembering again, Aurora utters: "It was my best friend, the only other Latina there, who betrayed me! Myra was the only one they couldn't convince to change her version of what she had seen! It was my loyal friend, Hilda, the Cuban! I swore, after that, to never let anyone convince me of something that I damn well knew was right or not. That single event was a catalyst, but give me a break! A psychological experiment, a cultural weakness. FUCK THEM!"

Remembering the incident about the homeless crazy lady on La Llorona bridge in Las Vegas, Aurora says, "Guess what the crazy lady asked? She wanted to know if I was doctor, or something, because they were the only ones that were nice and listened to her!" Laughing, I admitted to Aurora, "Well, Doctor Bustamante, I'm one 'crazy' lady that's grateful you're still there to help me figure out the 'nitty-gritty', and 'kick butt'!"

The lesbian daughter of your friend Meche calls you and says that she's read some of your manuscript. "I think you got it right on getting the gay issue out there, Pat, but there's one important thing that's wrong. I loved that woman first, through my head. It wasn't really the drugs or the alcohol. We fell for each other. I mean, if there was a seduction, it was 'cause of the things we could tell each other and all that she knew so much more about. And I fell in love that way first. What? Like La Malinche? Yeah, I told my 'amá that you needed to 'get it straight'! Ha, ha, yeah, that's a switch, isn't it?" You are already now tying the pieces together, and you remember that for many years you had resisted telling about what was prohibited and terrifying. So many memories.

And leaving us thunderstruck and bereft, we lost Jesús, my student, in a tragic accident as he was on the road to a patriotic fiesta one summer. Talking about what Jesús, the Movement, her community, and the university meant to her, his closest friend, Vickie Dee, recently said to me, "I miss talking to him, and his sense of humor. I know he wasn't perfect, like Cesar, he was just a man, but Jesús was my inspiration, and *he was* my 'sanctuary', you know?"

And now, not long after the loss of your father and Jesús, your mother is losing all her memories of her youth in New Mexico. You begin to miss her love and gift of recounting the stories of her mischievous children, her own struggles, and your hardworking but errant father.

Her being is slipping away, as it happened also to your father. "Mom! Do you know what day this is? Do you know where you are? What month is this?" She, head and hands shaking, stammers that no, "Eh? No, no, I don't know exactly, no. . . ." It stalks us, it awaits us.

This is what you gave me, Papá, the desire and will to keep on going to school, to the university, as far as my own faults and failings would let me. "I don't want you working in the fields! I told you, Woman, that I don't want them to be like us, let them go to school!" You remember all this anew, in the days just before your father's death. During the funeral, the mariachis you've arranged for play solemn songs. You and your companion Bob had arranged for them to play during the funeral service and at the cemetery burial. The only request you made was that the mariachi play "Cielito Lindo" and "Allá en el Rancho Grande," in memory of the songs that your father still remembered during those last years when you would travel to California to take Dad out from whatever place he was "asylumed" for a visit and a meal.

You all tried to visit him or take him out for his birthdays, and one of the last times, before that final year when he was bedfast and silently strapped to curb the last symptoms, you were sitting in the car with the radio on. The radio began playing *música* Latina or salsa, and your father started clapping his hands to the rhythm from his seat in the back. He was sitting between your daughter, María, and your sister Belita, and we all burst out laughing, because the faster the music got, your father accelerated his clapping rhythm perfectly with the beat: "Tatatá-tatá! Pas-paspás-pas!" and so forth. "Let's see, Dad, how does 'el Rancho Grande' go?" somebody asked. He started to sing right on pitch, Alzheimer's infirmity and all. We loved it, because he'd always whistled or sung, except if he was reading, talking, or really drinking hard. So it was that you requested his own music, that last day that you went to see him at the funeral.

After the service at the cemetery, they give you, the eldest of his children, the American veteran's flag, which had been neatly folded into a triangle and placed besides Papá in the coffin. He had been in the Navy during the Second World War, the first years of your life, you remembered. Your brother Samuelito takes the flag from the coffin, brings it to you with a fond smile, you take it startled, not expecting this, uttering "Oh! For me? Oh . . . Papá!" You began to sob, cradling this last final gift from your father against your breast. The mariachi began playing a joyful "Rancho Grande," followed by the wistful "Cielito Lindo."

In the old Betaville grammar school, that Georgian mansion in my memories, we still used to have to salute the flag, and I remember it hanging there, every day. . . . I didn't know what racism, exploitation, or even patriotism meant back then. Papá said he had fought to defend the flag, and he became naturalized in the service. "That's when I became a citizen, *sabes?*" And his own family had first begun toiling in the fields themselves, as young people, just like many of the farmworkers now do. Your mother, too, was out picking in the fields, and she would recall, "We'd wear bandannas on our head, long-sleeved shirts, God what sunburns we'd get ourselves, and your back, you can just imagine how we'd return home each night!" She and Dad met while she was also cleaning some big boss's house; like my Grandma before her, that's the work she did when she met my father down in the Imperial Valley, so many years ago. This was before the years when they ran the small businesses for my Nana Petra, and later as I've told you, they began working the agriculture business "from another angle," as labor contractors for braceros and campesino families.

After the funeral, we went to Monterey, to the wharf. There, in one of Dad's favorite restaurants, we chatted quietly and then began laughing little by little, making peace with our own memories of Don Samuel Leyva, the great and complicated man of flesh and bone. "He was something else!" we all agreed. We began to pitch in his acts of kindness and love, in spite of never being one to tell you that he loved you except in his last few years while he could still speak. We noted the change happily, because Esmeralda in fact had told us that Dad thought it was corny to tell people "I love you" all the time. We recalled their many acts of generosity. Even when they'd had to start over, back in the States from Mexico, they always had the heart and made room to take in needy friends or family. "Remember? Remember?" "Remember the time he gave me the old Ford Torino after I graduated college, that year Marisa and I were so broke?" Once, a *Chicanito* gas attendant admired the Torino, saying, "Hey, man, a stick-shift Torino! Cool low-rider material, lady!" "Remember the time he brought my kids some furniture 'cause he and Esmeralda knew we couldn't afford it?" "Remember the strawberries he'd give us when we went to Salmas to visit?" "Remember how he'd drive around with his favorite poodle on his lap?" Dad did love pets, and he adored children, talking to them, teasing them. One time, after one of my miscarriages, he and Esmeralda came to the county hospital to see me. Mom stayed downstairs, "out of their way" she said. Papá said very little, not even one joke; I was in grave condition, and his silence to me meant that he was very worried, seeing me feverish, still and pale. He left me some money, which I slipped under the pillow and gave to my grateful mother, who was housing me and my two small kids at the time. We both knew what being pregnant and out of wedlock and living off welfare food meant, at that time. Memories and secrets. Some good, some bad, but still some funny ones and all our own.

Vinnie said recently, "Dad would have thought it was hilarious, what happened in our sanctuary, the church I mean, last year." I asked her what she meant, although I knew full well Dad was familiar with the *alleleya* or "Holy Ghost" services from his own youth. His family had lived by such a church when he was in Brole, before they moved to Betaville. He joked about the shouting and music and clapping and screams heard during the neighboring church's services. Vinnie was saying, "Tom and I had just attended the police dog training academy championships, and we had really enjoyed them, over in that town where we live. Well, a couple of weeks later we were in the middle of a huge revival service, and the whole church was rocking, 'Praise the Lord! O thank you, God! Glory, glory, Shalala! . . .' and so on, really tearing it up in full-out worship. People just worshipping with the Holy Ghost in them, I tell you what, and then suddenly Tom and I saw this raggedy, dirty-looking guy run up the middle aisle, throw down some bags in front of the altar, right between two of the ministers up there worshipping. The guy clasps his hands in prayer, then starts to stomp on the bags which started blowing out whitish powder, then two dogs, police dogs, came running up the aisle and right up to the raggedy guy's legs. Then several policemen, some in uniform and some in street clothes, came running up, struggled with the crazy guy still trying to stomp on the powdery bags, grabbed him, and took him out of one of the side exits up by the altar! I told Tom, 'Look, it's Sandy, the champion dog from the police academy contests, up there, grabbing that skuzzy guy!'" Vinnie had us laughing by now, and as we're choking, saying, "I can't believe it, in church, really?" And stuff like that. Then she adds, "Do you believe it? Most of the people in that service didn't even realize what was going on, because they were so taken up in worshipping, the Holy Ghost in'em and all that, you know? Afterwards, some of us that had seen were laughing so hard, and Tom and I most of all, because I had recognized the police dog!" We all agreed that Dad would have loved the story. Mom, well, she was just aghast when she heard this one. "Don't people have any respect any more for the Lord? Humph!"

Actually, Mother had a funny story or two about priests and such.

This one has varied a little over the years with Mom, but she brings it up from time to time. "Once, your father and I took the priest, his Irish drinking buddy from the church across from where we lived in New-dale, to your Tía Lita's Mexican restaurant. He and your dad got plas-tered as usual, so I drove them home, setting a covered paper plate with a big fat tostada on the seat, next to the priest. Well, the two drunks were joking and laughing and trying to sing on the way home, which was only a few blocks. When we got to the rectory, where the priest lived, he picks up his hat, and what do you think? The whole tostada fell from his hat onto his head, and he had chile, beans, meat, and lettuce all over him. And the two drinking buddies laughed, too, but not as hard as I did, old stinkin' priests! And to think that the following year, I went to that same old drunk priest, to ask for understanding and coun-sel when I was thinking of leaving your dad, because I'd gotten fed up with his foolin' around! The priest said, 'Your husband, Sam, said you'd found a new man, some blond guy up in Masterton, izit so, me lady? Well, you're nothin' but a lying whore woman, that's what you are!'" So my mother soon after "got the Holy Ghost" at a new friend's church in a neighboring town, and since then, she's "been saved."

But it was my father who went to my spelling bees and most school functions. He took me, in fact, to my very first day at school, saying I was older than I actually was, so I wouldn't miss out on the new year in first grade. No kindergarten in that old Betaville school. Dad. Mother. He gave me the will to do more than work in the fields. I was pregnant and lived on welfare food for a couple of hopeless years. I know I had been a disappointment to both of my parents, but I have come to for-give them, not being "spotless" myself.

Dad gave me inspiring dreams. Mom tolerated my ambitions, then. Now, although she can barely reason, she respects us and our schooling. What they gave us was a will to live, that stubborn zest and persistence that ran in both of them.

Not death. Lust, secrets, love, memories, good intentions, challenges, change, what I can and can't, what I will, what I won't. *Life* is my business. Her/Your daughter in torment, her/your beautiful child, so now I can't forget and the clippings and notes and this testimony, this fictional autobiography, this RECORD, talk, talk, talk, and I fear their loss, I FEAR, I FEAR, still death is here all around, yet distant, until that very moment. YOU HAD WANTED TO, they lived life, they wanted to live BELOVED all our/my beloved and I begin to write "The Taboo Stories," and again set out to interview campesino/campesina students about their families, their fathers, mothers, brothers/sisters, amigos/amigas. Their beloved. And how and if their lives had changed. And you remember from the Movement something that reminded you, shook you out of, yearned to believe in: *For Life.* You say to yourself, writing, "I don't care what *you think,* all you *mother/daughter fuckers* out there. Just for today, LIFE is all I can handle."

And today, this new day, you recall your father and your other beloveds who have gone away forever except in your memory, the thousands of your *pueblo* of many colors who searched for what you searched—a safe place, a harbor, a sanctuary, a way to keep on forward, with energy, with love, and the words of your father that remote day, but as if it were yesterday, and you bust out laughing also your father's laugh, and it lifts you, renews you forward, the memory, *this new day:*

"Look at this damn pigeon without a leg, look how he jumps and eats and flies more than the rest of them, ha, ha, how cool. Look, *ay va,* there he goes, look how high! Ha, ha, ha!"

♥

This English version of *Sanctuaries of the Heart* was translated from the original Spanish by Barbara Riess and Trino Sandoval, in collaboration with the author. The Spanish version follows on the next page.

Sanctuarios del Corazón

Para mi padre fallecido, Jesús Cota, mi muy querida amiga, Tey Diana Rebolledo, y mi esposo, Tom Parrish, todos quienes me han dado apoyo e inspiración durante mis años de escritora.

♥

No rechaces al amor
aunque ya no creas
aunque ya ni esperas
Nos ronda
un abrazo tan ancho tan ancho
que no siente fronteras.

MARGARITA COTA-CÁRDENAS
Marchitas de mayo, 1989

La muerte no es mi asunto

La noche que mi papá quemó su casa, pues yo apenas coleccionaba trozos de periódicos y apuntes para mi novela, que iba a ser sobre el movimiento del Santuario. Me llamo Petra Leyva, me llamo así por mi Nana, una mexicana *fuerte*, de mucho carácter, de Sonora, y por mi Tía Leyva, conocida entre nuestros parientes por sus *witty retorts* ocasionales y su *sharp tongue* frecuente. Plática, plática, plática. . . memorias y secretos, tantas/tantos memorias y secretos.

El escribir, el tratar de resolver las inquietudes, lo que siento, por medio de mi papeleo, me ocupa muy irregularmente, casi siempre como remolinos de viento que me agarran, me estrujan pa'quí pa'llá y zácate! pas! de repente estoy frente a frente con lo que estaba queriendo no ver o reconocer. Y así con mi novela, salió no ser sobre el movimiento del Santuario mismo, sino resultó ser sobre lo que es "santuario," y en el proceso descubrí terribles, a veces cariñosos, memorias y secretos, y me trajo aceptación de la noche que mi Papá, borracho y vengativo, prendió un fósforo y lo tiró en el piso de su sala, destruyendo los retratos que allí tenían, tal vez nuestras cartas, y por seguro quemando los muebles *doilied* afrancesados de su difunta esposa.

"Pues, para empezar, mi padre no ha muerto todavía, pero como que se nos está yendo, así así. Nosotros eso lo podemos ver, cuando lo vamos a visitar. Sí podría decirles que está en un lugar como de descanso. Aquí les llaman *rest homes*. Son casas para ancianos, también les llaman asilos o santuarios. . . como donde ponen a la gente loca de a tiro, como *asylums*. El nunca había pensado, ante nosotros, sobre si lo iban a meter en uno de esos lugares o no. Me imagino que nos habría dicho, si lo hubiera pensado antes, que no le pegaba bien la idea. Cómo ocurrió que lo metieron, así como por fin fue, pues a ver si me animo a contarles. El ya lleva más de ocho años allí, y todo empezó por una serie de eventos raros y tristes. Pero de veras pienso que empezó todo hace muchos años, más antes. . . Yo sueño en poder sacarlo de aquel manicomio, digo aquella casa de viejos en marcha. Así como él vino y me sacó del Convento del Buen Pastor cuando yo tenía apenas unos siete, ocho años. Cuánto hace, cuánto hace, a ver. . . unos cuarenta-cincuenta años atrás, allá en Nuevo México, sí seguro, cuando visitábamos a los tíos por Las Cruces, Mesilla. Yo creo que, allá entonces, mi'apá sabía que yo los esperaba, que no aguantaba estar allí encerrada con aquellas industriosas, tercas monjas. Así, así, me gustaría poder hacerlo con él, como cuando él vino por mí. Sentía que me había *salvado*, sabes. . ."

Estás viendo que tu padre está contento esta mañana allí en el wharf de Monterrey, un día bonito de la playa en California, y los pichones volando y saltando hasta el brazo de tu papá que extiende una cajita de esquite. Todos se ríen, tu papá gozando los pichones, los pichones tan acostumbrados a los turistas que ni les tienen miedo. Tus hermanas tomando fotos del papá dándoles de comer a los pichoncitos, tu madre escondiéndose para que no platique tu padre con ella. Exclama jubilosamente tu papá, "Mira este carajo pichón sin una pata, cómo salta y vuela y come más que los demás! Mira nomás, qué suave, qué vivito, ja, ja!" Después se cansan con los pájaros, caminan por el muelle con sus tiendas de turismo, y tu hermana Vinnie pregunta, "What time do we have to get Dad back to the rest home?" "Not til tonight, but we have to leave him off on the way to take Pat back to the airport in San José" dice

Ben, el esposo de tu hermana Belita. Tu padre interpone, exclamando: Pues no se vayan tan temprano, you trying to get rid of the old man, ja, ja. . .?

Caminando hacia los carros, todos se van riendo, hasta tu madre que trata de mantenerse separada de tu papá. Se divorciaron hace más de treinta años, recuerdas, y tú vas pensando, qué tan lejos hemos venido todos, no siempre fue esto todo tan complicado y triste y lleno de rest homes para padres viejos y confusos y de divorcios y memorias agridulces.

Esa tarde, tu padre les ha contado, todos comiendo tacos de machaca y frijoles refritos, de cómo había venido su familia de México a Arizona y entonces a California. Lo contaba de manera ordenada, los pensamientos menuditos y diciendo chistes y riéndose de lo inocentes que habían sido todos. Tu, la mayor, has oído sus cuentos antes, pero siempre llegaba tu padre a recordar algo nuevo y chistoso, como lo que está contando ahora:

—Pos sí, cuando nos íbamos pa'l norte desde Brole hasta Bakersfield, nos íbamos por el Grapevine, el antiguo Hiway 99 por las montañas. Una vez nos fuimos cuando había nieve, y el camino se hizo resbaloso. Ah carajo, qué trabajo tuvimos con la carcancha! Nos adelantábamos un rato, y entonces el carro no subía más, y había que bajarnos y puchar, sí empujando así hacíamos un poco de camino, y otra vez nos subíamos cuando se podía. Híjuela, qué trabajos pasábamos a veces en aquellas cruzadas. . . Y todo para poder comer, vivir, unos centavos más; ja, ja, qué trabajos pasábamos, What a pain it was!-

Una nieta le ha preguntado al abuelo, "Grandpa, when did your family come to the United States?" Tu padre contesta, "I was naturalized when I went into the Navy!" y entonces, su mirada fijándose en los ojos esquivos de tu madre ". . . durante la Segunda Guerra Mundial, verdad. . .? Cuándo fue eso, eh. . .?"

—Fue en los treinta, cuenta tu madre, como 1936, '37, algo por allí, yo tenía once años y vívíamos en Nuevo México en el ranchito que era de los patrones, del Colonel Nelson y su esposa. Estaba yo bailando en la recámara, donde debía estar limpiando, pero tenían allí un espejo muy elegante, de esos largos y que se paraban sobre patitas de animal, de madera era hecho el espejo. Había un radio puesto por otra parte de la casa, y empecé a dar saltos y levantar las piernas, y daba una patada muy alta, levantándoseme las faldas cuando veo que traigo mancha'os los calzones! Pues me asusté, y corrí pa' lavarme en la tina de atrás. Yo creí que de dar tan fuertes las patadas, que me había lastima'o! Entonces, ai voy otra vez a la recámara para terminar el trabajo, pero como la música to'avía tocaba qué te crees pues dentro de poco me jallé dando otros saltos a la música ranchera, y pos otra vez los calzones mancha'os. Esta vez me cachó mi Tía Sara que trabajaba en la cocina, y me preguntó que por qué iba tan asustada y a las escondidas por el corredor. Llorando de vergüenza, le contesté; "Traigo sangre en los calzones, creo que me lastimé bailando." Y tu tía mi tía se rió fuerte, "Ah, tontita, se me olvidó decirte de algo. No te asustes, les pasa a todas!" Yo era tan de tímida que no le creí hasta después que le pasó a Loli, la hija de la vecina con quien jugaba yo a las casitas."

Tu madre siempre decía que no había tenido dieciocho, "de edad legal," cuando se casaron, pero no la podian fijar nunca en la edad que de verdad habría tenido. Sus antepasados, les decía, habían sido franceses y españoles pero los detalles habían variado por los años, y no sabían qué había recordado bien y qué le había compuesto un tantito. Un día te han regañado porque llamó la tía Rosalía riéndose y chismeando porque "la Pat le dijo a los otros primos que su madre es Apachi y su papá es Yaqui. Que tú le habías dicho! Ay, qué bárbara eres, ja, ja. . .!" Tu padre casi te da una azotada pero te escapas porque la tía Rosalía, la Tía Leyva, era entre ellas la más mentirosa y chismosa, y aunque le temían la lengua larga, tú te escapas porque eras de tu padre la consentida por ocurrente, en cuanto más escandalosa de niña eras, pues más te consentía. . . Tu madre, en frustración, por otra parte decía "Igualita a tu padre. . . Just like your father!"

Poco después de la muerte de la segunda esposa, tu padre apenas supo encontrar tu casa, que ahora quedaba en otra ciudad al norte de Southwest City. Deprimido, luchando con la tristeza, columpiaba entre necesitar la botella y una necesidad igual de fuerte de conectar con la vida. Respondía a tus preguntas, con sus propias memorias. . . "Trabajábamos en Arizona. Vivimos unos años en Arizona, la mayor parte le hacíamos en lo que había, en el campo, los files, lo que hubiera, pero allí tu tía Herminia también trabajó como cocinera en la casa de aquel ex-Presidente de México, cómo se llamaba? Pues, éste vivía en exilio por acá, digo, ai en Arizona, sí, en el mismo pueblito a donde había venido nuestra familia, y tu Tía Minia se acuerda que la ponían a hacer tortillas todas las mañanas, para el gran hombre. Yo apenas tenía tres años cuando nos trajeron tus abuelos, mis papás. Fue por los años de la Revolución cuando se vinieron, porque estaban muy duras las cosas por allá. Yo estaba muy chiquito, pero tus tías sí se acuerdan de aquellos tiempos. . . de Sonora, de aquellos otros pueblitos. Una vez, sí, sí regresé de grande, fuimos hasta Empalme, Ciudad Obregón, por allá, y vimos la casa donde dijieron que habíamos nacido los más mayores de nosotros. Qué sucia, que chiquita, un lugarcito así no más, de adobe. Has visto retrato de tu abuelo? Tu tío Pelón se parece mucho a él, pelo negro, prieto, así, muy indio y con bigote grande. . . Qué? Ay, mija, pero cómo se te ocurre que se parecía a Pancho Villa! Si te oyen tus tías, verás!

"These people have fled here because they fear for their lives, they are not only seeking economic solutions; when they state before you that they flee from death squads and repression in their homelands, they are appealing to you for their very lives. Call it political amnesty, call it sanctuary, but be assured that they. . . "Así defiende la abogada pelirroja de Nueva York al grupo sentado tras la mesa, los reconoces en la televisión, por los periódicos y las revistas; un grupo de tres que han trabajado con refugiados de varios países hispanoamericanos, ahora acusados por ayudar a algunos a cruzar ilegalmente la frontera. Aunque cruzaban para vivir y no morir, te dices entre dientes, aunque tenían que salirse aunque allá vivían con *la muerte* aunque. . . Pat! Pat! Hey wake up, what are you thinking about? Oh yeah, those people, well, why don't you go interview them, you know, start that book you'd been threatening me you were going to start. What? Really, there's already about ten books being written about them, the Movement? Oh, I don't know, what you said about that one woman, that really grabs you, I think," tu compañero Bob te dice, mostrando, estrujando sus propios borradores/papeles que ha traído a casa para editar en la computadora. No puedes evitar viendo que, en la cara te lo muestra. . . *In your face.* . .

Tu amiga Lulu Espinoza, quien trabaja contigo en la revista *Southwest Cities and Deserts,* te ofrece otro té helado con limón. Tú recuerdas, mientras Lulu regresa a su escritorio, a una periodista joven de Nuevo México, en otra gente que se puso a investigar y defender y ya ves lo que se encontraron. Recuerdas las palabras repetidas de tu madre aquellas otras veces, por qué te metes en lo que no es tu asunto? para qué andas buscándole? no son tus negocios, y qué te crees, siempre fuiste igualita a tu papá!

"This time it's different, Ma. Besides, why do I have to be like you or like Dad? Esto se trata de otra cosa, Mamá, no crees que si tú fueras aquellas mujeres, no ibas a querer salirte de allá, y qué crees les podría haber pasado que. . ." Los movimientos de los campesinos y de los estudiantes, le dices a Lulu, nunca van a desaparecer, pero el movimiento del santuario tal vez sea el hecho histórico de más impacto de los años '80 en el suroeste y para adelante, para los chicanos. "These women, le dices a Lulu, these women, the ones coming over and the ones helping them, well I think they really have *ovaries,* you know, *balls, ovaries!*"

"Yo me parezco a mi Nana," le dices tentativamente a tu tía Elsa un verano cuando estaban viendo fotos de la familia, que tu tía tenía montados en las paredes de su casita. A tu Tía, menor que tu padre, se le sale: "Tú Pat, ni lo pienses!" Así se le escapa a tu tía, que después trata de recuperar, "Eh. . . no, tú te pareces más a tu mamá, no crees?" "Ni me debería haber comparado," piensas decaída. Recuerdas que tu Nana, una mujer muy trabajadora quien había criado a sus muchos hijos solita, y a pesar de estar casi ciega. Había muerto en una explosión en el subterráneo del restaurante que tenía ella. Tú estabas en primero o segundo grado en Betaville, ocho millas al norte de la frontera mexicana en California. Te consuelas: Tú también tienes los recuerdos de tu nana, y recuerdas que fuiste querida. Y de los hijos e hijas de tu nana, todos amados, algunos mimados, tu padre era para todos ellos, *el predilecto*. Mientras tu nana bajaba al sótano con Humberto, el joven ayudante de cocina, para averiguar por qué el calentón del agua no trabajaba, cuando Humberto prendió el *fósforo*, la mecha que prendió fuego al gas que allí se escapaba, mientras ella y Humberto fueron echados contra el techo del sótano, pensaba en la muerte, pensó que pronto estaría afuera, sentada y descansando contra la pared exterior detrás del Nogales Café, diciéndoles a sus hijos hijas allí que procuraran por la hija menor, pensaba?

"Querida hija mía: que no te sorprenda que te conteste tan rápido tu última carta estoy muy ocupado vigilando estos cuates que no se escapen de este manicomio. No hace unos cuantos minutos que agarré a un cuate en su moto—su wheelchair, que se salia por la puerta. Qué tal han de estar los otros, que yo lo aiga catchado. No estoy tan tan como dicen, es pura vacilada mia."

Respondes a la carta de tu padre, hace cinco-seis años: "Pop! Cómo estás? Acabamos de recibir tu cartita. Oh, no te acuerdas. . . La escribieron por ti, o qué? Pues parece tu letra, pero como hace años que no recibo carta de ti, pues sólo la firma me puedo asegurar es. . . Sí, mi esposo anda bien, los chamacos ajá, sí también. Dónde vivo? Pues todavía, cerca de Southwest City. Oh, te trajeron tus pastillas y tienes que colgar. Bueno, okay, I'll call you in a few. . .'stá suave?"

Le dices que lo quieres, él dice que también, igual. Tú recuerdas que él no costumbraba decirles eso, "I love you," o "Te quiero," no era algo que él les decía. Será cierto entonces, te preguntas, lo que tanto dicen los sicólogos ahora, que había que decirse a cada rato? Cómo lo sabíamos entonces, que le temíamos en su seriedad o en sus tomaderas, creíamos que era chistoso, bromista y listo, sharp, so very sharp, pero estábamos conscientes de ello en aquel entonces? Pensábamos que el cariño y el temor iban juntos, pero que la muerte y el morir quedaban muy lejos? La pérdida, la respiramos todavía. Recuerdas que, estando en el mismo cuarto tus papás, se dirigían formalmente, hablándose de "usted" y no de "tú" con cada uno. Nos preguntábamos, es sólo un juego? "I wonder if they did that in bed?" le dices una vez a tu hermana Belita.

"No lo aguantaba a veces," dice tu madre, "era muy mujeriego y no lo quería." Tú te ríes, recordando a tus padres de jóvenes cuando eran niños ustedes, y abrazándola le dices quedito al oído, "Oh, sure, Mom, you had us kids, let's see, how many of us are there? And you were celosa híjole qué celosa. Ya, I know you had reason to be, time and again. . . pos no eran así ellos? Pero lo querías, que si lo querías, oh sure tell me about it. . . ja, ja, Ma, tú tampoco no te aguantas you're so stubborn and proud, man oh man ay mujer. . . ja ja ay qué chula eres dame otro besito! En años recientes, les ha dicho que él le pegaba, no siempre cuando estaba tomado, y varias veces fue por alguna vieja. . . otra mujer. *God you're so cute give me another besito!"*

"He was the Singing Rage of Brole," recuerdas que les decía tu Mamá cuando ustedes le preguntaban How did you meet? "Lo había oído cantar antes de conocerlo. Lo que sí puedo decir, que siempre fue buen proveedor para su familia, eso sí puedo decirles. Sí, eso sí. . ."

Tu esposo entra a la cocina, tú le pías: "Hi Honey! I talked to Dad just now. Sort of okay, I guess. He couldn't remember again, where we live. No, he didn't remember that either, I can't tell if he wrote it all or what. Yeah, I know, I know, but it's hard!" *Honey* come, prende el remoto a la televisión y en vez de noticias se pone a ver un programa sobre las Batallas Contra las Drogas. Hay un cuate que están entrevistando que dice que:

"No, I don't think the Drug Wars are being won; the American public is being lied to. Well, by their leaders, the 'suits', in the highest Government offices, that's right. By what authority do I? Well, I say it all in my book here, that the leaders of this country have their own agenda with these foreign governments in Latin America, those raids by the military to supposedly burn fields of all those drugs, cocaine, heroin, why for every one of *Borriega* there's dozens of other guys that our government has made deals with. Well, because they have bigger things to wheel-and-deal with those guys about, like these bank loans to these countries. Those places can't make payment on those huge loans if we really busted their drug crops. I was a DEA undercover agent for over fifteen years, and I'm telling you all right now, you're being lied to. Yes, I recognize this guy beside me from when I worked the Southwest Cities region, he's right, the DEA did what they could. And Immigration tried to cooperate along the border areas, he's right. But back to the main point of my book, the 'suits' have the power, and you're all being lied to."

Has leído que a una de las mujeres sentadas allí en la Corte, acusadas de violar las leyes de inmigración y no sabes qué más, fue engañada por un agente del gobierno americano, un chicano que trabaja con inmigración o la policía secreta o algo así. Le hizo el amor a la mujer, cortejándola en frente y con toda la familia de ella, por varios meses seguidos, sacaba a la mujer, a veces con los hijos o parientes de ella. La engañó haciéndole el amor, para que ella confiara *cómo* y *dónde* y *cuándo* y si sí ayudaba a aquellas gentes o no. Como *ingenue,* como *fool* cayó en la trampa la pobre, enamorándose besuquiando a un baboso mentiroso.

AGENT TESTIFIES IN COURT THAT HE TRICKED PARAMOUR INTO REVEALING cabrón, cabrones. "And you're all being lied to."

"People are basically good in this world," te dice Lulu. "You have to learn to trust people," te dice tu esposo. Tú le escribes a tu hijo, Ricardo, un evangelista que va a mudarse a México para trabajar allí por un año, ayudando a construir nuevas iglesias no católicas: "De veras crees que Dios nos quiere a todos, perdona a todos?" "Sí, creo que la gente puede cambiar, para su salvación, Mamá." Tú le preguntas a tu hijo si ha oído del "carnalismo," o sea, el espíritu simbólico del Movimiento Chicano.

"I don't know about their brotherhood, Mom, but I've heard about some secret society to overthrow the government." "No, no es lo que te preguntaba, Mijo. Y si sabes de ello, pues no puede ser una sociedad tan secreta, no crees? No, César Chávez se dedicó, como Martin Luther King, al modelo de Gandhi, al activismo sin violencia, no, no creo que eran sólo palabras. . . palabreo. Pues, sí, es cierto, yo misma no marché con ellos, es cierto. Seguro, yo sé que tuvieron huelgas cuando mi papá, tu abuelo, trabajaba en las fresas. Mijo! Nada más quería saber si tú crees en la absolución. . . que la gente puede cambiar!"

Y cómo tú trataste a tu propio hijo? como tú no estuviste allí para tus propios hijos/hijas, dónde estabas cuando los tuyos los propios tuyos te necesitaban entera no enamoradísima and not screwed up babosos mentirosos y tú pendeja and you a fool a struggling fool yet needy romantic wounded demasiado necesitada sin embargo was it ever way too late Qué pensabas qué pensaste cuando eras joven When you were young?

Mi hermanito Samuel era muy bien portado, de niño lo fue y ahora de grande también excepto por una época donde tomaba mucho y la hacía al gran Macho pero eso se le pasó y ahora ha luchado por muchos años, educándose él, y a sus hijos. Y como he tenido mis secretos, él igual ha tenido los suyos, *secretos* esperando acechando. Pues de chavalitos, íbamos seguido al mercado de Mexicali, al otro lado de la frontera, como lo hicimos esta vez, con nuestra abuela y mi mamá. Esta vez que les estoy contando, nuestra Nana y nuestra Mamá nos dejaron en el carro a mí y al Samuelito, sí en esos días todavía se podía dejar a niños en el carro y desatendidos, no es como ahora. . . Pues cuando regresaron al carro, mi mamá y mi abuela vieron que había alguna gente parada cerca del carro y algunos se reían y apuntaban. Al llegar adonde estábamos nosotros, muy calladitos, dentro del carro y en el asiento de atrás, vieron que había algo como excremento, sí caca pues, embarrado desde arriba hasta abajo en una *streak,* en la puerta del carro por el lado donde estaba el gentío y donde algunos de los hombres apuntaban.

Cuando espiamos a nuestra madre, mi hermanito gritó: "Mira, mamita, mira mami! Aquel hombre que va'llá se cagó aquí en la puerta!"

Pues la gente que caminaba o estaba allí cerca parada alrededor del carro, ahora sí se echó a reír y estornudar. Mi madre, muy avergonzada, se metió al carro, y despés de caminar un rato hacia nuestro pueblito que quedaba unas ocho millas al norte de la frontera, mi madre paró el carro al lado del camino. Cuidadosamente, las dos señoras nos esculcaron la ropa y calzones. No había señas de nada, no sabían qué pensar las dos señoras, y adelante hacia nuestra casa en Betaville.

Al ratito, posiblemente enfadados por el día largo, nosotros nos empezamos a pelear en el asiento de atrás. Pronto, me dice bajito mi hermano: —Pati, si no te portas bien, le voy a decir a mi'amá quién se cagó en la puerta.—

Pues entonces, oyendo esto las dos señoras, pregunta mi Nana en un tono divertido A ver, Samuelito, quién se cagó en la puerta? Nadie. . ., contestó mi hermanito, eh, aquel hombre l'izo. Pues tras unas millas más en el camino, y otros tantos minutos de pellizcones y pleito en el asiento de atrás, pos salió la historia.

Cuando llegamos a casa, mi madre me jaló pa'l bano pa' darme mis nalgadas sin que la viera mi Nana, pero luego entró mi papá, contándoselo todo primero mi Nana, y pos otra vez me escapé una buena. . . Sí, le cayó de gracia a mi'apá, y todavía, de vez en cuando, cuando se junta mi familia, se acuerdan entre todos ellos, de la puerta cagada en Mexicali. Seguro, entonces como ahora, todavía teníamos nuestros secretos. *Y los calzoncitos limpios, limpios.*

—Pues ya de grande, mija, no se puede cagar el palo sin que te den tus coscorones y tus buenas,- así todavía me dice mi madre, —de alguna manera, si cagas el palo, pues como decía mi padre tu abuelo, *"Pos adiós nena, se hundió el barco!"*

Tú le contestas esta vez a tu mamá que Give me a break, you gotta have hope you gotta believe in the goodness of people, tú sabes, la hermandad la caridad y todo eso y ella contesta con otro dicho de su gente que cuanto más te agachas más se te y tú dices que si también cree en cuando el chango sube el árbol se le ve el culo desde abajo? "What does that have to do with anything?" te pregunta, y tú te ríes que ay las mujeres cómo hay que aprender. *In your face. . .* allí, delante de ti.

No has estado aquí antes?, te preguntas, cuando Lulu te sugiere que vayas a entrevistar a las gentes del Santuario. No tuviste que dejarlo todo, la universidad con su política enredada, las intrigas, la falta de gente en quien confiar y la amargura, la tristeza de ver que ni el Movimiento, ni la promesa del carnalismo, de la hermandad, ni eso. Entonces qué?

"Remember when you met me, how all that other was, so we decided for then to let it go? I just wanted some peace. . ." Tu compañero te recuerda, en respuesta, "You also said you wanted what your campesina lawyer friend, Venus, offered, *another way.* Remember? *Peace. Love. Justice." Well then,* piensas, *entonces qué. . .?*

JUDGE SENTENCES NUN IN SANCTUARY TRIAL huelgas protestas *headlines* violencia DÉJA VU tell me, dime tú.

"Tell me about when you wanted to be a nun, Mom," dice tu hijo, para diversión de tus nietos.

"Dear *Mami,* please come to get me, pronto. Love, Patty." Por fin, fue tu padre quien vino por ti, cara seria, serio y determinado pero tú felicísima de verlo llegar, y fue él, él fue quien te pescó del Convento del Buen Pastor afuera de Las Cruces. Años después, ustedes se ríen de las muchas cartitas y notas de niña rogante que habías escrito, y que habías entregado a las monjas para que las mandaran a los parientes nuevomexicanos de tu mamá que vivían cerca.

Tu papá estaba que reventaba, dijo tu tía Sara, que qué diablos había hecho tu'amá?, llevándote al convento y tú apenas de siete años. . . pues te pasaste un buen mes y medio allí antes que llegó tu papá de California y te sacó, te pescó de allí, maldiciendo a las monjas que le'ícian *que entoavía no estabas 'lista'!*

Tu madre todavía lo recuerda, "Pos quisiste ser monja por una

película de la María Félix. . . y se te quitó, qué no? Aquellas viejas san-
titas, ni nos mandaron niuna nota tuya. Ja!. Seguro que se te quitó!"
QUISISTE SER.

Camino a Clarkston, el pueblito donde querías llevar unas cajas
de ropa usada servible a la iglesia protestante, empiezas a pensar de
nuevo sobre la pareja anglo que maneja el Centro allí. Ayudan y asisten
a refugiados, campesinos/campesinas sin documentos, a los pobres, a
los desesperados. La gente, has leído en aquel artículo en el periódico
hace unos meses atrás, viene desde México, Centro y Sur América. Refugiados, campesinas, campesinos/obreros, a veces familias enteras, les
aparecen allí, les llegan a la Iglesia. No sólo buscan una vida mejor, sino
muchas veces, el mero *tener vida*. Oh, aquí viene la mujer, sale de la
iglesia para saludarte, mientras tú estacionas, la reconoces de la foto
del periódico. "When the reporter came to do the story on what my
husband and I have been doing here, he brought a photographer that
kept taking pictures of everything. I had to tell them that they could
take pictures of me, of my husband, the Reverend Loyd, as much as they
wanted, but they weren't to take any photos of *la gente*. The people who
come here, well, muchos están en peligro, tú sabes cómo están las cosas
con nosotros aquí."

La gente le ha puesto "La Hermana Lizabet de *'Glareston,'*" y les
han llegado gentes, hasta familias enteras a veces a veces uno o dos o
tres solos, huyéndose de aquel lugar distante *desde allá nos vinimos nos
dijieron que Usté nos jayudaba. . .* desde aquel lugar de Terror Muerte
desde. . . *Hermana Lizabeta.* Y la Sister Lizabet y el Reverendo Loyd
ayudan de tal manera, que nuestro gobierno considera su trabajo como
acciones subversivas, peligrosas: encuentran hospedaje, obtienen medi-
cinas y ayuda médica, obsequian ropa, hasta buscan muebles, trastes y
ollas, traducen documentos, llenan formularios oficiales o documentos
pidiendo por ejemplo *la amnistía,* sí, cómo no, o la inmigracion, la asistencia social. . . Además, en su propio *van* o camioneta, ayudan cuando
pueden, con el transporte a estas gentes desesperadas, o piden ayuda

de algunas monjas voluntarias de las iglesias católicas de los pueblos cercanos. "We have to be careful, *entiendes,* who we let help us. *Nunca se sabe.*"

JOURNALIST INDICTED FOR TRANSPORTING ILLEGAL ALIENS.

Tambien pasó en Nuevo México, en Arizona, en . . . YOU NEVER KNOW. . . "This writer Guillermina that we met last year at that poetry reading, just made the papers today," te dice tu compañero Bob, quien lee el periódico, "Seems like the government got some women that testified your acquaintance drove them across the Border."

They said they needed help, and they told me about their children, their babies. Their stories touch and interested me, and I never suspected that. . . Nunca pensé que. . .

—Todo está muy feo,—le escribes a Aurora, una amiga mutua tuya y de Guillermina en Nuevo México,—pero por lo menos no la humillaron más mandándole a un hombre macho guapo y con bigotito y todo, a que la enamorara y así la espiaran mientras. Nada de *open warfare,* encuentran tus debilidades, y cómo y por dónde eres vulnerable, y desde allí, se meten para agarrarte. . . *para abrirte.* Well, sorry to be *gross,* pero desde allí 'montan la batalla' o montan el caballo/la yegua, o se meten adentro, *whatever.* . . Qué valiente es Guillermina, de veras que tiene *huevarios!* It takes a lot of guts, and you sure are some gutsy women!

—Y qué ingenua fui,—te contaba tu amiga de confianza desde tus años en la universidad, colega y crítica/escritora, Aurora Bustamente,— eran mis años de subgraduada en aquella universidad *elite* por allá en Connecticut, y me pasó lo que me pasó, por creerles. Sí también fueron los años sesenta. Fue una clase de psicología. *If you sometimes think you're going mad. . . Well let me tell you, I really got crazy.* De veras que me volví loca. . .— Entonces tú empiezas a imaginar cómo fue, que. . .—

Aurora, una de las estudiantes con beca porque su familia no era como de las otras, rica, entró en la clase, donde a mediosemestre dijeron que iban a tener un ejercicio de tipo examen, y que todas ellas, todas muchachas *anglo* excepto por una sola cubana, Hilda, y la única chicana Aurora, debían esperar a que las llamaran al cuarto del examen. Iban a entrar, una por una, explicó el profesor hombre anglo, por una puerta aquí y saldrían por otra puerta que daba directamente hacia afuera. De esa manera, no podrían regresar las ya entrevistadas para informar a las jóvenes que todavía esperaban. "We want this to be a *clinical, scientific* kind of test," les había dicho el profesor.

Myra Greenfield se sentó al lado de Aurora, quien escuchó divertida los chismes de su amiga, a quien Aurora admiraba tanto por ser aquélla tan directa, tan honesta. "You're the most forthright, outspoken person I know, aren't you ever afraid of offending somebody?"—Así le había dicho Aurora a Myra después de uno de sus largos argumentos políticos en la cafetería. Hilda y Aurora, las únicas dos hispanas, habían llegado a ser amigas íntimas, se sonreían sabiendo ya cuando empezaba Myra a discutir, argüir, contradecir y responder sobre cualquier asunto o tema en cualquier momento. Aurora quería a Hilda, pero abiertamente admiraba a Myra por la falta de temor de ésta: a cada vuelta, Myra se confrontaba con el profesor en las clases que llevaban. . . "Myra, I felt, was a muchacha fuerte. . . argumentativa, una cabrona rete suave, una *sharp cookie.*"

Reconstruyes de nuevo, que. . . Aurora, dentro de la sala del examen, se sentó donde le indicaron, y empezó a girar una proyectora. "Watch closely," instruye una voz, "and tell me which door the little cartoon figure ends up choosing and going through." Tú ves que la figurita tamborilea, tamborilea, y finalmente va hacia y por la puerta al lado izquierdo de la pantalla. Tú dices, *"Left!* Is that it? Is that the test?"

En ese momento, para la proyectora y entran por las dos puertas de la sala de examinación (verdadera y concreta) en donde está sentada Aurora, sus compañeras de clase, inclusive su amiga Myra, quien se sienta como siempre, al lado de Aurora, e Hilda se sienta al otro lado. Todas toman asiento a tu/su alrededor. La Voz ahora pregunta, *clínicamente,* "Which door did the figure choose, let's run that by once more quickly, and then each of you answer one by one." La proyectora repite las escenas, donde ves que la figurita tamborilea hacia y por la puerta... a la izquierda. Entonces, una por una, tus compañeras de clase dicen, the figure chose the door *to the right!* Y cada vez que, al horror y asombro de ti/de Aurora, dicen lo contrario a lo que habías visto tú/Aurora, pausan y te/le preguntan a Aurora, *"Are you sure? Aren't you mistaken?"* y entonces *"Don't you want to change your mind?"*

Cuando llegó el turno de Myra, pues yo sabía que por fin saldría la verdad, verdá, lo que yo también había visto, pero para entonces yo no me explicaba qué locura era ésta que estaban haciendo...?

"A la derecha, dijo Myra, the figure turned *to the right,* went through the right. I mean the door on the right!"

—Myra había mentido también! Entonces, por unos cinco minutos... qué locura qué horror era ésto... la clase entera trató de hacerme ver que yo me había equivocado, que *yo* había visto mal la película. Pues, como para entonces estaba tan fuera de mí, tan horrorizada de no sabía qué, y pues como tenía tanta fe en Myra, mi amiga fiel mi aliada siempre. Dudé, y por fin ya no pude contra esa opinión tan unanime, tan Myra. "I guess it was the *right,* I mean the door to the right. I thought, I guess not, but I... yo había pensado que..."

"My father, a university professor himself who had come to the Southwest from South America, later told me, How could you let the school get away with it? After what that incident did to me, fue cuando me empezó el coraje de veras, that's when I stopped being so tonta, so ingenua. Te imaginas, fue nada más un experimento psicológico, nada más, yo fui la única allí que no supo hasta después que había sido la chicana *guinea pig.* Me dijeron después, que probablemente era una debilidad *cultural,* no una falta intelectual. Me dio una rabia como te digo, una rabia que todavía, Pues no se me quita, y todavía a veces..."

Uno de estos días, tu papá no los reconocerá, ni por la voz. Qué y cómo pensará? Pensará en la muerte, le parecerá próxima? Seguramente tus tíos, ahora hay dos de ellos que están recuperando del cáncer, surely they must. O tratarán de no pensarlo. And Tío Pelón *ya se fue,* el año pasado, también colon cancer, después de la quimoterapia. Esteban, el mayor, murió de cirrosis del hígado hace tiempo, y su mujer la Tia Lita *se fue* el año pasado. Se fue como era, ocurrentísima, peleonera echando madres y padres, pataleando hasta el fin. La más joven también, ella y el esposo, casi se fueron varias veces, pero allí los tienes, retedevivitos to'avía. Su generación todavía representada, hangin' in, juntándose en los bautismos, bodas, aniversarios, más o menos viéndose la familia en los velorios y entierros. *Not gone, not dead, not yet.* En cada velorio y entierro, ha habido gritos, llantos, pero siempre en las juntas o comidas *después,* hijos hijas, primos, hermanos, hermanas, comen, beben, recuerdan, contándose allí las últimas noticias y chismes familiares. So and So also died, did you know? Sabías que esos dos primos allí tienen HIV? *Sí. Son jotos, probable van a morir.* Qué triste, verdá? get sad some remembering entonces alquien cuenta un chiste, laugh Man, these velorios those wakes are something else! *Papá, piensas en la muerte? Qué sientes?, quiero sacarte de allí y no sé la manera."*

"Grandpa's safer there than out," dice tu hija mayor María. Safety *un santuario,* sentirse seguros, no queriendo el caos, la violencia, buscando algo mejor, so tus abuelos nos habían traído pa'cá, eso tu padre lo recordó. *Ni muertos ni idos, todavía no.*

HABÍAS QUERIDO.

Habías querido, habías empezado, a escribir una novela sobre el Movimiento del Santuario, y *el camino* te llevó a *SECRETOS recuerdos muertes* pérdidas familiares seres queridos *Self.* Aurora, ahora también de unos cincuenta años, te dijo el año pasado, "It's weird, really weird, qué estraño, pero conozco a nueve, no, once, no, más gentes que han muerto en los últimos meses. I told mi compañero, Miguel Ángel that what was this, una brujería o qué? Anyway, I mean, couldn't it just stop right here? Qué ondas con mi vida? Geez!" Casi perdimos a Aurora misma, hace un par de años, pero qué bueno, todavía 'stá aquí, "Did I tell you about the crazy homeless lady on the *Llorona* bridge in Santa

Fe. . .? It was before all those *muertes* started, maybe it was *an omen.* What do you think, ha, ha?" Todavía luchando, vital creativa bromista, ALIVE, still telling people when to fuck you, ve y chíngate. *In your face.*

El mismo año de lo de tu padre y el asilo/santuario, también *metieron* a tu querida viejita francesa, tu amiga y la niñera de tu hijita Marisa, aquélla ya frágil y acabándose, en un "rest home," un lugarcito bonito cerca de Hannibal, Missouri, un lugar bonito (para ser asilo). Y uno de estos días, se nos irá. *La muerte,* debo pensar en la muerte?

La hija de una amiga le llama, agitada, sollozando: "Ma, encontraron a mi stepmother muerta en un hotel, she OD'd. They found out. Yeah, she was an addict. Oh, pastilles, heroína; no sé porque se entregó a todo eso. Pero también lo hacía su esposo, mi *real father.* Boy, qué familia, huh!" Entonces, ahora debería pensar en la muerte? "Ma, tengo algo que decirte." Esto también hace unos ocho años, estos últimos ocho años te pone a pensar te pica te pica Qué debo recordar? Qué debo puedo contar revelar? "Ma, lo siento, pero I have something to tell you. De mi padre." Sollozando, su/tu bella criatura her/your child que él/ellos llevaban en brazos cuando niña no su hija propia mas todavía suya desde la infancia hasta que UNTIL "About Dad and me, nosotros, yo. . . Cuando yo tenía dieciocho. . . *Nosotros,* I'm so sorry, Ma, I'm so sorry, no quiero lastimarte, pero ayer, when I was driving him back to those friends he was visiting, Dad trató de. . . And it brought it all back, all of it. Yo creía que eso ya se había acabado, pero no él no me deja. He keeps trying to. . . Y ahora no puedo olvidar."

"Será simplista pensarlo?" le preguntas a Laurel, una amiga pintora de Southwest City, "que de veras no tengo las fuerzas pa'star siempre de luto, esperando la muerte!" "That's what I told you years ago, when you were struggling with your *demonios, tu dolor.* Today, *hoy mismo,* is our only business. Death is not. . . no es nuestro asunto."

Vida muerte DRUGS SEX ALCOHOL INCEST *y ahora no puedo olvidar.*

parte segunda

Memorias y secretos: las historias *tabú*

CAPÍTULO UNO

Por el campo se decía que ese día habían reportado a los Menchaca. Habían dejado al más chiquito en el cuarto, encerrado todo el día. "Qué bárbaros," decían las mamás mexicanas; "Qué malos," dijo mi mamá; "Ya ni l'acen," dijo mi papá, "así que los pescaron." Oí a mis tíos diciendo que era muy feo lo que habían hecho los papás de aquel niñito, dejándolo solo dentro de una caja grande de cartón. Aquel chamaquito apenas gateaba, me acuerdo, y después de grande, me preguntaba yo si sus papás lo habían hecho por no tener quién les cuidara al bebito, o si lo habían hecho por malos, como decían en el campo el día que los pescaron las autoridades.

Los tomates crecían gruesos, se veían pesados y gordos, verdes, anaranjados y rojos. Los cogía y los olía primero, se me hacía que iban a reventar de carnita y jugosidad. De vez en cuando encontrábamos un gusano grande, y había que cuidar dónde pisabas porque se aplastaban los tomates en el suelo, los desechados o caídos por accidente. Sabían bien los tomates que me comí. A pesar de andar lonchando con la fruta, me pisqué una caja antes de que me encontrara mi papá. "Te dije que no quería que salieran ellos a trabajar en el fil, mujer, por qué no hiciste caso?" Creí que me iban a dar una buena, pero no, nada más me regañó mi papá con lo de "Quiero que vayas a la escuela, que no tengas que pasar las cosas como nosotros. Vale más que me hagan caso, a mis hijos, no los quiero en el fil, ni en el tomate, ni en la fresa. Que vayan a la escuela."

"We lived in tents once. . ." les dije a mis hijos. "No you didn't, Mom!" Pues así y como no me crean, es una de mis memorias curiosas del campo. Que se hace tanto escándalo de que cuando la gente tiene que vivir en carpas, por alguna emergencia o inconveniencia, y pues la gente del campo lo hacía, y por alguna parte, te aseguro que lo hace. Y muchas veces viven en lugares peores. Pues, no, como mi padre para ese entonces era uno de los socios del campo, "al que le tocaba el trabajo de burro" dice mi mamá todavía, a nosotros nos hicieron una carpa con piso de madera. Mi mamá la tenía bien desinfectada, me acuerdo, bien barrida, hasta *escrins* tenía la carpa, nada de moscas que se invitaran. . . La otra gente, pues no todas las familias ni los hombres tenían carpas con lados de *screens* o alambre, aunque todas las que vi tenían pisos de madera. El socio de mi papá vivía en el edificio grande a la entrada del campo, donde había un comedor, la cocina y los baños, además de una extensión donde tenían unos cuartos el Tommy y su familia. Andaban muy entusiasmados los socios, cuando empezaron. Se habían conocido de chavalos en Brole, en el Valle Imperial. . . después dejaron de ser socios porque "Nosotros trabajando como burros, y aquéllos fanfarroneándose de que eran los dueños." Más después, me acuerdo del pleito que tuvieron, mi papá y el Tommy.

Lo que hacíamos de *entertainment*, era hablar, pelearnos y escuchar la radio. . . Había un cine en el pueblo, y nos llevaban a las películas mexicanas. La gente mexicana, de costumbre se sentaba lo más atrás en el teatro. Así se costumbraba, así me dijeron que lo hiciera, y allí nos tocaba sentarnos. Pues ahora no te pueden decir ni jijo sobre dónde sentarte, ni en California ni en Arizona. A saber lo que te hacen todavía en Texas, pero así era en aquellos días. . .

La construcción de los campos en que vivimos, era muy parecida a los otros que conocí de niña. . . La famila Rosas vivía en un campo más elegante y más establecido. Había los edificios centrales, pero había casitas para familias, y algunas tenían cercos, y yardas donde las mamás habían plantado rosas y otras plantas bonitas. Siempre había una planta de yerba buena por donde goteara el agua de la manguera, o la llave de agua en el jardín. "Walnut Labor Camp," le llamaban, porque estaba en la calle Walnut creo, un par de millas del pueblito de Masterton. Alrededor de ese pueblito, me acuerdo que había no menos de tres "labor camps". Y éramos muchos los mexicanitos que andábamos por ai, y a través de los años, nos conocíamos por aquellos pueblitos del Valle San Joaquín.

La vieja de mi papá fue la causa de un pleito que tuvieron mis papás, en los entonces del campo con el Tommy. . . La vieja le llamaba a casa del Tommy, y una vez, después que ya no vivíamos en las carpas sino en una casa viejísima de madera allá en medio de unos files terrosos y a un par de millas del campo del Tommy, pasó lo del pleito de mis papás.

Habíamos ido todos juntos en el carro, porque había dicho mi papá que tenía que hablar con el Tommy sobre unos trabajadores. Mamá esperó con nosotros en el carro en la oscuridad, y mi papá se fue adentro para llamar. "¡Qué carajos estará haciendo éste, que no vuelve, y aquí nosotros en la oscuridad! Quédense aquí, chamacos, que 'horita vuelvo." Pronto salió llorando y gritando mi mamá, que no le entendíamos. . . Papá salió de balazo, le pegó a mi mamá quien lloraba y le decía cosas de que sinvergüenza y que aquella vieja y que llévame a mi casa y que yo trabajando como buey y tú rete. . . Duró enojada muchos días después, y no se le quitó lo malhumorado a mi papá hasta que sucedió lo de la operación de mamá. Pues pasó que le tuvieron que sacar el appendix a mamá, de emergencia unas semanas después de aquel pleito, y al rato ya otra vez se hablaban quedito mis papás.

"Esa misma vieja," me dijo mi mamá muchos años después, "aunque se casó con un viejo ricacho, andaba por allá en Gilroy, ya vieja, entiendes, cuando tu papá y Esmeralda se decían ya de casados." Por unas tías me di cuenta que la vieja, cuando estaban jóvenes y casados mis propios papás, era la mujer de un boxeador muy famoso del Valle. Y que la vieja, igual que mi padre, ni de joven ni con arrugas muchos años después, no se aguantaba. "Cómo se conocieron? En el fil, en la cantina, ya ni recuerdo."

"Esta le sacó al padre. . ." están diciendo unos hombres en la fiesta, tú recuerdas que es la fiesta de cuando se casó tu hermana, la que sacaron de México muchos años antes, tus propios papás la tomaron como suya, la trajeron a Estados Unidos, y ahora se estaba celebrando su matrimonio en casa de tu papá y tu madrastra: "Dicen que se ha casado muchas veces, y que tiene hijos de aquí y de allí. Mírenla. . . allí está!"De choque, te entra lo que estás escuchando, lo que están diciendo de ti, en frente de ti y de uno de tus hermanos, quien te está tratando de decir. . . Y tú piensas cómo fue que se me había olvidado cómo es la gente de. . . más cabrones serán que tú, que yo, te dices mientras tu hermano te está queriendo decir "We didn't think you could make it to the wedding, Sis. Why were you so late?" "El Charlie y yo nos perdimos, le dices. We had to come all the way into Gilroy, and then to the chapel here in Monterrey, Carmel-by-the-Sea, whatever. Yeah, we got lost. Ni entramos a la Chapel, en vez de entrar tarde, los esperamos afuera pa' que salieran. Qué vergüenza! A ver si sale el matrimonio, te dices a ti misma. Pues no tenemos muy buen "track record en esta familia." Quién sabe. . . "Let's go eat some tamales or something," le dices a tu hermano y a su novia, "I don't like it here" dices en voz más alta. Viendo a los dos supuestos amigos borrachos de tu padre, que todavía hablan y te siguen mirando a ti de vez en cuando, miradas lascivas, viejos cabrones me lastimaron y ni me conocen viejos bigotudos seguramente o retecatólicos o retevolados en su turno.

"De primero hacíamos tortillas todos los días, para cada comida," te está diciendo tu madre, "después empezamos a hacerles *sandwiches* y comida diferente. En vez de hacer las tortillas a mano, compramos unas máquinas y las hacíamos diario, pero no de a mano. Salían infladitas de todas maneras, muy calientitas."

De unos catorce años, me pusieron a ayudar en la tiendita del último campo que tuvieron mis papás. Yo me acomedía a despachar, cobrando los dulces, las sodas, el papel de escribir, jabones, cigarros, lo que había allí disponible en el puestecito al lado de la oficina del campo. Los hombres que venían eran de muchas edades, eran braceros ahora casi todos estos que había en ese campo, y casi siempre pedían y saludaban muy limpia y directamente. Sus diferentes personalidades se vislumbraban, porque algunos hacían chistes, otros no. Un día, vino un joven muy cortés pero callado, compró lo que quería, y le dije: "Trece centavos cambio." El me vio muy sorprendido, y me dice calladito que "No, son treinta." Pues yo terca y terca que eran trece, y así le di su cambio correspondiente; el pobre me miró por fin muy fastidiado, dio vuelta, y al rato volvió con otro bracero, un señor mayor que yo conocía, quien me dijo: "Mire, señorita Petrita, con la soda y el peine que Lalo se compró aquí, debe devolverle treinta centavos del dólar." Y yo, ahora asustada pero insistiendo que había dicho bien: "No, son trece solamente." Los dos hombres se miraron, se encogieron de hombros, y se fueron, hablando quedito y después riéndose. Y yo, respirando fuerte y libremente, retecontenta de que había despachado bien mis deberes, habiendo dicho bien lo que traía en la cabeza "Un dólar menos 'seventy' centavos, son 'thirty' de cambio. 'Thirty' se dice . . . trece. . . no, treinta!" Pero pues ya se habían ido los dos agraviados, y me quedé avergonzada que lo había pensado bien, pero me salió mal de la boca, el cambio que se le debía al bracero llamado Lalo. Pues, es un detallito nomás, pero no se me ha olvidado. Sentí un alivio enorme cuando regresó el Guayabera, otro trabajador que le ayudaba a mi mamá en el comedor y que les ayudaba con el puesto de tiendita. No se lo conté nunca a mis papás porque no sabía confesar cómo me había equivocado "30" con "13."

El Gallareta era otro bracero, sabía hacer pan, pan dulce, pasteles. Sabía de pastelería francesa. Yo nunca había conocido el "French pastry" hasta que conocí al Gallareta. Por un tiempo, le ayudó a mi mamá en la cocina del campo "del Tommy" en Masterton, y después se fue con nosotros a trabajar en el campo de Newdale. Antes que hicieran el segundo campo en Newdale, cuando todavía estaban los edificios en construcción allá en unos files lejos del pueblito, le pusieron una panadería al Gallareta. Se la hicieron en el garaje de la casa chiquita que habían rentado mis papás. Era un garaje viejo, que tuvo su propia historia breve en la vida de mi familia. . . Pues por un tiempo, allí vivía el Gallareta. Y le pusieron una estufa grande con comales enormes y dos hornos. Allí, el "Galla" hacía sus pastelitos y panes, y allí hacía, con la ayuda de mi mamá y la Marieta, las tortillas para los abonados y los braceros que trabajaban con mi papá y mis tíos. En el campo, ya había carpas con suelos, y baños, pero todavía, en ese entonces, no tenían hechos ni el comedor y la cocina, ni la oficina, ni las casitas donde después vivían unos tíos míos y donde pasaban algún tiempo mis papás.

La Marieta? La Marieta era la más querida de las señoras que vinieron para vivir con nosotros y a ayudarle a mi mamá con los quehaceres de la casa. Era también confidente de mi mamá, y me llevaba al cine cuando pasaban las películas mexicanas de vez en cuando. Después, ella iba hasta a las de en inglés, como nosotros empezamos a hacer. Había rifas y contests o concursos algunos fines de semana en el cine, y le sacábamos mucha fiesta al ir y ver y juntarnos con la otra gente del pueblito. Sí, lo recuerdo como un pueblito suave. Y allí, nuestras vidas cambiaron para siempre en muchos sentidos. . .

En el garaje "del Galla," una vez un borracho carpintero, cuate de cantina de mi papá, perjudicó a una de mis hermanitas, a la gordita. Digo que la perjudicó porque no la violó exactamente, pero sí le hizo algo que no debía. Fue en Newdale, aquel pueblito agrícola, y mi papá tenía como siempre, muchos amigos, entre ellos ese carpintero que trabajaba de vez en cuando para mi papá y otra gente del pueblo. El Ted, así de vez en cuando pasaba por nuestra casa para hablar con papá. Mi mamá nunca lo había querido, porque como dijo después "Viejo apestoso, es hasta más bebedor que tu papá." Un día que no estaban mis papás, nada más yo, mis hermanitas y la Marieta, vino el Ted a la puerta y preguntó por mi papá. Había venido en su camioneta vieja. Pues al ver al Ted, mi hermanita se le fue corriendo a saludarlo, como ella era y todavía es de todas nosotras, la más abierta y cariñosa. No sé cómo pudo haber pasado, pero el hombre se fue de la puerta, y nosotros nos ocupamos por otra parte... De repente, oímos un grito de niña de la yarda de atrás, y me fui por la puerta de atrás de la cocina, y vi que en la ventana del garaje, estaban parados dentro, el Ted con mi hermanita en los brazos, y ella estaba llorando. Me fui corriendo, y al entrar por la puerta del garaje, dije "Vinnie! Qué pasó?" Mi hermanita, quien tenía unos tres años, me sollozó "He took off my panties." Arrebaté a la Vinnie del viejo apestoso a licor y ni recuerdo lo que le dije al viejo, algo estúpido como váyase usté de aquí o no sé qué le dije. Me fui con la niña pa'dentro, le dije a la Marieta, en frente de los otros hermanitos, que el viejo le había hecho algo a Vinnie y que llamara a mi mamá, quien estaba trabajando en la cocina del campo, lejos del pueblo. Fui a la puerta de en frente, y vi que el Ted se tambaleó y se metió a su pickup, donde lo esperaban, sin haberse dado cuenta de lo que había pasado, su hija mayor con el nieto! Me pareció loco todo esto, y yo, enojada, asustada y llena de terror, fui al teléfono que me extendía la Marieta para decirle a mamá que sí, el amigo carpintero de papá, el famoso Ted, le había quitado los calzoncitos a la gordita, a la Vinnie.

Papá andaba por allá por Modesto en los files, pero mamá llegó pronto para llevarse a la Vinnie al doctor, "Pa'ver qué le hizo este apestoso, a ver si la lastimó." Después, me llevó mamá con el District Attorney para decir lo que había visto, de lo que le pasó a la Vinnie. Al viejo lo arrestaron y dentro de poco estaba libre, porque papá no quiso "press charges", que al cabo no le pasó nada a la Vinnie, que a lo mejor me lo había imaginado yo "Ya sabes que la Petra andaba siempre con sus exageraciones... No quiero que haya mitote en el pueblo. Mejor que no diga nada la Pat, ni la Vinnie." Pues, la verdad es que mamá casi mataba al viejo Ted, ella y papá tuvieron pleitos y pleitos sobre lo que quería hacerle al viejo mi mamá, y lo que no quería papá que supiera la gente. Mamá creo que se la guardó, otra vez, a papá. Y todavía, ahora a los setenta años, vale más que no le recuerdes de la vez que el borracho cuate de papá, el carpintero Ted, le hizo algo malo a la gordita. Ahora ha dicho cosas como, "Aquellos viejos borrachos ya sabes cómo se tapaban la cola." A veces, mi madre muy cristiana desde años, hasta ha dicho "Se tapan siempre la mierda. . ." o cosas así por el estilo.

Durante aquellos años en que vivíamos en los campos de Masterton, era cuando teníamos la familia de perros largos "salchicha" o "wienie". Como eran bajos y largos, mi papá les había puesto "los Chapos." El Chapo y la Chapa tuvieron muchos Chapitos, que los dieron por allí a conocidos. Pues la Belita fue la preferida de los Chapos. . . Ella, muy cowboyita siempre en sus bluejeans y camisetas y botitas, así le gustó vestirse por muchos años cuando estaba en casa. Así, "Marimachita" le decían a la Belita, y esto siempre hacía enojar a mamá, pero mi papá la adoraba a la Belita, siempre andaba con papá. Se la llevaba con él a veces al trabajo, en su camioneta o en el carro. Era de todos nosotros, la "güerita," y como decía, era la consentida de papá. Pues lo que contaba de la Belita y los Chapos. . . Ella los quería, pero porque tanta atención les ponía, a veces se le iba la imaginación en los juegos que les inventaba a los pobres perros. Ya les habré contado por otra parte que a un Chapo le quiso sacar la muela, con pinzas grandes de mecánico, verdá? Pues, esa güerita les hacía la vida terrible a los Chapos. El día que contaba mi papá a los tíos y a los abonados después con mucho brío, carcajándose todos, era cuando la Belita andaba jugando al doctor con otro de los Chapos. A este perro lo espiaron mis papás, que vieron que el perro se arrastraba y se arrastraba en la tierra. Pues cuando fueron a ver qué traiba el perro, vieron el palito metido adentro de, de la cola del Chapo. Era otro de esos "experimentos" de la Belita, que por curiosidad solía desbaratar relojes y juguetes porque "quería verlos por dentro." También le llamaban "la huilita, la Tijerillas" y otras cosas así. Valiente, terrible y ocurrente, así era mi hermanita la güerita Beli. Después, por algunos años de madre y casada mujer cristiana, llegó a portarse bien. Y ahora. . . Y ahora, según algunos en la familia, pues no se porta igual.

El amor prohibido, lo que no se debe contar, eso sí que es otra cosa en nuestra cultura. . . Eso sí que es *tabú*, más de lo que es *en inglés*.

CAPÍTULO DOS

Lulu te ha llamado, que tiene algo que decirte, de su hija y su padre/su padrastro, antes el esposo de tu amiga. Cuando Lulu entra en el apartamento de Stacy, la hija le cuenta que, "I have to tell you this. . . I'm sorry, Mom, I'm sorry, Pero Dad y yo, cuando yo estaba en la universidad, El, nosotros. . . él me dijo que al cabo no era mi verdadero padre, that he had desired me, desde que yo tenía cinco, seis años. Y me trajo marijuana, y a los once we started to smoke juntos, it was our secret. . . Y empecé a creer que teníamos una relación especial secreta. . . Me confundí, y no sabía lo que sentía por mi Dad. . . He was the only Dad que conocía. . . You know?" Después te dirá lo más feo y terrible. . . Y le habían dicho *que no dijera a nadie*.

A Aurora le has contado hace tiempo, de tus primeras relaciones: "Me puse gorda la noche antes de graduación de la high school, a la orilla de un canal cerca del pueblito rural vecino." Lewis no fue ni mi primer novio, y ya a finales del año siguiente, tuve mi primer hijo, y sin casarme, y ya a Lewis le habíamos reclamado la paternidad legal de la niña. Yo había empezado el College, tiempo completo y estudiando drama como especialidad, y pronto conocí a quien sería mi primero esposo en el primer baile de ese primer semestre. Me puse encinta dentro de unas semanas, con mi segunda criatura. Pero de lo que de veras quería contar ahora, son las cosas que *esa gente* me dijo que no contara. Sí, what someone or somebody told me, "Don't tell anybody. . . No digas nada. . . Porque si sí dices, algo malo pasará. . . a ti, a alguien. . . No le digas a tu papá, tu mamá, a. . . nadie."

"*No digas nada,*" Don't tell anybody, me está diciendo el vecino de quince años de edad, bajo los bushes al lado de su casa. No digas nada, y me tocaba allá abajo, en la oscuridad, agachado a mi lado. Y yo, estremecida de susto, miedo y alboroto a la vez, murmuré, "Sí," y él me preguntaba, "Te gusta? Don't you like it?" Serge, el vecino, era nuestro babysitter frecuente, un joven guapísimo, pelo rizado, muy simpático, y mi madre confiaba mucho en él, probablemente por su manera respuestuosa con ellos. Le ayudaba a su propia madre divorciada con sus ganancias de los varios trabajitos que hacía después de la escuela, y durante los fines de semana. Me encantaba ir por "pomegranates" de su yarda. . . Yo apenas tenía cinco o seis años, and he loved babysitting me. . ."Súbete, Get on top of me," me decía, y cuando yo pregunté, "Por qué estás todo mojado aquí, qué es esto?" He told me después vas a saber. Me engaratucé con él, y después de un tiempo, finalmente me evitaba. . . *No le digas a nadie*. . . Y yo nunca dije.

Mi primo Huesos sólo tenía catorce-quince cuando vino a visitarnos en El Centro, pero para entonces yo tenía siete-ocho años, and thought he was muy guapo. Una vez, debajo de mi cama, me quitó los calzoncitos. . . and then he *got off,* estrujándose contra mí. Era el sobrino favorito de mi mamá, from New Mexico también. Años más tarde, afuera de la casa de un tío nuestro y durante una fiesta de familia, el Huesos se me acercó a donde yo esperaba en el carro de mis padres. "Do you remember, Pat? Lo has hecho todavía? Te pondrás toda caliente. . ." Le dije que todo aquello había sido en el pasado, y volteé la cara para no oler su aliento fuerte a cerveza. No le digas *a nadie.*

Tu madre te está explicando, "Esto es como tú estás, allá abajo adentro. . . Así, como esta media. It's a thin film like this nylon. Y cuando te casas, el hombre la rompe. . . Sí, sí sangrarás. . ."

Tu padre, borracho otra vez, te está pagando otro "midnight raid", y te despierta esa noche como en tantas otras, su voz rasposa, "Tengo que decirte algo. . . Tu mamá no fue virgen cuando nos casamos. Your mother wasn't a virgin. . ." Tratando de evitar sus olores de whiskey, das vuelta hacia la pared para no mirarlo, pensando, "Qué quiere decir? Dad. . . She's not a saint, I know. . ." Tu madre ausente, pecadora y errante según él, no era la Virgen María? Yo no lo entendía nada, ni hasta mucho después.

"Que no se te acerquen los chamacos, sólo quieren una cosa. No olvides, es un mundo de perros. . . Just remember, it's a doggey-dog world, mija, a doggey-dog world. . . And men, boys, they want only one thing. . ." Se te habían olvidado algo los consejos de borrachera de tu padre, pero ahora te está diciendo tu hermana la Vinnie que "Dad me despertaba a veces durante la noche, y me decía cosas extrañas. Qué edad tenía? About six. . . eight. . . No me acuerdo. It was stuff about boys and sex. Me daba mucho miedo, y. . . I didn't know what he was talking about for the longest time."

"Me quieres decir algo, mija. . .? Is there something you want to tell me, baby?" le preguntas a Vinnie, y ella dice, "There's some things I can't remember full-out, but hay como retratos o sentimientos que recuerdo como relampagazos. I get glimpses of some things. . . What? Sí, el primo Gonzalo sí, me sentó, and took off my panties and. . . sí, me acuerdo que me dolió. Y no me acuerdo del Ted, aquel viejo borracho. . . Oh? Tú sí te acuerdas. How old was I? Three? Lord, I don't believe it. And then, creo que me acuerdo, una vez nos quedamos con Dad, en su apartamente de soltero esa vez, and I was about twelve or so. . . y tuvimos que dormir todos en su cama grande. Two of us, I think. Pero no me acuerdo exactamente qué, hay un 'blackout' de lo que fue esa escena, when I try to remember. . . Me queda nada más como un sentimiento, alguna vaga memoria. But I try to forgive him now, digo, sí lo perdono ahora. Sí, a lo mejor andaba tomado, sí." *No digas nada. . .*

Estas son algunas de las cosas que no querían que. . . Les tenía que contar, como plática, como, de lo que me dijeron, nos decían. Don't tell anyone, it's our secret. *Es nuestro secreto. No le digas a nadie.*

Haciendo se aprende, me decían en casa. . . Yo nunca supe cocinar bien, bien. De chiquita no me hacían que ayudara en la cocina, y así lo que aprendí de cocina mexicana fue por ver y recordar y luego hacer mis chascos hasta que saliera bien lo que estaba cocinando. Tortillas? Siempre me salían chuecas, aunque a veces muy tasty. Tamales? Los hago ahora con carne de turkey. Tacos? Puro estilo chuppie (Chicano yuppie), con tortillas hechas y ya fritas en forma, carne de guajolote, ensalada comprada, queso ya raspado, todo toditito low-calorie, non-fat. Y salsa? Cuando se me antoja, pues hecha de scratch: tuesto los chiles, etc. Pero por lo general, salsa hecha, de Don Juan's, el Pato, la Rosita, la marca que sea, pero toda ya lista para echar. Y cuando vamos a casa de mi mamá, pues qué es lo que se nos antoja? Todo home-made, de tortillas a salsa, guisado y frijoles. Pero somos una gente de mucha invención, yo creo, y así, si el gusto se complace, pues por qué no, y no se pasa tanto tiempo en la cocina, al cabo que nuestras mamás, tías y abuelas eran las que estaban metidas allí, sobre el comal y la parrilla, para lo que les sirvió después. . . Mientras que aquéllos, tranquilitos y esperando que se les sirviera. La tradición, los valores transmitidos, creo que sí nos importan todavía, pero give me a break. De todas maneras me río de mí misma, yo sé que mis cochinadas, ajém, cocinadas, todas son estilo gringo, pero también yo sé bien la realidad en que vivo, y digo, por qué no? No me digas que no andamos todavía retechonchitos y contentos, con comer nuestros platos típicos, habiéndolos preparado al estilo rápido y de prisa? Y al que no le guste, pues. . . "Este es el show, el que estás viviendo. No refunds."

Ellos? Ay, cómo los quiero a ellos. Pero véanlo bien; lo que—según ellos—les corresponde: saben tomar, sobresaliente. Saben verse con mujeres, sobresaliente. Saben llegar a la hora que quieran, cuando quieran, excelente también. Cocinar? por lo general, nones; lavar ropa, limpiar suelos, ayudar con los platos, tampoco. Pues ahora hay excepciones, pero por lo general, según ellos, no les corresponde y a nosotras sí. . . Limpiar al niño, cambiarle las zapetas? Pues qué te crees? Nel, nones, ni modo. . . y qué se va a hacer?

En tus clases, un par de veces, un par de varoncitos murmuran

"Llorona. . ." y se ríen otros. Tú te fijas, te lastima, porque los has querido a ellos también. "Perdónalos, que no saben lo que hacen." Nel, ésa, sí saben, y les gusta, segurón que sí. Sin corazón, sin corazón, we're, *Alguien* is produciendo masticándolos churning them out that way.

En el campo de Masterton, tu prima Tere te hizo el amor. Qué edad tenías? Pues, tú unos 8-9 años, ella once o doce, y te hizo, que tú hicieras, lo erótico. Es cierto, no era "el amor'," sino un episodio sensual, que tú recuerdas, con vergüenza y rencor, cuarenta años después. La habían dejado a la Tere, cuidándote a ti y a los hermanitos, mientras trajinaba tu mamá por allá en el pueblo, haciendo mandados o algo así. La prima era de Nuevo México, la habían dejado "encargada" de ustedes. Era la hermanita del primo Huesos, y tú en tus pocos años no sabías nada de "incesto" o "abuse". Eran tus primos, parientes de tu madre, y estaban allí, cuidandote, como era costumbre dejar a los parientes cuidando a los hijos. "Ven, acuéstate aquí en el catre conmigo. . . Quítate la ropa. Ven. . ." Y te besó, y te gustó. Y se untaron contra sí, y se besaban besos calientes, y te sentías toda caliente, como que ardías. Y tu prima te dijo, al fin del largo rato aborotado y tú sabías—prohibido—*No le digas a nadie. . .*

El refried bean sandwich? Fue una comida que yo inventé un día que, estando yo sola con algunos de mis hermanitos, vino un señor pobre, vestido en garras y pidiendo limosna de comida, nada más quería algo de comer: "Tengo hambre," dijo en español simplemente, "me da algo de comer?" Pues yo, niña adolescente, traté de ayudarle, y fui a la cocina, donde encontré unos frijoles refritos, fríos y duros, y una barra de pan seco. Todo lo que se me ocurrió darle al señor, no sabiendo cocinar nadita, era un sandwich de frijoles. Y fue lo que le regalé. . . Tomó el bultito de sandwich que le di, me dijo sencillamente "Gracias," y se fue hacia la calle principal del pueblo. Miré por la ventana de la recámara, y vi que el señor, padeciendo de hambre, seguramente, como había dicho, se sentó a comer lo que mis manos inexpertas le habían obsequiado. Y vi que el pobre tomó un bocado, lo escupió, y tiró mi sandwich al suelo. Pobre señor, se levantó y se encaminó a la casa que quedaba directamente enfrente de él, y en la calle principal donde estaba, allí a la esquina del lote de nuestra casa. Y pidió limosna, una caridad, de algo bueno que comer. Yo todavía recuerdo eso, y recuerdo después que me dijo la Trudi González, "Teníamos una carne guisada y verduras, y le dimos al señor unos taquitos." Con qué gusto se ha de haber comido esos taquitos, mi pobre señor que solamente quería algo bueno que comer! El refried bean sandwich? Entre todas mis confecciones, no lo recomiendo.

En el campo, les hacían tacos con tortillas, frijoles y carne guisada, o chorizo con papas o algo más o diferente así guisado. Y les daban su fruta. Así fue hasta que algunos de los abonados y braceros empezaron a pedir comida americana, para variar. Y empezó la época de los sandwiches, los lonches americanos. Así que terminaban de cocinar y limpiar lo del desayuno—o almuerzo como decíamos nosotros entonces—empezaban a preparar el "lonche" de los trabajadores. Pura línea de asamblea. Todo ordenado, así lo organizaba mi mamá con la cocina con sus ayudantes. El Galla, en el campo de Masterton y el de Newdale, era su ayudante principal. Después a la Marieta la llevaban de vez en cuando, cuando había algo especial o cuando mi mamá no se sentía bien, pero por lo general, eran el Galla y otros dos o tres braceros los que trabajaban allí. A veces oí decir a mi mamá, "Se quejan ahora de tacos siempre. . . se quejan después que comida gringa."

Por algunos años, mi padre tuvo un negocio de "bail bonds". . . Así llegó a tener algo que ver con algunos representantes de la Unión, porque de vez en cuando a él le llamaban para que sacara a uno de los del Sindicato de Chávez de la cárcel. Años antes, en los primeros años de las huelgas, le habían tirado un ladrillo o un piedra grande por la ventana de la casa de mi papá y mi madrastra. Como mi padre estaba entonces como reclutador de personal del fil, de la asociación de rancheros de la fresa, pues no se veía él muy bien con la Unión. Pero ya después, le llamaban a él, para sacar a los sindicalistas de la cárcel. "Ya ves cómo da vueltas el mundo," decía la Esmeralda, "la gente de *tu amigo Chávez* nos echó una piedra por la ventana, cuando las huelgas, y ahora tu papá sacándolos." Esmeralda, pícara, bien sabía que yo tenía *mis secretos*, y que yo *no* había sido buena amiga de la Huelga, sino mostré, en los '60s, ser buena hija de contratista. . . *Y no hija buena, tampoco y además. . .*

CAPÍTULO TRES

Mi tío "Toro" era mi tío favorito. . . Llegó a casarse unas seis veces, y todavía nunca fue con la mujer que realmente quería. En su memoria de hombre maduro, recordaba a Chelita, la muchacha de Nuevo México, a quien de veras había querido. Todavía, me dijo, cuando iba a Mesilla, "Voy a verla, a la Chelita. She's got real nice skin, todavía," me dijo. Cada vez que va pa'llá, dice que va a divorciar a su esposa que tiene, pero hasta la fecha, no lo hace. Y lleva ahora más de veinticinco años con la última, una mujer portuguesa grácil, fuerte y paciente.

Mi Tío Toro era tan travieso como lo era atractivo. Un día que iban al fil, mi tío Toro alborotó al Gallareta a que fueran en busca de miel de abejas. Iban al fil de fresas, a dejar los lonches. Habían visto, allá por Modesto, en las afueras donde estaban los files de fresas, que había, bajo unos árboles enormes de nueces "walnut," unas cajas blancas en columna, casitas de abejas de miel. Algún ranchero las estaba cultivando, y a mi tío y al Gallareta, les entró la codicia por la miel de abeja, fresquecita. De alguna manera, fue el Galla el que se eligió para ir y abrir una de las casitas/caja, el abejero que quedaba más cerca al troque que llevaban ese día. Y lo atacaron, en masa hervidera, las abejas enojadas. Lograron salir de allí, pero tuvieron que venir unos hombres del fil para ayudarles, porque el Galla andaba bien picado, y empezó a hincharse mientras gritaba "Ay, ay, auxilio!, Ay, me duele, ay!" o algo por el estilo dijo mi tío Toro, riéndose después el travieso, "Anda tan hinchado el Gallareta, que parece tomate listo pa'splotar," así dijo mi tío

Toro travieso. Era muy suave con nosotros los sobrinos, pero yo supe que él había sufrido mucho por enamorado. . .

Una de las "esposas" del tío Toro nunca llegó a ser su esposa. Iba a ser la tercera, creo, o la cuarta. En esos tiempos, yo no le ponía caso a la serie, pero sí me dio lástima porque al tío se le "fue el sueño" por una chavala. Ella era de Mexicali, de una familia "decente" como me dijo mi mamá. Yo había visto al tío ponerse muy guapo, preparar sus maletas, y subirse en su carrito "convertible" para ir, desde el Valle San Joaquín donde vivíamos en Masterton, a Mexicali. Le había estado mandando dinero a la novia por muchos meses. . . El se la había conocido en Mexicali, cuando él todavía vivía por allá en El Centro o Betaville, y se había venido después para ganarse unos centavos y poder ir por ella. Mientras, la novia estaba guardando el dinero pa' la boda, y pa' su vestido y la luna de miel. Después de dos días, el tío Toro regresó, todo callado, y no quiso hablar ni con nosotros los chiquitos ni con mi papá. Llegó sin novia ni esposa, le dijo algo a mi mamá quien había salido al carrito convertible pa' ver qué traiba el tío. "No se casaron," dijo mi mamá, "lo dejó plantado." Así nos dijo a nosotros y a la Marieta, "Gastó el dinero, que pa'unas deudas del papá o algo así." También nos dijo después que la Choli, la novia, le había dijo al tío que no lo quería siempre. El no quiso vernos por unos días, y supimos que se fue a vivir en el hotel chiquito del pueblo, y que anduvo de "parranda" por unas semanas.

No me quedé triste que mi tío no se había casado con la Choli. Me habían llevado de visita, visita muy corta me acuerdo, antes del desastre, y la conocí. Lo único que tenía de impresionante la muchacha, para mis ojos adolescentes, era que tenía ojos grandes con pestañas largas, y un lunar negro y grande, merito en medio de la frente. Sí, pues, en la cara, merito en la frente. Años después, me subí con mis dos hijitos en un autobús de Modesto a Stockton, en el mismo Valle San Joaquín, y vi a una señora maciza y seria, sentada con una muchacha del mismo pelo lacio y ojos grandes. Era la Choli, ya de vieja, muy seria, y el lunar negro y grande, merito en medio de la frente. Me acordé que mi mamá, aquellos muchos años antes, había dicho cuando volvió mi tío, novio frustrado, "Verán, si algún día llego a ver a ésa, la voy a'garrar del chongo!"

Mi papá ahora no se acuerda de nada. Dicen que tiene Alzheimers, pero sospechan tus hermanas y tú, que fue por el alcohol. . . De joven, fue un terror. Una que tu madre no puede olvidar, fue la del pescuezo sucio. Esta era "del otro lado," de Mexicali, que quedaba a unas ocho millas del pueblito donde vivíamos todos nosotros. "A tu viejo lo vimos en la corrida de toros el domingo. Andaba con una muchacha, se veían muy enamorados" fue lo que le dijo mi tía Rosalba a mi mamá. Mi mamá dijo que algunas noches, llegaba bien tarde y borracho mi papá, especialmente los fines de semana, y una vez que él había ido a Mexicali con unos compadres, no llegó hasta el día siguiente. "Y ni vergüenza tenía. Traiba los calzoncillos con la sangre de la vieja. Era bien cochina, *y él.* . . No se aguantaba." "Por qué se quedaban casados, Mamá? No lo querías?" "No sé. . . Nadie se divorciaba." "Pero no lo querías?" "Pues sí, cuando nos casamos, pero, no sé. . ."

Tu padre y tus tíos, toda esa familia, era muy festejera, se juntaban mucho de jóvenes, por muchos años todos los hijos vivían primero juntos, luego en la misma vecindad, aunque ya tenían marido o esposa. Todos muy bien parecidos y de buena disposición, el más galán había sido nuestro papá. Y les gustaban las bromas, decían chistes, se hacían jugaditas. En el campo de mi tío Mingo, tuvieron una fiesta una vez que duró por la tarde y toda la noche. No recuerdo bien la ocasión, si una boda, un bautizo, o nada más pa'comer y beber. Se habían puesto bien cuetes mis tíos y mi papá, y allí andaban los chavalitos bailando y corriendo en el comedor lleno de gente. Estaban tocando discos, guitarras, cantando, y se aparecieron mi papá y uno de mis tíos, vestiditos de mujer. Como dijo después otro tío: "Esos dos locos, con chichero y naguas de hawaiiana. Y debajo, apenitas calzoncillos."

En Salmas, un camión llevando a muchos braceros, fue destrozado por un tren cuando cruzaban el traque. . . Murieron muchos, se lastimaron gravemente otros. Y hasta el gobierno federal se metió en la investigación de cómo había pasado. Mi papá tuvo que ir al sitio, poco después de haber sucedido, para ver qué se podía hacer. "Estuvo bien feo," dijo, "fueron muertes de oquis. No saben por qué trató de cruzar el troque, así lleno de hombres. Alguien la va'pagar. . ." Desde México, se dejaron venir otros oficiales para hacer su parte en la investigación, después de hacerse quejas y gestiones oficiales.

"Hello, mija. I'm in Puerto Rico," así lee la tarjeta postal que te manda tu padre desde Puerto Rico, donde lo habían mandado desde Salmas, de parte de la sociedad de rancheros y patrocinado por el gobierno, para ver si se hacía un arreglo de un programa de trabajadores campesinos. Sí, querían traer a trabajadores agrícolas para Estados Unidos, desde Puerto Rico. "Aquí está muy bonito. Love, Your Old Man," dice la tarjeta. Después, dejó la asociación de los freseros, porque trajeron "Some young punk. Has a degree in Agriculture or something, trying to tell me what to do. Cabrones dueños gringos, no agradecen. . ."

Mi papá? A mi papá le gustaron los *ojos verdes*. La vieja del pescuezo sucio, aquella de Mexicali, la llegó a espiar mi mamá. La llevó mi tía Rosalba, muy atrevida ésta aunque mi mamá en ese entonces era algo tímida, y se fueron a los toros de sorpresa un domingo. Por allá vieron a mi padre guapo jacalero, bien abrazadito "Con aquella vieja. Era bien prieta, bien prieta, pelo chinito y grasoso, y de ojos verdes. Traiba el cuello bien sucio, y el pescuezo se le veía manchado, como que no se lo lavaba. Y cuando él se iba a verla, pues yo metida en el restaurante, trabajando. Ustedes estaban muy chiquitos, no sabían nada. *Y lo que sabíamos, no decíamos a nadie.*

El último campo que tuvieron, el de Newdale, donde llegaron a usar las máquinas para hacer tortillas, lo perdieron mis padres debido a que "Tu padre por mujeriego y volado. Porque le gustaron los ojos verdes de esta güera de Juárez," está diciendo tu mamá, "por eso lo perdimos todo, y después ellos se arreglaron cómo sacarle mis propias ganancias, para llevárselas ellos. . ." En caso de la ausencia de mi padre, mi mamá manejaba el campo en Newdale, como siempre levantándose temprano y regresando tarde, a veces ni podía regresar a casa para pasar la noche con nosotros. La Marieta vivía todavía con nosotros, y mi mamá de vez en cuando tenía que quedarse en la casita que habían construido en el campo. Y así pasó que, mi mamá se quedó encargada de este campo que tenían, y mi papá se fue allá cerca de Visalia donde corría un campo en un lugar que había sido una base del gobierno, con comedor, barracas con camas, todo en un lugar árido. Esa base se había abandonado por algunos años, y mi papá, tíos y otros socios, habían tenido la idea de poder emplear a más trabajadores por aquella parte del Valle San Joaquín. . . quedaba a una distancia de Fresno, en el mero centro del Valle.

"La Esmeralda era una vieja cantinera. Trabajaba por allá cerca de donde tenían el campo en la base abandonada. La conoció por allá. Y ella empezó a mandarme postales, de los moteles donde se quedaban. Después supe que tenía ojos verdes y era güera, aunque se pintaba el pelo, así casi colorado." Tu madre, quien por años se pintó el pelo anaranjado, te está contando, otra vez, de cómo "se había volado tu papá, con esa Esmeralda."

CAPÍTULO CUATRO

"Habla el gran señor Leyva? Sabes quién soy?" "Aló, . . . Pat. . . seguro, es la. . . Petra. . . Aló, mija. . ." Y empiezan sus esfuerzos de tratar de hacer bromas, chistes. Llega a ser un juego tuyo, esto de llamarle a tu papá, y empezando así, confirmar que todavía te reconoce la voz. Hasta cuándo, te preguntas, hasta cuándo?

Tú te acuerdas de la última vez que fueron a ver a tu papá, fue hace seis meses, ahora lo tienen en San Mingo, en un lugar de nombre curioso: Lugar de la Casa. La primera vez que te dicen, "allí vive ahora," tú les discutes, pensando que se han equivocado, pero después te dices

"Another dumb translation of Spanish, so what's new?" En el muelle de Santa Cruz esa tarde, van caminando más en frente el marido de la Vinnie y Bob, tu esposo. En frente de ti, tras ellos, van Vinnie y tu papá, enlazados del brazo. Pasando un puesto de barquitos para rentar, sale música fuerte y rítmica de rock and roll. Ves que tu padre de repente da dos o tres saltitos al ritmo, hace un paso de baile, pa'quí, pa'llá, y siguen adelante, riéndose la Vinnie y abrazando a tu papá. Todavía está para hacer muñecadas y vaciladas. . . Ay, qué viejito éste. Y todavía, todavía le sigue la corriente. Pero va perdiendo el hilo, ya muy poquito sabe dónde está. Por teléfono? Todavía te reconoce, bueno, excepto una sola vez, hasta ahora. Pero en persona, cuando lo ves y cuando salimos juntos, es otro cuento. Se nos van yendo nuestros viejitos, nuestras vidas así, piensas. . .

La viejita francesa, la que te conoció y te ayudó y te crió a Marisa en Southwest City, también está en un lugar como santuario. Es un rest home, pero es realmente una casa antigua remodelada y rehecha muy bonita, en un pueblito de cerros por allá por Missouri. Vive muy lejos ahora del desierto, pero su vida ahora es un desierto. . . El caso de ella, diferente al de tu padre, porque tu viejita francesa no camina ya, ni puede escribir cartas porque le fallan la vista y las manos para guiar la pluma. Pero razona y todavía rezonga, perfectamente bien, casi, casi. "I haven't heard from you in a long time, I tink you lost or somezing. Wher' you bin, Pat, wher' Marisa?" en su acento fuerte francés y extranjero, la viejita te dice que nadie la viene a ver, que por qué no han escrito, que si se han olvidado de ella, como sus propios nietos lo han hecho. De más de diez nietos y muchos biznietos, solamente una nieta viene a ver a la abuela en el resthome. El hijo que allí le queda, pasa una-dos veces por semana a verla, y pa' pedirle dinero. René es el hijo que nunca llegó a nada, el otro hijo se jubiló de la fuerza aérea. Habían vivido por muchos años en Southwest City, porque allí lo habían estacionado en la base enorme que había allí. Hace unos cinco años, la viejita todavía vivía independientemente, entonces se cayó y le descubrieron una enfermedad que la afectaría como ahora, que no puede caminar, ni apenas con un "walker." Años más atrás, en Southwest City cuando todos ustedes estaban más nuevecitos, esta viejita refunfuñaba y le daba las madres a cualquiera que la ofendiera. De carácter fuerte, de todas maneras era una dama "a todo dar." Me contaba de cómo había conocido a los dos esposos, allá en Francia. Y cómo había venido a llegar a Illinois.

Santuario. . . El convento del Buen Pastor, en Las Cruces, Nuevo México, así era, lleno de santos y santas. Pero no llegó a ser mi santuario. . . Las monjas nos enseñaron a bordar. Llegué a saber dibujar, con aguja y la hilasa, florecitas, caracolitos, hojas finas o grandes y esponjadas, pajaritos, corazoncitos, listoncitos, you name it. El fin de mis enseñanzas. Y no recuerdo que ese verano que pasé allí, hubiera aprendido otra cosa más práctica. Era para ayudar en la "assembly line" de las monjas. Todo el trabajo bordado que producíamos nosotras las internadas, y sólo tenía unos siete-ocho años, era para venta en los "kermeses" que según entendía yo de niñita, eran un tipo de "bazaar" que hacían en algunas de las parroquias. El dinero era para el Convento, o la Iglesia, a saber. También, en la sección del Convento donde estaban las más grandes y las novicias, había una dulcería y una lavandería. Bueno, lo de la dulcería a lo mejor me lo imaginaba yo, pero sí había una lavandería grande. Qué hacían? Pues yo de veras no sé, sé que creía que allí había "industria," y que de alguna manera tenía que ver con mantener limpios los trapos católicos, o como diría Sabine Ulibarrí, escritor humorista de por aquellos lares: "de católicos y apostólicos."

Tan católicas nos hicieron, como les he dicho por otra parte, que nos ponían a dar las gracias a Dios por el café que nos daban para echarle al mois. Sí, al cereal, en vez de leche.

"Ask my Dad what the Sanctuary Movement means," te apuntas, para ver si te puede contestar algo tu papá, sobre el movimiento del santuario. A tu madre le preguntas. "Tú sabes si tu iglesia le ha dado santuario a algunos refugiados, o a gente indocumentada. No, no son la misma cosa, pero querer hacer buenas obras. . . Tu iglesia se ha metido en eso?" Y tu hijo, que ahora va de evangelista extranjero a México, qué hará él. "Que no te metas en política, stay out of their politics. . ." le amonestas a tu hijo. Tu hijo, alto, pelo café, ojos castaños con flequitas verdes, te contesta que él no, ellos nada más van "To spread the word of God," para decirles, a los mexicanos, de la palabra de Dios. Esto te parece a la vez absurdo, triste y chistoso. Para decirles de la palabra de Dios. A ja jaaaaaay!

Pues eso sí que hace falta, que a los mexicanos—a los latinos—vengan y se les explique, la verdadera palabra de Dios. Vamos terminando por donde empezamos, te dices, qué vueltas. . .

"How long will you be there, mijo?" le preguntas a tu hijo el ministro pentecostés apostólico. Y tú, a pesar de las palabras de tu madre que le salen de la boca, sabes bien: Lo quiero, a este muchacho, lo quiero. "Pues que Dios te bendiga, mijo. God bless you, and take care." Todo lo que dice tu hijo, lo podría haber dicho tu madre, o cualquiera de tus otros hermanos criados así como pentecosteses. Pero tienen buenas intenciones, nada más algunas opiniones conservadoras por una parte, y extremistas por otra. Así es el mundo: Escucha la palabra de Dios Todopoderoso por una parte, y contando chistes sobre los negros por otra. "And Rastus said, you got big-lips, black boy. Ha, ha." Cómo, te preguntas, cómo se puede ser buen cristiano por una parte, y racista/misoginista/elitista etc. etc., por otra?

He visto, en nombre de su mensaje, que alguien diga algo como que "O me dejas que te salve, o te mato. O te dejas salvar (por mí, por nosotros), o te cuacho los dientes, o haces lo que yo te digo (quiero, recomiendo, predico), o te desmadro, te doy en los huevos (las chichis, el culo, el zunfiate). Nada más, conviértete (a la fuerza, ni a tu causa). . . Así, no? Pues, así, no.

"Los hijos de la tía Marta, dos de ellos, los que eran raros, te acuerdas, pos dizque los dos hicieron test HIV-positive. . . O sea, si tenías dudas de que si eran o no eran, pos desquítate ahora. Qué harán nuestros tíos, los papás de ellos? Pos que Dios los ampare." Así te decía tu prima, visitando desde Los Angeles. Aquellos primos enfermos, y los papás, todos, siempre fueron muy buena gente con nosotros. La tía como que, después del divorcio de tus padres, no quería ser "desleal" a tu papá, y no quisieron tener nada que ver con tu mamá. Tu mamá había dejado a tu padre años atrás, y todavía le guardaban rencores... Hasta hace poco, no tenían nada que ver con ella. No sé cómo pensaban, pero como que tu mamá había sido la culpable, por haberlo dejado, aunque todos los hermanos de tu padre sabían de sus "mocedades y vejedades." Si tú les preguntabas, se hacían... Pues, todo eso aparte, tus tíos ahora iban a pasar de lo más horrible que pueden pasar unos padres, ver morir a uno dos hijos. Y de la SIDA, que será una muerte prolongada, empezando ahora que no se les ve nada de malos.

"Y el hijo de la prima Chayo, también hizo test HIV-positive. Qué te parece? Es bien feo, verdá...? No, el chamaco no, lo que le pasa, eso está bien feo, verdá. Isn't it awful? Le ruego a Dios que no nos pase a nuestros hijos." Ni a nosotros, le contestas. Pero, ver a un hijo morirse, así despacio y en agonías a lo ultimo... Que no tenga que pasarlo con nuestros hijos, o hijas.

Tu amiga Mercedes te está contando algo, algo muy serio... "Qué qué decías, Meché, Quién es homosexual! Qué? Que bisexual, tu hija?" Tu amiga te está diciendo, entre sollozos y lágrimas, "Me dijo que siempre sabía que era diferente, que a pesar de haberse enamorado varias veces, y se iba a casar aquella vez, te acuerdas? Pues, así y todo, me dice, esta bomba que me ha dejado caer, pues... La primera vez, me confesó, era cuando estaba under the influence, emborrachada y endrogada. Y la agarraron. Por fin me admitió, que la primera vez, la seducieron. Una mujer amiga de la universidad, con quien estudiaba, estudios de mujeres de la Raza algo así..." Así que, la hija de tu amiga es gay. Y tus primos son gay. Así que los chicanos, y las chicanitas, también pueden ser de esos, gay.

"You can't be gay and be Chicano!" Así insiste un viejo nervioso en Albuquerque, una vez que has ido a hablar de chicanas en la literatura y cosas de libros. Vienen tras de él, un par de chicanitas calladas pero atentas, y después les preguntan a ustedes los profesores, "Is that guy for real, or what? Qué disparates, el cuate!" Simón, ése, ésa. Son de tu sangre, son tus gentes, son de tu familia. . . "Homosexuals are an abomination. That's why God has sent AIDS. . ." Así te han dicho tu mamá, tu hijo. "Por eso van a morir todos los raros. . . Dios los está castigando, mandando el SIDA."

"Mijo. Esa enfermedad, el SIDA, aparece en la población entera, no solamente entre los homosexuals. . . Pues, por muchos descuidos, sí, pero no siempre por pecado." Estos son de los temas prohibidos en las discusiones familiares. . . Tu hijo te ha platicado mientras estaban solos una tarde. Te parece que no es tan eficaz lo que aconsejan muchos "Just say NO." Cómo hacer que la juventud no sienta pasiones? Cómo hacer que se cuiden, y se protejan, de tanto, tanto peligro? Nada más con decir NO, y hacia la salvación?

Ya sabes lo que dirá tu madre. Eso de que "Son los últimos días, por eso, estamos en los últimos días." Me canso de oír eso, Mamá, piensas tú. . .

CAPÍTULO CINCO

Just say NO. Es el camino, la solución que se ofrece a tantos problemas. . . Por qué entonces, no dijo NO la cuñada de tu amiga Lulu, la mujer que murió antes de cumplir los cincuenta, de alcoholismo? Tu tío, el mayor que estaba siempre de buen humor contigo, pero padecía de esa enfermedad también. A los dos, los llamarían algunos, "winos," porque el vino era su alcohol favorito. Por qué tuvieron que beber hasta matarse con la bebida, teniendo tanto talento y posibilidades? Y tu padre, que ahora no se acuerda de la cara de sus hijos, no reconoce, aunque todavía recuerda sus voces? Oh, cómo se miente con la propaganda. Que faltándoles motivación espiritual, "Sólo decir NO!"

"Las hermanas Simón, las conoció en el fil," dice tu madre, "Algunas de esas viejas, en el mismo trabajo las encontraba. A las Simón, por allá en los files de Fresno, en aquel campo que manejaba tu papá con tus tíos. Por allá andaban. Pues se la llevaba grande tu padre, dos hermanas y una vieja de pelo rojo y ojos verdes." Te acuerdas después, que tu padre trata de convencer a tu mamá que no lo dejara. El era piloto, pide prestado el avión del ranchero de fresas, el japonés Hakagachi, y en compañía de la hermana mayor de tu padre, te llevan hasta Reno para "quitarle la idea a Lorenza." En Reno, la hermana mayor, tu tía, le dice a la portera de la residencia donde vive tu madre mientras finalizan el divorcio, "Tell Lorenza that, that her youngest child has been in an accident with her husband and they need her at home." Después te darás cuenta que entre muchas familias, así son, se ayudan como debe ser, incluyendo las leperadas de los varones. Y cuando llega a los disparates o equivocaciones de las hijas/primas/cuñadas, pues depende, y pobre de ti.

"Tu hermana Lupe es una. . . bareta," te está diciendo tu madre. Esta hermanita la trajeron de México. Sí, es la única mexicana, de México mero, entre ustedes los hijos de Lorenza y tu Papá. Y la que menos quiere ser mexicana. Ni una palabra de español, dice que no quiere. Hace unos años, te escribe Lupe: "I want to go find my real mother. I want you to go and interpret for us." Tú le responds que sería imposible, tú no quieres ir en busca de otra madre para tu hermana, que su madre natural, según las condiciones en que vivía, probablemente ya no vivía, y otras cosas por el estilo. "Tu hermana Lupe era cuate. . ." Tenía un hermanito-cuate, y el médico del pueblito, cerca de Truenos, allá en las montañas de Sonora, el médico fue quien le contó a tu madre de una señora india que acababa de tener unos gemelos. "Por allá vivía, en un jacal allá en las afueras del pueblo. Entré al jacal, y estaban los dos bultitos en el suelo. La niña estaba enferma, y la mamá, pues le dimos dinero, y nos llevamos a la niñita." "Llévesela, señora. . . a ver si sobrevive con ustedes. . ." y lloró la madre indígena, "Lloró al darme la niñita, y lloró cuando le di los cien dólares. 'Yo sé que esto no le paga por su hijita, pero la cuidaré. . .' Esa mujer era la querida de un viejo ricacho del pueblo, dicen que todo güero, y la mujer, pues era india. . ."

"Tu hermana Lupe me odia. Vieras cómo me habla. . ." "Mamá, tú le dabas escobazos. Como que no la querías, porque tenías ya a mis otros hermanitos con el segundo viejo. Ella sí te quiere. Pero a lo mejor, no se le olvida." "No, no, tu hermana se acuesta con hombres por todas partes, los trae allí a la casa estando sus hijos. . . Me gritó el otro día: 'You weren't such a saint!' Fíjate, decirme así, que yo no había sido ni tan santa. Es una bareta, esa huila!"

Supieron mis padres después, unos años después que regresaron con Lupita de Truenos, que un jabalí había entrado al jacal de la señora india, y le había comido parte de la cara al hermanito de Lupe, al geme-lito. "Esa señora tenía otros hijos, todos en escalerita de edades, más grandes que los gemelos." La familia Sosa, quienes trabajaban en los files donde andaba tu papá, le habían dicho lo del gemelito y el jabalí. Esa fue la misma familia de la boda grande en el pueblito allá en las montañas, por Truenos, donde se les habían atravesado las gallinas y los perros, en camino a la iglesia.

Una vez que regresábamos del Valle San Joaquín hacia el Valle Im-perial hacia el sur, mi hermanito Samuelito y yo éramos lo únicos que íbamos atrás en el troque grande. . . Allí teníamos cajas y costales y muebles y sacos de comida como frijol, papas, cebollas, pero también llevábamos un lonche, agua, y había muchos colchones en la parte más cerrada y protegida del camion. Pues nos pusimos a pelear, mi her-manito y yo. Nuestros papás iban en frente con la bebita, Belita, y no vieron cómo empezamos a pelear allá atrás. Pues en nuestro combate, le saqué sangre a mi hermanito, dándole un cato así ZAS! en la nariz. Quise darle en la cara, pero estábamos bien enojados por no me acu-erdo ni qué, y pues conecté con la nariz. Unos días después, ya que estábamos en El Centro, mi mamá me llamó al cuarto donde estaba lavando la ropa. Allí tenía el vestidito mío, que había usado para pararle la sangre a la nariz de mi hermanito. Yo creía que ella lo sabía todo y me iban a dar una buena nalgada, cuando me preguntó mi mamá, "Petrita. Tú sabes lo que es *menstruación?*" Yo le dije que no, no sabía lo que era esa palabra. "Pues estás todavía muy chiquita, pero, esta sangre en el vestido. . . Qué puede ser? Mija, tú te acuerdas?" Yo le dije, en tono de confesión, que me había lastimado en el troque. Pero no le confesé hasta mucho tiempo después, cómo le había dado "bloody nose" a mi hermanito, en un momento de coraje y pleito. Él, claro, por su parte no dijo nada tampoco, como era bien machito y no quería que supieran que una mujer le había sacado sangre de la nariz. Los dos hermanitos, teníamos nuestros secretos "inocentes" también.

Pelearme con mis hermanos? No, de veras que no. Fueron solamente dos los pleitos que recuerdo con mi hermano. . . Y el último fue en lo que resultaron ser los últimos días del matrimonio de mis papás. Ellos estaban separados, uno en el campo en el pueblo donde vivíamos, y el otro trabajando en el otro campo, el de la base abandonada cerca de Visalia. Pues habían empezado ya las llamadas a casa, a veces contestaba yo, a veces mi hermano. Eramos los mayores. La Marieta todavía estaba, pero la largó mi papá cuando lo dejó mi mamá, "Porque esa Marieta era una vieja chapucera, alcahueta de tu mamá." Pues, tras unos días de llamadas a la casa en voces de mujer, ahora diciendo "Tu madre está saliendo con otro hombre. . ." o diciendo "Tu padre se acuesta con una vieja de ojos verdes. . ." o algo como "Tus papás se están poniendo cuernos," empezábamos a entender algo de lo que oíamos, y andábamos nerviosos mi hermano y yo. Teníamos ya unos catorce y quince años. Y por algún motivo, nos pusimos a darnos unas bofetadas y unos porrazos. . . Pues yo traiba uñas largas, de las pocas épocas cuando me había dejado crecer las uñas y no comérmelas. Para acortar el cuento, mi hermano me ganó esta vez, dándome unos buenos sonazos en el estómago. Como siempre, ni me acuerdo de lo que fue. Solamente me acuerdo que me había rompido mi uña más larga, mi predilecta. Y aunque mi hermano llevó las cicatrices de mis uñas por unos días, nunca les dijimos a nuestros papás que "los dos hermanos ideales" nos habíamos agarrado "de la greña." Y lo curioso, cuando trato de recordar el último pleito, fue que nos peleáramos nosotros dos, dos hermanos que mucho nos queríamos y siempre nos llevábamos bien. Nunca se me olvidará la fuerza, la violencia, con que nos peleamos la última vez. Nos propelaba un odio, un sentimiento enorme, enorme, violento y feroz.

CAPÍTULO SEIS

Tu madre también tenía sus secretos, te dices. "Tu madre no fue virgen cuando nos casamos. . ." "Yo me debía haber casado con otro hombre, con el Felipe de Nuevo México. Pero él se fue al army. Después, pues me casé con tu papá, y Felipe nunca volvió. Murió en la Guerra. Con él fue con quien me debía haber casado. . ." Por allá en otro estado, tienen ustedes un mediohermano que no conocen. Bueno, la Vinnie lo ha visto, y tu mamá. Lo tuvo una prima de tu madre, cuando estaban recién casados, la prima visitó y tu papá, pues el cuento de siempre. El, guapo y platicador y volado, le hizo la chapuza a la prima, y adiós, Nena, se hundió el barco! Es triste la historia, y tú ya no averiguas nada por allá porque todos lo niegan. El mediohermano? Pues creo que no sabe. Creo que le contaron algo de que el papá había muerto en la guerra. Sí, son muy raras las cosas en la vida real, más que en los cuentos. Pa'qué te cuento. . .

Pues prometí contar los cuentos prohibidos, de los secretos. Sí, voy seleccionando, pero es mi opción y como se dice, al que no le guste. . . Pues allí está la puerta y todo eso.

Después de hacer lo de "bailbonds" por unos años, tu padre vuelve a trabajar en la agricultura. . . Lo convence un socio a que manejen unos terrenos fuera de la ciudad, camino a Santa Cruz, donde habrá un sistema de "sharecropping." Los campesinos que allí vienen, compartirán en las ganancias de la cosecha de fresas. "It's a better deal for them," dice tu padre. Es allí donde está trabajando cuando empiezan a notar ustedes, que tu padre ya no dice los chistes como siempre, que se ve inseguro y algo frágil, cuando ustedes lo van a ver. Han ido, ese año, para que él conociera a tu esposo. También iban Vinnie y su esposo, y la Belita. Habían llamado el día antes, y habían arreglado con tu papá que él los encontraría en Monterrey, en el motel de ustedes, pero la mañana siguiente, tu padre no llegó. Entonces, ustedes fueron a buscarlo en su trabajo, en la oficina de los terrenos de fresa, allá yendo pa'Gilroy. . . "Qué pasó, Papá?" "Nada. . . por qué. . .?" Lo invitaron a comer, y sentados allí al lado del mar en un restaurante en la bahía, ustedes pueden observar que ha habido un cambio en tu padre. Los mira nerviosos. Y dentro de tres años, tu papá se vuelve más distinto, cohibido, introspectivo, no reconociendo o recordando detalles.

De una de tus hermanas, sospechas que es. . . de las otras. Las que se gustan entre ellas. Sí, mujer, es bisexual. Te acuerdas haber leído años atrás, unos poemas que tu hermana había escrito, en un tipo de "diary." Escribía de "Y te beso en ese lugar. . . Amor secreto. . ." Duró unos quince años de casada. "Tu hermana y la amiga gorda, dicen que pasan las mañanas juntas. Que tu hermana se pasa los días libres, allá con la amiga gringa, la gorda. . ." Tú dijiste, "No puede ser. La amiga, la Ginger, trabaja en el Bible College. Y mi hermana y su esposo, pues están casados, qué no?. Tienen hijos, qué no? No puede ser, no le hagas caso a los chismes de las cuñadas, están celosas. Pues porque mi hermana es tan lista, tan de buen corazón con todos. . ." Y de fuerte carácter, así como tu papá, recuerdas bien que siempre la llevaba por todas partes. "You were Dad's favorite, le dices a tu hermana. Tú siempre fuiste la favorita de mi papá." "You're mom's favorite, tú es a quien mi mamá más quiere, ja, ja. . ." Así se burlan y se hacen broma entre ustedes los hermanos. "Y si supieran el secreto. . . Y si supieran quién quiere a quién, y cómo y dónde, en detalle? Entonces, te iban a querer, igual como antes. . .?

Cuando el divorcio, el marido la acusa del amor contra la naturaleza. A tu mamá, a los otros hermanos, les parece absurdo. Después, atan hilos y se van acordando de detalles, de cositas que no habían notado. Y así, los hijos "perfectos," como los papás, y las mamás, pierden su aspecto de santo. Es lo que te pasa por idealizar, te regañas tú misma por querer que salga todo según el molde. "Pues mírate tú bien primero, y no juzgues," a cada uno su gusto, y no hay que pensar que algo les va a pasar por hacerlo. . .

Algunos de tus amigos están muy en contra de los gays y bisexuales. "Es un joto. Se declaró en un congreso literario, que era uno de esos, doblados. . ." "Conoces a Tal-y-Tal? Es uno de los raros. No te has fijado cómo habla (cómo se viste, cómo anda), sus gestos. No te parece afeminado?" Y, "Es una marimacha. . ." "Una mujer muy hombruna." "Esa es, tú sabes, de ésas. Lesbianas. Fíjate!" Y ni sus padres lo sabían. Secretos. Tú le dices a alguien, tú ahora emancipada, seguro, "You can't tell by looking!"

Otro día, estás leyendo, que las monjas en algún hospital en Chiapas, están en peligro ahora. . . Porque dan alivio, ayuda y hospedaje al que llega a su hospital. Les dan santuario a todos los que llegan allí, pero los rancheros del lugar acusan a las monjas que manejan el hospital, de ser cómplices en la rebelión de los campesinos indígenas. Allí, según los rancheros, hospedan y esconden a los "malhechores" campesinos, los llamados "Zapatistas." Según las monjas, dan ayuda y suministran a los heridos o enfermos. Los Zapatistas dicen que los ranchos grandes les han robado de sus terrenos, hectárea por hectárea. Los rancheros acusan a los Zapatistas de haberse tomado propiedades privadas. Los dos lados se acusan de expropiaciones, etc, etc. Entre los rancheros, hay quienes son oficiales del PRI, entonces el PRI va tomando el lado de los rancheros. Según las monjas enfermeras mexicanas, "No nos metimos en política. Sólo damos santuario a cualquier herido o necesitado. . ." Hacer una obra de caridad, tratar de hacer bien, ayudar al prójimo, dar santuario. . . entonces, eso es meterse en política? Así te preguntas, dando vuelta al periódico para ver dónde continúa la descripción del levantamiento entre los Zapatistas, el nuevo orden que ha resuscitado en México. Cómo hay gente valiente, te dices, cómo hay mujeres retevalientes. . .

"I feel sorry for Chicano politicians," te dice una estudiante chicana cuando estás todavía en Southwest City. "Ellos, los políticos chicanos, muchas veces simplemente no pueden lograr lo que necesitan, o lo que quieran hacer para el pueblo, porque son precisamente eso, son el pueblo, la minoría. Y no pueden, a veces después de largas sesiones y argumentos, no pueden votar en masa, porque son la minoría. Y votan en contra de nuestros casos o derechos, la mayoría. Así lo veía aquella muchacha, que quería ser abogada después de graduarse de la universidad. Había visto un programa con los oficiales chicanos que se habían elegido para el gobierno estatal, y quedó entristecida. "A fin de cuentas, el político chicano es una voz en el desierto, y muchos se sienten frustrados. Que hasta se ha elegido un gobernador chicano? Pura paja, y por encima. . . nomás. Ahora, hay un político chicano en Washington, desde nuestro estado, pero este estado es bastante difícil."

"Should I go into Spanish in graduate school? Somebody told me that I couldn't get a job later, if I had a degree in Spanish. Because I'm not a minority female," esto te pregunta un alumno en su último año en español. Cree que solamente las mujeres de minoría, hispanas, reciben puestos en las escuelas y universidades. Por lo del famoso Affirmative Action, la llamada legislación de programas para terminar la descriminación religiosa, racial, de edad y sexual. Le dices al muchacho que de verdad, da igual, los hombres siguen logrando puestos y consideración, y que siga adelante si esa es su meta, su sueño. Y tú bien sabes, el ser chicana no te protege de la mitad de las injusticias que puedes pasar como mujer y como chicana. Tú eres el huarache del totem pole, arriba de ti van las latinas y las españolas. . . o las queridas de los que administran en todos esos trabajos. Esto sucede, especialmente, en la universidad. Pregúntenles a las chicanas que allí andan tratando de sobrevivir. Frustraciones y malos encuentros. "Maybe there's some solutions," dice tu colega, lingüista chicana, "a lo mejor debemos seguir con los Chicana caucus. Júntate a nojotras." Tú, quien no eres para socia en las organizaciones, resistes y después dejan de invitarte. "Cómo les va?" preguntas, "Diles que se encuentren a alguien quien las guíe. Como *mentor*... pero que no les mienta el mentado *mentor*. Y que no se dejen *chingar*."

CAPÍTULO SIETE

En el Valle San Joaquín todavía cuando tenías unos trece años, el primo Cheno murió camino a Masterton, en una carretera afuera de Firebaugh, que queda por allá por Fresno. El y otro primo venían de regreso de por allá donde habían ido a ver a *unas güisas*. Ellos eran parientes de mi mamá y eran originalmente de Nuevo México también. Pues el primo Chenito, alto, moreno, pelo grueso y un bigotito, tan buen chavalo que era siempre, allí se quedó en aquella carretera. Habían venido de noche, y de noche murió. Trabajaban también en el campo, en los files con la gente de mi papá, y vivían con mi abuelita Lencha, la que fue la abuela de mi mamá. Te despertó la Marieta, diciendo "Petra, venga porque algo le pasa a su mamá. Está llorando y su papá no la puede consolar. Qué? Algo con su primo, uno de sus primos..." "Aaaaaayyyy...! AAAAAAYYYY NOOOOO!" Así, así gritaba mi mamá por su primo el Chenito, como si fuera su propio hijito, como si hubiera sido su propio hermano. "Lorenza, si no te calmas, tendré que llamar al Doctor Harrison. Qué quieres que haga?" Dentro de un rato, ha sonado el teléfono, y después de hablar tu padre, dice que tiene que ir por unas botellas de sangre, para el primo aquél que sobrevivió, el Huesos, porque sin la sangre, no iba a aliviarse. Estaba muy grave el sobreviviente, en condición mala, grave condition. "Ven conmigo, Pat. Que venga la Petrita conmigo. Así tengo con quien hablar, y no me duermo..." Nos pasamos el viaje hacia el hospital más grande en Modesto, hablando de mi mamá, del primo Chenito, y de cosas sencillas como que no se veía ven a esas horas. Eran las dos, tres de la mañana ya, pero por lo menos no había neblina como en invierno.

Poco recuerdo del viaje que hicimos esa noche, mi padre y yo, yendo por sangre para el primo Huesos. Tuvimos que ir, de regreso, hasta el pequeño hospital del pueblito donde vivíamos todos, para entregar los frascos de sangre. Esto para el primo Huesos, el mismo primo que había "jugado" conmigo debajo de una cama, cuando yo era niña. *Y yo nunca dije nada.* Ni aquella noche que yo fui con mi padre, para platicar con él y que no se durmiera durante el viaje.

Después, hubo el funeral del Chenito, y vinieron muchos de los vecinos como las señoras portuguesas y americanas que conocían a mi mamá. Fue la primera vez que yo conocí la costumbre de que se trajeran pasteles y comidas a la casa donde había luto para un muerto de la familia. Mi tía Lita lo hizo de otra manera. Ella fue por muchos días, acompañando a mi mamá, a la iglesia donde rezaban por el primo Cheno. . . A mí me llevaron un par de veces, y mi madre me dio un velo negro para que me pusiera. Mi tía los había traído, y también dijo que teníamos que ir al restaurante de ellos, que allí tuvieron por un tiempo en el pueblito, y que mi mamá no debía andar cocinando para tanta tribu en estos días. Así, con los recuerdos de la muerte, del viaje de sangre, del velorio y el funeral de Chenito, también tengo recuerdos de ir al restorán de mis tíos, donde comimos comidas "de fiesta" por muchos días seguidos. Allí tuvimos menudo, tamales, tacos, enchiladas, chiles rellenos, chorizo con huevo, papas con chorizo, "Lo que se les antoje, ándele mijita. Coman, mijitos. Aliméntate, Lorenza, tienes que ponerte fuerte, anda, come bien, lo que tú quieras." Todo preparado con cuidado y cariño por la tía Lita, quien quería mucho a mi mamá. "Me daba lástima tu mamá. . ." después me dijo mi tía, "todo lo que aguantaba, ella trabajando como burro acá, y él por allá. Y tu mamá, una mujer muy, muy trabajadora, ya vieras como era cuando todos vivíamos juntos. Allá cuando estábamos jóvenes, en Betaville, en aquel ranchito. . ."

De los secretos, a lo mejor uno ni debe recordarlos, ni tampoco contarlos a nadie. A lo mejor. Así, tú sabes, lo quieren muchos. Prefieren que tú, que ustedes, no digan nada. Y también, te preguntas, si hay algún bien en resuscitar los secretos, los agravios, los malos recuerdos? "Fueron parte de lo que pasó, parte de lo que compone, con todo lo bueno y los recuerdos agradables, lo que te pasó, lo que hiciste, lo que hicieron. . ." También recuerdas, entre todo esto, eventos chistosos o pícaros, algo así como ocurrieron. "A ver, abuelita, cómo va lo del hombre que se cagó en la puerta del carro, aquella vez en Mexicali. Cómo va, cómo va. . . O, sí: Pues, 'había una vez, un par de hermanitos. . .'"

"Tu padre se fue a México, con la de ojos verdes, ella era de Juárez y la conoció por allá por Visalia," te dice tu madre. Tú sabías que tus padres no iban a durar juntos, cuando ella, de regreso de Reno, viene a vivir con ustedes. "No te vas a quedar, verdá, Mamá?" Ella te respondió que cómo sabías, que *smart* eras, y tú le dijiste que nada más sentías que ellos no iban bien, y que no estaban igual ya las cosas. Ninguno de tus padres, tú lo veías, era como antes, riéndose o diciendo chistes simples, detalles así, cosas así. Después, viene un abogado de tu papá, quien le habla a tu mamá, y ella te pide que te sientes con ella para hablar con el abogado. Ni tu madre ni tú, con tus quince años, entienden por qué ahora el negocio de tus papás, el Campo, se tiene que vender. Y que solamente pueden pagar eso, lo que piden, que les está diciendo el abogado. "You won't get any money, though, because the sale price will just pay off the debts on the business." La casa, también, se tendrá que vender. Tu padre se ha ido a México con la de ojos verdes, y a tu mamá le han quedado las deudas, y "ningún otro remedio" como me dijo ella. Ella, con lágrimas, me mira y me pregunta, "Qué crees. . .?" y yo soy la que, en el momento, tal vez impresionada conmigo misma porque me han invitado a presenciar el trato y como siempre, algo confundida con el trajín en el mundo de los grandes, respondo en inglés, algo como "The amount being offered for the labor camp is quite COM-parable to. . ." Y así contesté mis babosadas, para impresionar al abogado/contador con mi pronunciación en inglés, de *comparable*. Y de esa manera, yo la mayor, y con mis quince años de vida, les ayudé a que le robaran el negocio a mi mamá. . .

CAPÍTULO OCHO

Empezó nuestra vida sin mi padre, con los cambios inevitables. El campo ya lo vendió mi mamá, y ella tuvo que preocuparse sola por vender la casa, las cuentas que había, y cómo sostener a todos nosotros. A la Marieta, ya la habían mandado a México, cuando mi mamá se fue a Reno. Fue cuando mi papá dijo lo de "Esa Marieta es una alcahueta," y despachó a la amiga de mi mamá. Llegó la navidad, y mi mamá no tenía con qué darnos "Regalos, como manda la gente. . ." Una mañana, mi mamá abrió la puerta de enfrente, y allí en el porche, había una caja llena de regalitos, frascos de *jams* y conservas, unos panes dulces como esos hechos de calabazas o plátanos y nueces, los panecitos formados en unas barritas y envueltos en papeles bonitos y listones, y naranjas, manzanas, y un costalito de nueces. Mi mamá todavía recuerda que también habían metido en la caja, un pavo, listo pa'a cocinar. Yo no me acuerdo del guajolote, pero sí recuerdo lo de los regalitos, los dulces y cómo siempre, las otras golosinas que comer. Nunca supimos quiénes habían sido nuestros benefactores. Mi mamá trató de darle las gracias a nuestra vecina, a quien queríamos mucho y que siempre nos platicaba. Su hija era una de mis mejores amigas, y ella también negó que ellas habían sido los que le hicieron de Santo Clos. Después de unas semanas, mi mamá y mis hermanitos se fueron a Modesto a vivir, y empezó nuestra época con el Welfare.

Mi hermano y yo, los mayores, nos quedamos en el pueblito, para poder terminar nuestros años escolares en la high school. Era mi último año, y él, muy activo también en la escuela, no quería perder la oportunidad de continuar con los deportes. Como yo, estaba en la banda y la orquesta, y era presidente de su clase, de esto y aquello otro también. El año siguiente, mi hermano se quedó otra vez con la familia que lo había recogido. A la señora de esa familia, familia de unos amigos de escuela de nosotros, mi mamá le había dado nuestro freezer. Una caja congeladora grande que teníamos, antes siempre llena de carnes, fruta, verduras, etc. y que ahora se encontraba casi siempre vacía. "No es mucho, pero les agradezco," le dijo mi mamá a la señora que recogió a mi hermano, para que éste acabara la high school. Finalmente, a mitad de su último año, la novia de mi hermano, una portuguesita muy pequeña y curiosita pero quien, según algunas amigas chismosas, "Dice palabrotas. . . She swears like a sailor!" resultó gorda. Se casaron, con bodita suave y todo, y él dejó la high school. No terminó entonces. Pero mi hermano, terco como nuestro papá cuando se proponía algo, a los cuarenta y pico años, empezó otra vez la escuela, y se graduó de la Universidad. Trabaja como "Coach," un director y consejero de varios deportes, en una "universad de la comunidad," un Junior College, en el Valle San Joaquín. Dicen que mi hermano sigue logrando mucho debido a la buena mujer que ahora tiene, pero yo digo que más bien fue por terco o *persistent*. Así como nuestros padres. . . Mi hermano, como mi mamá especialmente, solía ser de carácter reservado, pero después de muchos golpes y caídas, se levantó arriba. Para eso, sirve ser terco y *persistente*.

Mi padre fue quien me llevó a mis "spelling bees," los concursos de deletreo oral que en nuestras escuelas se hacían. Yo llegué, siempre muy "adelantada," a ganar el concurso en mi escuela primaria, en el grado octavo, y fue mi papá quien me llevó al concurso del distrito, en Modesto. Y iba yo, viento en popa, cuando me dieron la palabra "squirrel." Dije, respondiendo inmediatamente, "sqee-r-r-e-l" y me sacaron del concurso por querer pronunciar la palabra, en vez de deletrearla letra por letra. Así hice muchas veces, metiéndome en algo sin pensar. Y me sacaron. A veces sí, y a veces por suerte o por terca o simplemente cabeza dura, no.

El día de mi graduación de la primaria, del octavo, allí estuvo mi padre. A mi madre no le interesaban mis cosas de la escuela en esos tiempos. Ella "andaba hasta el copete" con la vida que tenía. Pero mi padre, como he dicho, tenía metido en la cabeza que teníamos, sus hijos, que ir a la escuela y hacerle combate a los libros. Así, yo me animaba mucho en salir adelante en mis clases. Al principio, para hacer bien en la escuela, como lo insinuaba mi papá que quería que hiciéramos, y después por mi propio gusto. En casa llegué a ser niña privilegiada por mis report cards y mis premios y buena fama entre los maestros y maestras de la escuela. Y mis papás me dejaron libre, en casa, para estudiar y seguir con lo que algunas de mis tías llamaban "las fanfarronerías de la Petra."

Tuve muchos días felices debido a mis días en la escuela secundaria, y pasé de querer ser médica, a querer ser actriz. . . De muy temprano, jugaba papeles en los espectáculos y programas, hasta canté en la radio un par de veces, aprendí a imitar a personajes como la Jayne Mansfield, Marilyn Monroe, Elvis, Tallulah. Cantaba, actuaba, me invitaron a ser "Master of Ceremony" para algunos eventos, pintaba murales en el gimnasio para los bailes, me elegían por aquí, por allá, y yo retecontenta que no me importaba que no me querían todos, porque me querían tantos. En el desfile de Homecoming, y esa noche en el partido de fútbol, fui, el último año de mis éxitos en la secundaria, la Reina más feliz. Esa noche, hasta vino mi papá para verme por un instante cuando me subieron al convertible. Yo lo miré allí parado entre un montón de espectadores, con cara seria y ojos orgullosos, mientras me arreglaban la falda de mi vestido blanco de olanes de encaje, alrededor de mí. "Viniste, papá," pensé, y le sonreí, pero no nos dijimos nada.

De mis parientes, en mi graduación de la high school, solamente vinieron mi mamá, el tío Toro, mi hermano, y otro tío que era el hermano menor de mi papá. Papá no vino por no verse con mi madre, según mi tío, que la de ojos verdes no quería que se vieran, según mi madre. Todos esos eventos, de días malos, días felices, los premios y todo, me han quedado tan grabados, como si fueran ayer. Como la noche antes de mi graduación, la noche en que empezaron en serio, mis años de "mujer perdida." Así llegó a llamarme mi padre, por haber empezado a hacerle caso a los "boys", a los muchachos. La noche antes de graduarme de la secundaria, quedé encinta de mi primer hijo, en un Oldsmobile viejo a las orillas de un canal. . .

"I'll marry you, but I don't love you, Pat," me dice el muchacho güero de ojos azules, explicando que su madre no quería que él se casara conmigo. Que por qué no me había quedado con el primer novio, éste que sí era de mi gente. "Why doesn't she marry that Mexican boy. How do I even know it's your baby? Maybe she's a whore; nice girls don't sleep with boys when they're not married!" Y así cosas por el estilo había dicho su madre, según nuestras amistades. Yo, lastimada pero orgullosa, le respondí que "I don't want to marry you if you don't love me, you don't have to. . ." Y a pesar de las amenazas al chavalo de parte de mi padrastro que era entonces un diputado de los sherifes del condado en seguida, no nos casamos. Después, el muchacho reconoció a su hija cuando mi madre me llevó a que le hiciera pleito legal, que había que hacer que "el chavalo mocoso cabrón gringo, contribuyera a mantener a la niña." Esa güerita llegó a ser la consentida de todos los nietos de mi mamá, "Por todo lo que pasamos con aquel chamaco gringo y su mamá la cabrona. Qué dudas tenían! Mira que la criatura es el puro retrato! No l'y hace, mija, despúes pagarán. Vas a ver." Rencorosa mi madre? No. Digo ahora más bien, que era bien terca.

En la televisión, en uno de esos "Talk Shows," programas donde los entrevistados hablan sobre una variedad de asuntos, algunos serios como AIDS o el SIDA, el aborto, el matrimonio y el divorcio, etc., y otras veces resultan simples, necios, o cómicos. Hoy están entrevistando a mujeres de varias edades, preguntándoles sobre los asuntos primordiales "When was the first time you had sex? What about your first orgasm?" Más adelante, las preguntas se desmoronan en otras como, si tuvieron su primer orgasmo la primera vez que "lo hiciste," si siempre tienen un orgasmo en un encuentro sexual, si los orgasmos múltiples son más gozados que un sólo orgasmo fuerte. Y así por el estilo, y te pusiste a recordar, que tu primer orgasmo no fue ni tu primera vez, ni con tu primer novio. . .

"We didn't know what had happened." dijo tu amiga, de la pareja que acompañaban a ti y a tu novio, el güero de ojos azules. Habían ido los cuatro, a "the boonies," un bosquecito entre los lugares que podían escoger para ir a besarse. Le llamaban "necking" por entonces. Era donde a veces los jóvenes perdían los estribos y las muchachas "se dejaban, perdían sus virtudes, etc., los muchachos se aprovechaban, etc." Nos habíamos separado, yo y el güerito, de la otra pareja que también eran una chicanita de mi pueblo y otro gringuito del otro pueblo. Y de noche como era, fuimos caminando entre la parada de árboles que allá se encontraba, lejos de nuestros dos pueblitos. Nos acostamos en una cobija que el chavalo, bien preparado, había traído. No, no era "mi primera vez," pero tampoco lo "habíamos hecho" más de unas dos veces hasta entonces. Pues, beso tras beso, estrujo tras estrujo, y yo empecé a sentirme caliente, me ardía la cara, las piernas, las uñas... Y de repente me dio, como golpe o relámpagazo, el gozo, "YAAAAAAAAYYYYYY!" Y después, todavía atarantada por el gusto, le pregunté al chavalo. "What was that...?" Que si qué fue lo que acababa de pasarme! El otro, tan ingenuos e inexpertos a pesar de que no habíamos sido "vírgenes," solamente supo contestarme "I guess it felt good?" Cuando salimos del bosquecito, mi amiga la Dora me dijo, tomándome por el brazo, "Qué pasó? Creí por un momento que se habían encontrado a La Llorona!" Yo, bien pendeja todavía, le hice whisper, "... He said *I came!*" Y regresamos los cuatro al pueblo, todos callados. Yo creo que a los chavalos les había dado más susto que vergüenza. Yo y la Dora, sofocando nuestras risitas y miradas avergonzadas. Muchachas perdidas... *y me gustó.*

En nuestro pueblito, cuando yo estaba en la secundaria y que empecé "de bareta," las parejas jóvenes que conocíamos tenían otros lugares como opciones, cuando querían encontrarse solos con el novio o la novia. O cuando se encontraban a una muchacha que "se dejaba o se dejaría." Esos lugares eran "los boonies" o "the trees," "the chickens" o "the canal." Yo estuve, en esa época, en los tres lugares, y creo que el más aislado fue el de "the chickens," sitio de un rancho abandonado donde habían criado a gallinas y pollos. Allí veíamos, parqueadas, a otras parejas calientes y en sus mocedades como nosotros. Una que otra de las muchachas después salió "gorda" como yo, y tuvieron que casarse. Eso es lo que se hacía en esos tiempos, y yo fui, de las varias muchachas que después escandalizaron por esos pueblitos, la primera que no se casó primero. Y como resultó, no me casé hasta después. . .

CAPÍTULO NUEVE

Tu madre está, a los setenta y dos años, tomando lecciones en el violín. . . Sí, sí, para aprender a tocarlo. "Me encontré un violín en una segunda, cuando iba *junkin*. Y el violín nuevecito, nuevecito, me lo jallé en veinticinco pesos, dólares." Unas semanas más tarde, te dice cuando le haces una de tus llamadas semanales, "Mija, te puedo llamar más tarde? Me'stán dando mi primera lección en el violín. Ajá, más tarde, o me llamas tú." Cuelgas y te ríes, qué chistoso te parece, sorprendida que tu madre tuviera tantas ganas de enseñarse el violin. Qué madre ésta, cuando creemos que ya le jallamos, Zas! una vuelta, y otra sorpresa!

Tu padre tocaba guitarra y cantaba, muy bien lo hacía, hasta por un tiempo de joven tocó y cantó en la radio, allá en el Valle Imperial, en Brole. Tu hermano, el que te seguía en edad, tocó corneta y trompeta, y le dio a los deportes aunque nunca fue grande de estatura o peso. Tus otros hermanos, ellas y ellos, han tocado el piano, ellas habiendo tenido algunas lecciones de jovencitas, y ellos, con las tamboras y las guitarras todo aprendido por sí mismos. Le daban bien suave a estos instrumentos, en los servicios pentecosteses, en la iglesia de ellos. Y ahora hay nietos y nietas que le dan por tocar o guitarra o piano, y recientemente, una que aprenderá, por su gusto, el saxofón. Pero hasta ahora, ni entre la familia de tu papá ni en la de tu mamá, que tú sepas, habrá tocado algún pariente, el violin. Tendrás que averiguarlo, para saber. Es cierto, es una familia muy, muy grande y a lo mejor por allá habrá alguien con un violín. "Es posible, es posible, que mi abuelo tocaba, entre otras cosas, el violín. Era muy viejero y volado, pero creo que por allí oí que tocaba muchos instrumentos," así concluyes, y te prometes preguntarle al tío Toro, a ver quién se acuerda.

"We have ministers in Chiapas, too," te dice tu hijo, recién vuelto de México, comentando sobre el asunto de los indígenas y los rancheros en el sur del país. Les han matado a ministros en el Perú te dice él, el grupo "Shining Path" que está peleando contra el gobierno. "They kill anybody who opposes them, or helps the soldiers. Even when our ministers only gave food. Pos dan santuario, sí, y según su conciencia." El querer jugarle de buenos samaritanos, a dos ministros en el Perú, les costó la vida. Recuerdas tú que tu profesor antiguo en California, el que había estudiado la historia de Latinoamérica, siempre decía de las revoluciones. "En Latinoamérica, un chingón remplaza a otro chingón." En México, te dice tu hijo, están hambrientos por la palabra de Dios, especialmente en las ciudades grandes, donde hay tanta pobreza. Tú piensas de las ciudades satélites de la capital, "Por lo menos, es cierto que están hambrientos." Para qué, le preguntas a tu hijo comprometido, para qué quieres ir a un país tan católico con tus nuevas ideas, para qué. . . "One thing, Mom, I won't attack the Virgen de Guadalupe, that's for sure!" "Por lo menos sabe algo de estrategia," te dices de tu hijo ministro aleluya, y te despides de ellos por el momento, "Let me know where you're going after you leave Texas" porque de Texas se irá, familia y todo, a Guadalajara, por un año. "Mi misión es, ahora lo sé por seguro, irme a México para evangelizar y convencerles de la Palabra. . ."

"Murió de 'cirrhosis of the liver' o algo así," te cuenta tu madre de la muerte de un tío de ustedes. Toda la vida trabajó, y toda la vida tomaba. Le dio bastante duro a la botella, los últimos años, a pesar de que los médicos le decían que no debía beber. Lo internaron algunas veces, para curarlo. Y todavía, le daba duro, eso es lo que entiendes de por qué murió tu tío. A pesar del alcoholismo, tienes buenos recuerdos de él, uno de los hermanos de tu padre. Mejor llegaste a conocer a

su esposa, la tía Lita. Sí, la que defendió a tu mamá contra todos ellos, cuando el divorcio de tus padres. Ahora, la tía Lita está en un *rest home*, el segundo que están "probando" sus hijos exhaustos de tratar de complacer a la mamá. Siempre de personalidad y carácter fuerte, la tía Lita manejó hábilmente su casa, los negocios de la familia y a su esposo, y según los hijos "Nosotros no nos dejamos ya controlar, y no le gustaba a Mamá. Ahora está donde está, porque no pudimos darle gusto. Ya no se le'allaba, Pat. We really tried." Una mujer siempre independiente, quedó 'lisiada' de un stroke que le dio hace unos años. Después creo que le dieron otros strokes. "No me querían con ellos, Pat. No tengo dónde vivir. . .!" "No es cierto! No queríamos que estuviera sola después del stroke, entonces la trajimos a vivir con nojotros. And she ran off the housekeeper-nurse that we hired to come and look after her during the day!" "Me tienen sola todo el día. No tengo a nadie, Pat." "No sabíamos qué hacer, después de ponerle un apartamento, porque insistió que quería vivir sola otra vez, pues allá cerca de sus hermanas, le pusimos apartamento. Y no se cuidó. No comía bien, creo que tomaba un poco o algo, pero pues, no la pudimos dejar vivir ya desatendida. I tell you, Pat, we tried, we really tried *everything*. Y siempre se está quejando. . ."
Tú te acuerdas de la mujer fuerte que te invitó a vivir con ella y los hijos, cuando tú tenías quince años. Tu tía tendría, entonces, alrededor de la misma edad que tú ahora. Platicando, allá en Betaville en la casa de tus tíos, haciendo galletas o antojos, y viendo películas mexicanas. Cómo se reían de los personajes, cómo lloraban con las historias melodramáticas de las películas viejas mexicanas. Empezaron, jugando, a hablarse como las inditas en las películas, "Yo mezma qu'eroquimi'aga'un favol. . ." "Posusté mezma, hág'lo. . .!" Después, cuando regresaste a tu casa al norte, tu padre te dice "Qué gorda te pusiste, Pat! Qué hacías allá con tu tía?" Con la tía Lita, tuve el calor de un hogar donde se me ofreció el cariño y apoyo, templado por la compañía, el humor y el carácter fuerte de mi tía.

"My teacher said I know how to hold the violin, very well. That

I'm an excellent student," te llama tu madre para contarte de su primera lección con el nuevo instrumento. Un violín viejo, que según ella, está en "very good condition, it's like new." "Sabe Dios dónde habrá encontrado ese violín," le dices a tu esposo y a María. "Pero mi mamá anda she's really happy these days. Como si fuera niña de dieciséis." Tu madre-chavala no se ha quejado en varios días del esposo, tu segundo padrastro, así tan contenta anda. Después, te dice durante otra conversación del violín y cómo le va haciendo los dedos pa'tocar, "Tengo un perrito! Se me olvidó decirte, y espera! Sorry about that, el perrito se quedó afuera y no me vio, y empezó a ladrar como diablito. Quieto! Ya, ya, ahora lo metí y está contento, digo contenta. Sí, it's a girl, es perrita. Qué? O, es una d'esas, dachshund, perritos-weinie. Sí, ahora tengo otra Chapa, Chapita, tienes razón, se me había olvidado. Ja, ja. Pues ahora tengo quien me cuida cuando él anda en su trabajo de noche. Sí, la perrita ladra, újule que si ladra." Pues allí, por ahora, está tu madre, hablándote del esposo comelón y dormelón y flojo, con perrita weinie y un violin...

Aurora, tu amiga desde tus días en Southwest City, te acaba de decir que la van a operar del cerebro. "I have fluid on my brain... They don't know from what!" Dentro de unos días, de las más valientes de tus amigas, está en casa, recuperando. Esta es la amiga quien ha luchado contra demonios e injusticias, desde la vez que le hicieron el "experimento sicológico" en los 60s, la que pelea, como tú en tus escritos, contra el "mind control." Ahora, ella se encuentra en peligro de poder conservar su ser y la inteligencia. En las semanas que siguen, tú reconoces cuánto contabas con el apoyo, moral y professional, de tu amiga. La echas de menos, su sentido de humor especial y las largas conversaciones, conversaciones que usualmente son de tus asuntos, tus preocupaciones, y no de ella. Rara vez, que tú podías escucharle sus problemas, enojos y reniegos. De vez en cuando, ella te contaba a ti de alguna buena conversación, de algún triunfo personal o en el trabajo. Tienes celos de las amigas que allí tiene, en su propia ciudad. Tus amigas más íntimas están todas, a larga distancia. Ella sabe siempre de tus proyectos. "Debes ser quien maneja mi carrera," le has dicho, mitad en broma. Y ella, dispuesta siempre, "Oh, sure, como no tengo nada que hacer, verdad. Ja, ja." "Como si tuviera 'carrera'. . . ja, ja," respondes tú. La madre de ella murió de algo relacionado al alcoholismo, así como tu tío. "I like to drink, "le dices a ella, y ella "I guess if a couple of glasses of wine with dinner makes you an alcoholic, I'm one too!" Deciden, en una ocasión, que entre parientes y amistades, casi todos podrían calificarse como alcóholicos. "Vendrá con la cultura?" le preguntas a Aurora.

Una amiga chicana de Texas, la Chavela, te había contado que cuando llegó a hablarles por primera vez en Yale, el gran escritor chicano XX, lo primero que dijo al entrar al salón donde se juntaban los estudiantes chicanos, fue "'Ontá el pisto?" Diciendo así, el escritor fue recibido de todo corazón por la chicanada. Pues era como estar en casa, no?

En las fiestas pentecostesas, te dice tu hijo, no hay alcohol. "You don't need alcohol, Mom, when you have the Lord!" Ni drogas, ni pastillas, ni sexo. Just say NO! "Let's say 'no'," le dices a Lulu en una ocasión cuando estaban platicando sobre las soluciones simplistas de la gente, se levantan, van a la puerta, y gritan "Nooooooo!" Después, riéndose como locas, vuelven al cuarto y se beben otro vaso de vino.

En tu ciudad, acaban de arrestar a más de cien indocumentados en el aeropuerto, en diferentes garitas de bordo. Los agentes federales del INS, inmigración y naturalización, dijeron que en los *boarding gates* se había visto mucho tráfico de personas que parecían ser refugiadas o indocumentadas. Que en muchos vuelos, no bastaban los asientos por este tráfico. Los vuelos yendo, por ejemplo, a Chicago, Los Angeles, Nueva York. Y después, según los periódicos, aprehendieron a varios de los "coyotes." La mayor parte de los indocumentados o refugiados eran de México, según las autoridades, el resto de Centro y Sur América. Tú te acuerdas de la película aquella, donde a los refugiados de Centroamérica les dicen que digan que son de México, y que digan, para confirmarlo con un detalle cultural "Chingar, chingazo, chingado," o cualquier variantes del verbo-expletivo tan "típicamente mexicano." Te ríes tú, a pesar de lo serio de lo que estás leyendo y oyendo, "Habrán inventado que eran mexicanos? Habrán dicho algo como 'Tú chíngate' o peor, 'Chinga a tu madre!" algo así para convencer. . .? A lo mejor preferían volver a México que a su tierra, a lo mejor pensaban que les iría mejor. "A lo mejor vuelven *mañana*."

CAPÍTULO DIEZ

Secretos. *Los tabúes.* Lo que no se debe, nunca, contar. Te han empezado un par de sueños *malos.* No son solamente pesadillas, sino que tú sientes, al estar soñando y al despertar con un salto, que son malos. . . Te asustan, te acongojan, los sueños. . . Tú y tu padre, desnudos en frente de un altar, una misión así algo como algo como, San Juan Bautista, o el Álamo, algo así. Tú con tu padre, besando, haciendo. . . lo que tú y tu padre saben que no deben, pero están como hipnotizados, endrogados, controlados por otros. . . Estos otros, allí viendo, riéndose? Tomando fotos, tomando fotografías o películas o videos. Y así controlarte, haciendo que tú y tu padre. . . AAAAAAAAAYYYYY, Mamaaaá!

Despiertas, tratas de respirar normal, te dices "Es un sueño, nada más. It's just a bad dream. . ." Solamente le confiesas a tu esposo, "That time we went to San Juan Bautista, I felt like I had been there before, with Dad. Remember? And I got so anxious. . ." Tu esposo te dice que solamente son, "Anxiety-pill dreams. You sure have some whoppers!" Puras mentiras, lo que sueñas, de todas maneras, te estorba porque sabes que adentro de tu cabeza, hay sueños malos, secretos. *No puede ser, te convences, no puede ser, esta vez, no.*

Otras veces, tus sueños son simples, invenciones de tus más enterrados deseos, de tus fantasías truncadas sobre lo que no se cumplió. Sueñas, una mañana como a las tres, poco antes de despertar para ir al baño, de Vittorio. Estás tú con Vittorio, su hijita perfecta ahora grande y bella y rete inteligente *como ustedes dos,* estás con Vittorio y él te rompe la blusa, o el camisón. Y te saltan las chichis, punteaditas y calientes. Y tú le quitas, de un jalón, la camisa bordada de seda. . . o el piyama rayado de seda. . . Y se abrazan con zeta, y entonces se abrasan con ese. . . Y entonces. . . despiertas, haciendo soniditos como acurrucando la almohada, y tu esposo levanta la cabeza de su almohada y te dice, "Petra, what are you doing? It looks like you're humping the bed!" "Oh, hi. Honey, I was just having one of those weird, erotic dreams. . . What? Oh, I uh, I don't really remember now." Ay, Chihuahua, piensas, qué sueños bien "vaqueta" tengo! Mi mamá diría que soy una bareta!

"Esa Petra es bien volada, cuidado. Hasta se volaría con sus propios primoshermanos." Así pensaron algunas primas de ti, creo con el consejo de las mamás. En una gran fiesta de reunión familiar hace unos veinte años, recuerdas que, al acercarse un primo para saludarte y darte el abrazo, lo jaló pa'trás la hermana. Como pa' que no se dejara llevar por mí. Ni que fuera yo tan así de bareta, o puta. . . como lo creían. Nunca manoseé a mis hermanos, ni con mis primos. Excepto aquéllos que me lo hicieron a mí de chiquita, cuando ellos nos dominaban a nosotras por ser las chiquitas y bajo su dominio. Pero no, no estoy hablando de esos eventos de abuso sexual, cuando nos hicieron cosas a nosotras. Estoy diciendo que, en la familia, me dieron fama de ser mujer tan suelta que hasta con sus propios primos. "No puedo creer que hicieron eso," le dices a tu mamá. "Cómo han de creer que, por nuestros errores, bad judgment, o relaciones, que pudiera yo. . . I thought *I* was 'mal pensada'!" En fin, desde niña, no lo niego, empecé a enamorarme, pero de todos modos, no era tan "volada" como me lo acreditaban mis parientes aquellas. Sí, por unos años, hasta mi propio padre me llamaba así. Es cierto que desde niña también, soñé que volaba. No, digo, que podía volar, como los pájaros.

Mis "vuelos" tienen variantes, así como los temas de los sueños, los buenos y malos. A veces, y es mi versión favorita, estoy contenta de algo, doy un salto y me voy volando sobre todo y todos. Todo el mundo queda pasmado, y yo, muy impresionada conmigo misma… Otras veces, estoy en peligro, me van a agarrar, me van a matar, me van a arrestar, me van a golpear… escupir, pegar, desnudar, etc. Y salto PIIINNGG! y así, suave, me escapo del peligro. A veces me llevo a alguien conmigo, y funciona muy suave el vuelo de todas maneras. Ah, y hay otra variante a los vuelos: muchas veces, cuando estoy soñando algo malo y quiero irme de allí o salirme rápido o escapar, nada más lo deseo así y hago algo como fruncir las cejas o hacer una mueca "mágica," y mi propia voluntad me salva. PIIIINNNGG! Salvada, y en libertad! Y se acabó el mal sueño, estoy en un lugar seguro y sin peligro, y a veces… hasta despierto. Salvada y en libertad.

Cuando me enamoro en los sueños, tienen un detalle fastidioso para mi yo despierto. Casi siempre estoy esbelta, demasiado atractiva como ninguna de las otras mujeres en la escena. Joven? No, no estoy joven siempre, pero casi, es cierto que casi siempre, me veo fabulosa, y nadie me resiste. Despierta, me recuerdo que "No creas en los sueños, son eso, nada más. Productos de tu conciencia, sub-in-conciencias nada más." Me convence más y más mi compañero de que mis sueños son mis pendejadas. Los sueños buenos, de todas formas, los trato a veces de recoger… Trato de recoger el hilo, de reinventar, pa'lo que sirva, yo misma ahora practico mi propio "mind control" de mí misma. "Estudiando los sueños, se puede liberar una…" así te ha sugerido uno de tus psicólogos. Aquel psiquiatra rubio de los pantalones de vaqueta apretados, de Southwest City. Tú prefieres no ponerles caso… Pero haces inventario.

Lo que has aprendido de la frontera, te estorba en los recuerdos. De vez en cuando, como fotografías instantáneas sueltas y desconectas, se te aparece una imagen en la cabeza. El médico del diente de oro, que te está escarbando el vientre, diciéndote entre las piernas que solamente te iba a picar un poquito. Después, él, el médico de diente de oro de Nogales, te dice, "Ya estás bien, sólo te va a sangrar unos días. Y tú sabes que somos todos hermanos, allá al otro lado, y aquí por éste. Debemos ser discretos, y...," y, cerrando los labios, hizo como que los cerraba con llave, y que tiraba la llave. Lo llamaron a la puerta, salió un momento, y desde otro cuarto oyes que le pregunta una voz masculina, de su hijo, el dentista en el despacho en seguida supones, "Quién es ella...?" Y tu médico mexicano, una de las luces del pueblo fronterizo, responde, "Nadie, nadie, una de esas muchachas que no se asean bien." Tú sacas de tu bolsa el dinero, las treinta monedas de plata... No, no, sacas de tu bolsa, los trescientos dólares, lo convenido en tu llamada telefónica la semana anterior, desde Southwest City. Así fue como supiste que hasta los médicos de "tu propia raza" también te podían engañar, porque para la tarde siguiente...

CAPÍTULO ONCE

Esta vez, tu padre apenas camina recto, anda encorvado hacia un lado, como que le ha dado un stroke. No las reconoce, pero reconoce sus voces cuando dicen, "Papá, soy Pat... Aquí están la Vinnie y su esposo. Te vamos a sacar por unas horas. Vamos a Santa Cruz, al wharf, okay?" Vinnie lo toma de un lado, tú del otro, y caminan con él por los corredores del "asilo." Han tenido que firmar un archivo, una lista donde los visitantes de tu papá dicen quiénes son, cuándo lo sacan, y cuándo lo devuelven. En el restaurante del wharf, donde tu padre ha saboreado la comida de clam chowder, pescado y papas fritas, tú le preguntas, "Dad, te acuerdas de César Chávez? Sabes quién es?" Tu padre hace pausa, repite "César... Cháv... Sí... sí..." "Sabes quién es, fue?" preguntas otra vez, y tu padre, con mucha dificultad, trata de completar la frase y decir lo que está pensando. Sí, sí conoce el nombre, te dice, pero no sabe quién es, no recuerda quién es. "Tú trabajaste con él después, en los bailbonds," le recuerdas que así te había dicho. Pero tu papá, los ojos vacantes, nada más dice, sí, sí, conozco el nombre. . . Después que terminan de comer, le dices a la Vinnie, I want to ask him something else, I'll explain later why, it's something I'm working on. Y le preguntas a tu papá, antes de levantarse los cuatro de la mesa, "Dad, do you know what the Sanctuary Movement is? Has oído del 'Santuario'?" El los mira a los tres, se ve confuso, y con esfuerzo contesta, "No, no sé. . . qué es. . .? No me viene. . . qué. . .?" "Don't worry, no te preocupes, nada más te quería preguntar ahora. No te preocupes."

Dentro de veinticuatro horas de tu segundo aborto, los dolores del vientre y las contracciones habían llegado a tan fuertes que Vittorio te tuvo que llevar a la sala de emergencia del hospital. El médico americano que te examina, te dice "Who did this to you? You've still got parts of the fetus in you, and it looks like whoever did this, did it halfway on purpose, so someone else could clean it up! Who did this half-assed job?" Tú, permaneciendo "leal a tu gente," no le dices el nombre del doctor mexicano que te ha dejado, ahora lo sabes, la mitad del feto abortado, dentro del vientre. El medicastro sabría que tú tendrías que ir a un médico de este lado, para que te terminara la "operacioncita", sabiendo que tú, como te veías asustada y domeñable, no ibas a querer decir el nombre. Qué no le habías prometido no repetir su nombre, por discreta? Discreta o indiscreta a fin de cuentas, no le dices al médico americano, quien furioso, llama a Vittorio a que presencie la operación, habiéndole preguntado también a él el nombre del malhechor, y negándole Vittorio la información por no querer líos con la ley ni nada, y pues te hicieron la operación de manera más higiénica y completa. El médico americano, regañándolos a ustedes dos, por ayudar a toda esa industria de aborcionistas ilegales. Tú ya le habías respondido una de las veces, que "Well, we couldn't get a legal abortion here!"

Una de las veces que tu padre, de macho renegado, quiso deshacerse de tu mamá, fue cuando la mandó en el bus hasta Gilroy. Él los puso a los tres, a tu mamá, a ti de un par de años y tu hermanito de unos meses, en el camión. Una amiga de tu madre le ha dado a tu mamá el número de unos parientes en la ciudad al norte, y así llega tu madre a quedarse unas semanas con esta familia, "Era una de las veces que andaba enamorado, y lo hizo de borrachera. Yo había sabido que él se traiba a aquella otra vieja, la prieta de ojos verdes, y que la mostraba a todos los compadres, en la cantina. Yo a veces trabajaba en el restaurante de la cantina. No, no el Nogales, el restaurante de tu Nana, sino en el 'Águila,' la cantina. Pero parece que cuando él sabía que yo no iba a estar, pues traiba a las viejas. Un día, habían llamado a la casa un par de veces, y él no me dejó contestar... Pues de repente, decidió que él iba a abrir la cantina, y me dijo que yo me quedara en casa ese día, que uno de los tíos haría de cocinero esta vez. A mí se me hizo rara la manera de tu 'apá, cómo me decía y no me miraba, y para el mediodía, yo estaba ya que reventaba. Pues, me arreglé y me fui a la cantina, dejándolos con la cuñada que vivía enseguida. Cuando entré como huracán en la cantina, me vieron, asustados, tu tío que guardaba la barra, y unos dos, tres compadres que allí se encontraban. Yo, enojadísima, vi que no estaba tu papá, pero sabiendo que debía andar por allí, dije, Y él...? Dónde anda? Y viendo que nadie me decía nada, le pregunté a la comadre que atendía la parte donde servían comida, No me dices tú tampoco? Pues tu tía, que a nadie la hacía tonta y no era para cubrirles a ninguno de ellos, apuntó hacia atrás, donde estaban las mesas de billares. Yo me fui recio, y no lo veía todavía, pero cuando llegué hacia la parte de atrás, oí risas y voces bajas del cuartito que estaba arriba, sobre el refrigerador enorme que tenían atrás. Subí las escaleras, y allí estaban, abrazados tu padre y una vieja... Todavía se me pegan las caras, asustado tu padre y la mujer, burlona y riendo, los dos parecían estar borrachos o algo, viéndome, bien pendejos los dos. Tu padre finalmente se levanta y viene hacia mí, diciendo, "Y tú, qué haces aquí? Vete a la casa y me estrujó del brazo, sacándome así y yo gritándole cosas, de la cantina. Al rato llegó a la casa, me dijo que me arreglara un velís, que no me quería y que era entremetida y no lo dejaba en paz, y fue como me mandó, con ustedes dos niñitos, nada de dinero y un velís, hasta Gilroy. Después, vino por nosotros, diciendo que todo había sido de borrachera. Qué? Por qué lo aguantaba? Oh, mija, yo apenas era una chamaca huila, no sabía qué más hacer, y así yo regresaba, a estar con él. Qué? No, no siempre, no siempre andaba con las otras viejas. Porque cuando no tomaba, pues era muy trabajador, muy inteligente, tenía buena cabeza para muchas cosas. Sí, a lo mejor, a lo mejor, yo lo quería como tú dices. . . Pero cuando se juntaba con aquellos babosos, los compadres volados, y aquéllas, pues era otro."

CAPÍTULO DOCE

La primera vez que yo vi a una pareja desnuda, tenía como nueve años. Habíamos ido, desde el Valle San Joaquín al norte, de visita al Valle Imperial, donde todavía vivían los tíos. Fuimos a quedarnos unos días con mis tíos Martínez, que tenían un campo unas cinco millas fuera de Betaville, allá donde había files y ranchos. Mis padres habían salido para Mexicali, de parranda con unos amigos doctores del otro lado, que habían conocido por mi tía Martínez, la Tía Tacha. Nos dejaron con los tíos, allí en el campo, a mí, a mi hermanito y a Belita, quien estaba bebita todavía. Yo no quería quedarme, quería ir con ellos, y tenía un poco de miedo quedarme con mis tíos. Ella era muy habladora y nos caía bien excepto que hacía, como mi papá, muchas bromas y yo no sabía cómo tomarlas ni creo que entendía la mitad de lo que hacía reír a ellos. Pero él, mi tío, era muy callado con nosotros, y así que no me sentía muy a gusto quedarme atrás con ellos. Pues, me entró el sentimiento, y cuando salieron mis papás, empecé a llorar, y lloré a todas ganas, hasta que mi tía se enojó, cansada de tratar de contentarme, y me regañó bien duro. Más al rato, callada pero no contenta, me dormí con mis hermanitos. Por la noche, me despertaron las ganas de orinar, y salí para la sala, que también era donde dormían mis tíos, y vi que la luz estaba puesta. . . y que ellos, mi tía Tacha y su esposo, estaban desnudos. . . Yo no pensé, "Están desnudos," porque no sabía esa palabra, sino pensé "Están bichis. . ." y caminé, fascinada, hacia el bote grande que tenían allí durante la noche como bacín. No, todavía no habían puesto un baño con *toilet, sink, shower,* y todo eso, ni tenían su propia cocina. Nada más, en esa época, tenían unos cuartos pegados a la barraca donde tenían el comedor grande y la cocina de los braceros. Allí era donde dirigía mi tía el cocinar para braceros y para su propia familia. Por lo general, se comía lo mismo. Pues como decía, de la noche que vi a mis "desnudos," yo me senté en el bacín, y miraba, miraba a mis tíos. . . Y me empezó a dar vergüenza de no sabía qué. Tenían un color muy bonito, ella toda igual, yacía bocarriba, las chichis (así lo pensaba yo) enormes, caídas hacia los lados, el vientre infladito, piernas largas, y negro donde yo no sabía que había. Mi tío, bocabajo, se veía grande y muscoloso, bronceado y oscuro, excepto más claro en la espalda, las nalgas robustas, tostaditas apenas, y las piernas, peludas, peludas. Se veía donde le terminaban las camisas cortas, porque los brazos eran de dos colores, más claros arriba, y prietos, oscuros para abajo. Fascinada, pero sintiendo que yo no debía estar mirando esto, y que a la vez quería y no quería mirar, me levanté quedita y me fui a mi cama con mis hermanitos. Esa noche, también oriné la cama, y por muchos días no podía ver a mi tía en la cara. . . Y no entendía cómo ella podía andar igualita como siempre, diciendo chistes, burlona y sonriente, coquetona con sus pechos enormes, y tratándonos de buen corazón como siempre, "Ven, mija, come de este arroz. Toma esta tortilla, verás qué buenas salieron," mientras yo sabía que los había visto, así, sin ropa, y seguramente, habían hecho algo raro, para dormirse así, tan bichis, tan así, tan lejos de mi poco entender. Allí, en mi pecho pueril, me nació la sospecha que mis tíos habían hecho algo malo en haberse dormido así, para dejarme como quedé por muchos días después, sientiéndome avergonzada, confusa, y de alguna manera, traicionada. No estoy segura, pero me he imaginado que si fuera a contarle ahora, tantos años después, a la tía Tacha lo que hice aquella noche y que los había espiado, a lo mejor soltaría la carcajada, riéndose y haciendo burla de mis cavilaciones infantiles.

Empiezas a hacer el plan de entrevistar a mujeres del campo, o venidas de aquella vida campesina, así como habías querido recoger datos sobre el santuario. . . Preguntarles qué hacían ahora, dónde y cómo habían vivido en las cosechas, si habían cambiado debido a sus experiencias entonces cómo y de qué vivían ahora, y así otras preguntas por el estilo, empezarías a hacer. "Cuando pueda pescarme a una, le haré las preguntas que se me ocurran, a ver qué aprendo."

La madre de una amiga te ha llamado, "Me dejaron sola, y me cansé, y dije "A quién puedo llamar?' y pues, dije, a la Pat, aunque no la conozco muy bien, pues quería hablar con alguien. Es local esta llamada, usté sabe?" Tú le aseguras que pueden hablar todo lo que quieran, como la llamada no es de larga distancia, y la madre de tu amiga Laurel te dice "Ya sabe cómo le gusta estar sola a la Laurel pues ya ni tiene teléfono, que mejor pa' que no la molestara la gente." Así hablamos largo rato, en torno lo que estaba haciendo ahora la Laurel, dónde trabajaba ahora, sus animalitos, etc., y de qué dedicada era Laurel a su pintura, su arte. La mamá menciona, mientras la escuchas y maravillada de que te haya llamado a ti, que ella era de aquella región de ranchos donde vivía ahora Laurel. Te encanta escuchar el hablar de la señora, al principio más inglés que español. Le dices que estás recogiendo historias sobre la vida campesina, y le hablas en español, para ver que tendría que contar. Y ella, la mamá, te explica, despaciosa pero limpiamente en español, que "Nojotros éranos de allá, dónde está ahora la Laurel. Dónde? Ai, cerca di'ai, mi papá tenía un ranchito."

"Farmworkers? Sí, pues piscábanos algodón, sugar beets, tomates, maíz. El algodón? Oh, ése lo vendía, mi'apá. Sí, nos pagaba a nojotras. Tenía munchos hermanos y hermanas. Juntaban el algodón en pacas, y del dinero qu'ice, me hacía vestidos, vestidos largos, pa' los bailes. . . Me gustaba muncho el baile. Despés de más grande, cuando se casaron mis hermanas, me llevaban al 'baile de los viejos' Qué? Oh, pos así le decíamos porque era el baile de los viejos. . .'onde iban los casados. Y me llevaban a mí ai. Y después de casada, yo también iba con mi esposo, anque él no baila ya, casi no. Oh, sí, a mí me gustaba bailar, ahora, bailar al estilo. Pues no le sabemos, pero entonces, pues el jitterbug y cosas así, yo lo sabía. El. . .? No, él nunca era muy bailador, y tampoco sabe cocinar. Pues, era el mayor, y el primer hombre, y así le hacían todo por él, y lo curioso, que a los hermanos de él después, los menores, les enseñaron a cook. Pero él, el no hace cook, ni hervir agua. Bueno, cuando me enfermo, a lo mejor me hace unos huevos. Pero para él, él no hace cook, sale al restaurante. Oh, pues si hay una fiesta o algo, a lo mejor me saca a bailar uno, dos bailes. Pero no le gusta, nada. . . hacer cook."

Una noche sueñas que vas a tomar parte en un foco, una junta de chicanos interesados y comprometidos en mejorar la situación de la comunidad chicana. Tu sueño se convierte en surrealista, qué cómico, verdá, puro sueño onírico, como redundancia. Vas a tomar parte en tu primer foco, cuando. . . empiezan un juego de pelota, softball. O hardball, no recuerdas al día siguiente, al despertar y examinar lo que soñaste. Pero, en tu sueño, sí recuerdas esto, que iban a jugar un juego de béisbol, y tú ves que otros van al bat y pegan bien fuerte, para ganar unos homeruns para tu equipo. Te imaginas pegando fuerte la pelota con el bat, pegando fuerte, fuerte, un éxito fabuloso, retegrande, y todos te admirarán. Tu turno llega, y tú temes no poder pegar fuerte y bien, y tienes miedo como digo, cuando alguien te dice, "Do it, you'll feel better," y llega tu turno, cuando. . . hacen la llamada al lado izquierda del campo, de la pista digo, a que convengan para tu primera junta y reunión. . . al foco, tu primer foco, cuando. . . tienes que ir a hacer pi. Sí, tienes que ir a orinar, cuando, a la vez debes asistir a la primera junta del foco y, a la vez, orinar. Despiertas. . . de tu sueño digo, y. . . tienes que ir a orinar. Adiós sueño, adiós foco, hay que hacer del chi.

Santuario y resolución

"Quiénes son ustedes? Son comunistas? Qué quieren?"

Así evocando tus propias memorias de la Huelga de 1965, cuando pasó Chávez con la Marcha de Delano y sus campesinos, sabes que te queda un último paso más. Ya has ido recogiendo conversaciones y recuerdos de amigas y estudiantes campesinas a través de los últimos años trabajando en la Universidad, inclusive uno que otro muchacho. Muchas veces, el caso era que el o la estudiante o amiga eran de los Valles en California también, o habían venido de por allá desde Yuma o algún pueblito agrícola. "Hay que cumplir ahora," te dices, hay que saldar las cuentas, darles voz, dejar que se sepa por tus recuerdos de aquellas voces el cómo se puede lograr un sueño, una meta que muchas veces se les niega hasta en su propio hogar.

Santuario, lugar seguro, donde pueda brotar la esperanza, dar germen a actitudes positivas, dónde se encuentra, encontró, sigue encontrándose, por otras y otros como tú. Tú, Petra, que ahora tienes que participar, no quedarte dormida, tienes finalmente que escupir a la nada, negar la negatividad de la muerte, de lo malo que les pasó a ustedes. Así y con propósito empiezas la pieza final de está búsqueda y jornada.

Mi padre vivió por muchos años en esos asilos, más o menos se puede decir así. Su sentido de humor, su ser verdadero entraba y salía mientras lo fuimos perdiendo con cada día. La noche que mi papá quemó su casa, había andado tomando. Su segunda esposa, aquella hermosa mexicana de ojos verdes he loved OJOS VERDES había muerto también el año anterior, y la casa de ellos había pasado a la posesión de otro miembro de la familia. Sospechamos, nos preguntamos: Cuándo? Quién firmó eso? Había estado tomado Papá? Qué era lo que no recordaba ahora? Agarraron a Papá más tarde el día del incendio, orgulloso, doliente, tomado vengativo afligido por la pérdida, sentado en frente de la casa humeante, una botella abierta de whisky a su lado sobre el asiento del carro. "Pat?" Tu hermanastra Cecilia te llama, ". . . Dad. . . mi. . . tu Dad está en la cárcel. Bueno, es un lugar hospital y cárcel a la vez. Estuvo tomando, hubo un pleito, trató de quemar la casa de ellos. *Vale más que vengas.*"

Inexorablemente de nuevo, nos azota la muerte. Tras más de diez años de temer los resultados de su enfermedad, perdimos a mi padre a una muerte últimamente esperada, tal como un alivio.

Años atrás, cuando tu padre quemó su casa, apenas empezabas a escribir un libro que iba a ser sobre el movimiento del santuario, pero te había traído a este camino. Años después, viaje al funeral de tu papá en Salmas, te agobian las memorias de tus padres, momentos felices también, memorias aliviadoras ahora que había llegado la hora final. Tú recuerdas las muchas veces que él, todavía sano y robusto, los invitaba a ustedes a ir por comida china, o a Monterrey Bay a comer mariscos en el wharf. Cuando ustedes eran chamacos allá hace mucho en Betaville, era "Vamos a Mexicali pa'cena china en el Shangri-La," o "vamos por tacos de caguama 'al otro lado'." Esta última comida era carne de tortuga grasosa, las tortugas enormes se importaban al interior desde Ensenada o alguna bahía más cercana. A ti no te caía la caguama, pero así como con el menudo para las crudas que se traían, a tu papá y a tus tíos les encantaba ir por caguama a Mexicali cada cuando, en un domingo.

Mexicali quedaba cerca, al lado mexicano de la frontera, "el otro lado" como le llamaban. Y esos viajecitos y salidas festivas de familia, tus padres juntos, a veces acompañados por tíos o primos, eran algo que tú mucho después recordabas. También recordabas siempre, los juegos de palabra, los chistes o cuentos divertidos que Papá tenía o inventaba en su "repertorio" lleno de humor y siempre variando.

También recuerdas que a tu padre le encantaba el boxeo, y de vez en cuando llevaría allí a tu Mamá, a veces también con uno o más de tus tíos o amigos. Una vez, tu madre recontó un pleito de boxeo al regresar. "Uno de los boxeadores parecía tener un catarro o algo, no sé qué, pero le'mpezaron a salir mocos. El público se empezó a poner fastidioso, enfadado y pendejo, y empezaron a gritar un montón de cosas. Pues, como que el boxeador quería sorberse los mocos pa'trás, mientras se movía pa'quí, pa''llá, pero pues no podía con la moquera. Finalmente, alguien por ai le gritó, 'Dale un cato, pendejo mocos de yo-yo!' o algo así." Mamá nos hizo reír con esto, y aunque "el box" no era de su gusto, y estamos seguros que sólo lo hacía para andar con mi'apá. Y todavía, entre Mamá y nuestros hermanas y hermanos, nos da por decir, "Entrale, dale golpe, mocos de yo-yo!," o "Límpiate la nariz, mocos de yo-yo!," algo así, o simplemente "Eeiit, tú yo-yo mocoso!" etc.

Uno de los estudiantes que más tarde entrevistas para un libro sobre estudiantes campesinos que llegan a estudiar en la Universidad, Jesús, te dice que "Cesar Chavez" (lo llamaban por su nombre pronunciado en inglés, no 'César Chávez' en español) también había sido aficionado del boxeo. Es un detalle interesante, le dices a Jesús, que a un pacifista practicante, creyente en las filosofías de Martin Luther King y Mahatma Gandhi, le gustaría un deporte tan sangriento como el boxeo. Pero en fin y al cabo, te recuerdas que a muchos mexicanos o chicanos les encantaba o encanta el boxeo, y por cierto en tu propia familia, había muchos aficionados. "Así que Papá y César Chávez tenían en común, algo además del trabajo en los campos y los 'bail bonds,'" te dices.

Tu amiga, Ana G., trabajó veinticinco años con una compañía eléctrica y fue entre las primeras de tus entrevistadas. Te dice que por muchos años, fueron campesinos. "Ibamos pa'llá, pa' Fresno, pa' California, pa' piscar raspberries. . ." Tú le preguntas, no sabiendo dónde se encontraban raspberries en California, que cómo sabía ella, y dice "Se nos manchaban las manos, por eso mi acueldo. Yo era la más chiquita, pero mi acueldo. Qué? Oh, sí, mi'apá era minero jantes, pero se jue pa'Coolidge, y jue ai qui nos quedanos, trabajando muncho tiempo, jen el algodón. Qui'acía yo? Pos, estaba mu'chiquita, me gustaba. Me dejaban que juera en frente de mi'apá, jaciendo bolitas del algodón que se'abía caido al suelo, en los rows. Cómo? Así, mira, así. . . agarraba los pedacitos, y los jacía en bolitas más grandes, y se los daba a mi'apá pa' su bolsa. Ellos, los grandes, pescaban de las plantas. A mí me'ijeron qui'iciera las bolitas, de lo del suelo. Por muchos años, allí en Coolidge, mi'apá trabajó con mis tíos, jaciendo cosas en el rancho. Manejó tratores, si mi'ace. Jue en Coolidge, que aprendí a manejar yo sola, cuando si'mborrachaba mi'apá. That was fun! Mi'apá, tú sabes, quiél jera tomador. Si'mborrachaba cada rato, y yo estaba sola una vez, tenía como once jaños. No jé cómo no'staban mi'amá ni naide, pol ai jan di'ber visitando a las comaldes, piro yo'staba solita con mi'apá y jel'staba borracho y dormido. Entré mu'suave y l'saqué las llaves del pantalón, polque jel siempre jandaba en camiseta y calzones en casa, no sé polqué. Y jai'staba el carro, y me subí. Pos me jui así, a jalones y saltos y paradas, tratando di'acer como'vía vido a mis'apás jacel, con el gear shift, pa'rriba era adelante, pa'l lado jera más recio. Esa primera vez, no le supe jacer el revés, y pensé "Cómo le voy'jacer. . .?" y entonces, nada má di güeltas y jui por cuadras la primera vez, y entonces me golví a la casa. Naide supo, ni sabían despés polqué yo me asomaba, brazos sobre los asientos di mis'apás, pa'ver cómo le jacían pa'manejar. Y así les vi jacer el revés. Me aprendí así, jaciendo nota en la cabeza, de cómo le movían el gearshift y jacían los cambios del carro."

"Jue asina, que yo jui por la, cómo le llamaban, la partadora? Ajá, la midwife era americana. Pues mi'ermana que vivía con nojotros, no'staba casada, y empezó a. . . sí, tener el baby. Y mi'apá, no sé, no mi acueldo si 'staba borracho, o polqué no'staba naide más qui yo, mi'amá y mi hermano. Y cuando mi'amá dijo 'No la puedo dejar sola. Quién va por el doctor?' Y yo brinqué, mu' excited, polque yo sabía manejal. 'Yo sé, yo sé, yo voy pol la partadora!' Y jui yo, di mis jonce jaños. . . Qué? Oh, yo sabía 'onde si'ncontraba la partadora. Pos Coolidge jera mu chiquito entonces. Pos, yeah, la partadora. . . oh, se dice partera. Oh, whatever! What's funny, jue que llegaron jotros de mis hermanos o primos o something, y nos pusieron a vel la TV, y no contestaban nuestras preguntas, de que qué li pasaba a Berta, mi'ermana, polque era una casita de unas tres recámaras, pero chiquita. Well, we were poor, I guess, but we didn't think about it. Pues, ahora que mi acueldo, no sé cómo no querían que nos diéranos cuenta de lo que pasaba, polque jabía ruidos, no, no munchos gritos, pero sounds, you know, so, nos dinos cuenta anyhow, polque después oínos al baby, y salieron con un paquete de newspapers y nos dijo 'amá, No miren esto, no miren pa'cá. Pero éranos chamacos, y juinos al rato, desatendidos, aver ónde'vía enterrado el package. Pos lo desenterramos, pero vinos que jabía cosas sangrientas adentro, y no quisinos vel más. Lo tapamos con tierra oltra vez. Pero qué funny jeran, veldá? Creiban qui no íbanos a dalnos cuenta, y jai 'stábanos, al otro lado de una coltina, haciendo que veíanos la TV! Después, nos vinimos a Guadalupe, pa'cá, y desde'ntonces, la familia 'stá aquí."

A la Ana, la maltrató el único esposo que tuvo, durante unos diez, once años. Lo divorció, y después de todos los contratiempos, con el padre alcóholico que las hacía que le empinaran la botella pa' que tomara el hombre, ya enfermo, y ella siendo chiquita todavía, y los años con el marido mujeriego, tomador, y enojón, pues, pasó lo que a muchas les ha pasado por su historia personal. Y no por la genética, no señor, no creo en todos los casos, yo sé que no es lo que pasó con todas ellas. Me duelen, sé que en el fondo, ellas sufren. La Ana llegó a ser bisexual, o lesbiana, en fin. Y la quiero mucho, es como nuestra familia misma. *Y no le digas a nadie.* Oh, sí, en su propia familia, hubo quienes chismeaban y se llegó a saber por su mamá, y finalmente, la Ana tuvo que, pues, decirle así nomás a su mamá, "Has oído algo, má. . .? A ver, dime qu'as oído? Pos sí, soy juna de aquéllas. . . Es verdá. . . má, má, don't cry!" Ana me dijo que lloraron las dos buen rato, se abrazaron, y despuesito, aliviadas por el llanto, sentimiento, y la rutina de tener que llevar a la mamá a la tienda por su mandadito semanal, empezaron a platicar, chismear de gente que vieron en la calle del pueblito, y de regreso a la casita de la mamá, ésta le dice a Ana, en voz tentativa pero bajita y dulce: "No vas a comel'jalgo co'migo? Jice toltillas jayer, no quieles, Mijita. . .?" Y de esa manera, sin explicarse más, se acabó el mitote sobre lo que era o no era la hija menor, la más trabajadora, responsable y cumplida de sus hermanas/hermanos, entre los familiares de Ana, y su mamá.

Ana dijo, que lo de estudiar más allá de la "high school," su padre no quería que fueran, para nada. "What for? Nomás pa'salil goldas con un baby? Pa'qué necesitas el college? Váyanse a trabajal!"

Mari L., otra chicanita muy inteligente, y gordita como tú, estudia contigo el segundo año que se encuentra en la universidad, y te ha dicho otra cosa. Ella, algo callada en clase y como su hermanito también, te han dicho que su papá, todo lo contrario, quería que ellos se educaran, que se prepararan, que vinieran pa'cá. "Sí, trabajamos en el fil, es muy duro. Y mi'apá dijo que debíamos seguir adelante, ir a la escuela." Tú les preguntas, "Y tu mamá? Quería tu mamá que fueras a la Universidad? No querían que te quedaras con ellos, ayudar con el trabajo, sabes, como en muchas familias. . .?"

Varios estudiantes te han dicho, "Eso es lo que todavía hacemos, durante las vacaciones, al fil pa'cer los gastos de la escuela, pa' la renta. . . Pues ya sabe. . ."

"Y qué hay de nuevo?" le preguntas a otra chicana, una estudiante morenita, alta, de Parker, un pueblito agricultural también, al lado del

Colorado, "Qué tal las otras clases? Les puedes preguntar a tus papás sobre el español, lo que estudiamos. Por qué llegaste tú a la universidad? etc. etc." Estela D. contesta que "Qué va! Mi papá nunca me quiso ayudar para na'! Y tiene un negocio allá, tiene tierras y files y vende las cosechas. Mire, aquí está la tarjeta de su negocio, ve, A & Z Farms, ése semos nojotros, *somos* nojotros. Sí, y qué va! Ni un centavo extra le da a mi'amá, qué cree usté, no, él se lo clava, ya ni l'ace, así es con mi'amá. Y yo me peleo con él, sí. Mi'amá, yo no sé por qué no lo deja, de veras, no sé por qué no. . ."

El hermano de Estela, pues también lo tuve en clases, antes y despúes, y él habló de sus orígenes campesinos sin desprecio ni enojo. Los dos, hermana mayor y hermanito, animados en clase cuando querían, el hermano parlanchín y travieso, "Fíjese," te dijo Estela, "na'más fíjese, que el piso de la treila en que tiene a mi'amá, podriéndose, y mi'apá tan codo que no li da pa'rreglarlo, así la tiene, que traime la comida, que ontá mi camisa planchada tengo que salir, así. Qué va! Sabe Dios 'ónde tiene el dinero, Maestra, yo no sé! Pero pa'mí o pa' mi'amá, qué va!" Estela y su hermano, ambos activistas, ambos apoyan el sindicato de campesinos de César, el UFW. "Pero qué va, Maestra, fíjese usté!"

Algunos años antes, viene Emilia C., para hacer estudios graduados en cultura y literatura chicana, y la invitas a tu casa, la encuentras para una soda y papas fritas, y así llegan a hacerse amistades. Una muchacha alta, en sus treinta y pico años de edad y de un carácter brusco y sencillo, era de Nuevo México pero había vivido y trabajado con la Unión en California. "Fui organizer," me contó, "y conocí a César, y a otros de ellos que vivían allí en headquarters. Por qué no hablo muy bien de ellos? Pues, la verdá es que no me llevaba bien con la Pasionara, la Líder. Y empezaron, algunos de ellos, a jugar mind-games como pasatiempos, en algunas juntas allí en el cuartel, las headquarters. Y pos yo no me quedaba callada, y me pelié con algunos d' ellos. Bueno, yo sé muchas cosas, que no me parecían bien. Y me salí, sí, sí seguro, yo los conocí, first hand, a César, Pasionara, a los mero-meros. Pos, y por lo que le'ije, me golví a mi tierra, a Nuevo México. Aquí, como ya le he contado, me vine polque me'ijeron que ustedes estaban aquí, y me la recomendaron. La tesis, el trabajo que tengo que escribir, los exámenes, pol'eso, vine a'blar con usté. . ."

Después de los exámenes escritos, se pelea con su director, y viene a pedirte que le ayudes a completar el título, que ahora lo quiere cambiar a los corridos. Y así, después de jalones, puchones, y coscorones que pasó, la chamaca organizer completó el título. Me han contado que todavía es activista en la comunidad; así, brusca, peleonera y todo, dando berrinches y patadas, *kicking ass.*

Nikka L., bajita, morenita y de pelo corto rizado, te llama cuando está en su último año en Wellesley College, al este de EE.UU. Me cuenta que es originalmente de California, del valle San Joaquín como yo, y dice "I'm doing my senior thesis on your novel, and I'd like to interview you. . ." A través de esta primera plática contigo, te cuenta ella que "My family was also against the huelgas in the Valley. Yeah, I remember they called us 'scabs.' It was like a really bad word. . ." Eran esquiroles, *strike-breakers,* dijo, pero en sus clases en Wellesley leyó mucho, y ahora con tu novela, pues había cambiado su posición sobre el UFW, y ahora quería hablar contigo como escritora chicana, etc. si le hacías el favor, etc. "I teach in the same school the farmworkers' children went to in *The Grapes of Wrath,*" te cuenta tu nueva amiguita. Dice que esta escuelita, modernizada, está al merito lado del campo laboral, sí, el labor camp, donde habían vivido los de Grapes of Wrath. En los años aquellos lejanos de la Depresión americana, del Dust Bowl, los campesinos de este lugar que te cuenta Nikka, los campesinos no eran los chicanos o mexicanos, sino *Okies,* gente empobrecida que había emigrado también, pero desde Arkansas, Oklahoma, desde allá. "I like teaching there, but it's hard because my family needs my help, my salary. I just got them a little house, at least it's their own. But it's hard to get along with my dad, and my mom, she doesn't help me much either. . . Yeah, they're proud of my education, but I think the relatives are jealous, I don't know now what to do." "Like me gustaría estudiar para el título de maestría, pero, pues, a lo mejor. . . Maybe we can talk sometime?" Entonces añade, "Sometimes, those little kids, they really make me feel good, a veces, when they learn, and they look up to you, you know. . .?"

Le respondes, "Sí, *yo sé. . .*"

"*Si tiene alguna otra pregunta, maistra, pues ya sabe. . .*"

Tú, a los cincuenta y tantos, gordinflones, arrugados, cansados años, sabes que sí, tienes muchas preguntas todavía, y que *no* todo es posible, que *no* se puede hacer todo, o por lo menos, no en el momento exacto en que insistes. Pero a pesar de eso, ja ja ja ja, Yo he cometido errores algunos grandotones y yo bien sé que no todo se puede pero, por qué no hacerle la lucha? Hacerles la lucha? Por qué no insistir en que se haga el bien, y no el mal, hacia al prójimo, la prójima. . . Y no con drogas, alcohol, y violencia, como tantos de nosotros aprendimos en nuestro barrio, en la escuela, o en nuestra propia casa.

Pablito, el hermano menor de tu padre, está recuperando de cirugía por un cáncer. Aunque él mismo anda débil por la quimoterapia, empieza de nuevo sus visitas a tu papá, y recientemente te reporta: "*Mija, tu papá se ve muy mal, a lo mejor no dura mucho ya*". Tu padre, le dicen a la familia, no tiene el Alzheimers exactamente, pero sí algun tipo de demencia. Falta de memoria, señas de locura ocasionales momentos de lucidez, de repente una violencia. . . Débil cuerpo, miradas vacantes, y luego puede salir, "All the way from Southwest City, huh?" "*Papá, sabes quién soy?*" ". . . Seguro que sí!" "Sabes quién habla?" "Why sure!" Ahora, las más de las veces, silencio, y una de tus tías te dice, "Last week, your Dad didn't even talk, he just stared ahead. . ." Demencia, demente, ya ni habla. Empezó todo hace tanto tiempo ya. Una de tus hijas expresa tu propio temor titilante: "*Me pasará a mí?*" Hace años. . .

Aurora? Aurora ahora es una de las más vocales, activistas, *Chica-*

nas *mujeres fuertes* en la región del suroeste. Recordándole de lo que ella te había contado, y que lo habías escrito, me dijo recientemente que así había sido lo del experimento sicológico, excepto por un detalle, un detalle terrible: No había sido su amiga, Myra Greenfield, la muchacha judía y quien acababa de ver en París este verano pasado, quien la había traicionado con el resto de la clase aquella vez. . . Había sido la cubana, la amiga Hilda, hija de *una familia aristócrata cubana*. Recordando de nuevo, Aurora explota: "Fue mi mejor amiga, la única otra latina allí, quien me traicionó! La Myra, la Myra fue la única que no pudieron hacer cambiar su versión de lo que realmente había visto! Fue mi amiga fiel, la cubana Hilda! Juré, entonces, nunca dejar que nadie me convenciera of something *que yo bien sabía que sí o que no*. Ese evento singular me lo cambió todo. . . But give me a break! Un experimento sicológico, una falta cultural, *que se chinguen*. . . FUCK THEM!"

Recordando el incidente de la "homeless crazy lady" en el Puente La Llorona en Las Vegas, Aurora te dice, "A que no sabes lo que me preguntó la viejita loca en el Puente? Quería saber si yo era doctora, o algo así, porque éstos eran los únicos que la trataban y le escuchaban!" Riendo yo, le admito a Aurora, "Bueno, Doctora Bustamante, yo misma soy una crazy vieja loca que está rete agradecida que todavía estás allí, ayudándome entender la 'mera-neta' y animándome que 'Dales en el culo!'"

La hija lesbiana de tu amiga, Meche, te llama y te dice, que ha leído algo de tu manuscrito: "Creo que le diste al clavo al sacar afuera el asunto gay, Pat, pero. . . there's one important thing that's wrong. Yo me había enamorado primero de esa mujer, through my head. . . No fue por seducción de las drogas o el alcohol. Nos ilusionamos, I mean, if there was a seducción, it was por todo lo que nos contábamos y lo que ella sabía más que yo, y la quise así primero. What? Como la Malinchi? Yeah, I told mi'amá you needed to 'get it straight!' Ja, ja, yeah that's a switch, isn't it?" Tú ya vas atando hilos y recuerdas, que habías resistido contar lo prohibido y terrible. Cuántas memorias. . .

Y dejándonos a todos anonados, se nos fue Jesús mi estudiante, en un accidente trágico, camino a una fiesta patriótica. Te dice Vickie Dee, la mejor amiga de Jesús, "Echo de menos sus pláticas y humor. I know he wasn't perfect, he was just a man, but he was my inspiración and *he was my* 'sanctuary,' you know?"

Y ahora, ni dos años después, tu madre está perdiendo todas sus memorias de su juventud nuevomexicana y los recuentos de las travesuras de ustedes de niños. Se le va su ser, así como le sucedió a tu papá. "Mom! Sabes qué día es hoy? Sabes dónde estás? What month is it?" Ella responde, manos temblando, que no, "Eh? No, no sé, exactamente, no. . ." Nos acecha, nos espera.

Esto es lo que me diste, Papá, el deseo y voluntad de seguir con la escuela, la Universidad, hasta donde me permitieran mis propias faltas y debilidades. "No quiero que trabajen en los files! Te dije, Mujer, que no quiero que sean como nosotros, que vayan a la escuela!" Recuerdas todo esto de nuevo, en los días poco antes de la muerte de tu padre. Durante el funeral, los mariachis que has comisionado, tocan canciones solemnes. Tú y tu compañero Bob habían arreglado que tocaran durante la misa y también en el entierro. Lo único que pidieron, era que el mariachi tocara "Cielito lindo" and "Allá en el Rancho Grande," en recuerdo de las canciones que tu padre todavía sabía en esos últimos años cuando viajaban a California para sacar a Papá de donde estuviera "asilado," para una comidita y visita.

Todos trataban de visitarlo o sacarlo de paseo para sus cumpleaños, y una de las más recientes veces, antes del año final que lo tenían atado a la cama para controlar los últimos síntomas, estaban sentados en el carro con música de la radio. Empezaron a tocar música latina o salsa en la radio, y tu padre comenzó a imitar el ritmo, dando palmadas desde su asiento atrás. Estaba sentado entre tu hija María y tu hermana Belita, y se nos soltó la risa, porque en cuanto más recio la música, tu padre aceleraba su ritmo, imitando con las manos perfectamente: "Tatatá-tatá! Pas-paspás-pas!" y así por el estilo. "Let's see, Dad, cómo va 'El Rancho Grande'?" preguntó alguien. Papá le entró, armonizando y todo, a pesar de su enfermedad Alzheimers. Nos encantó, porque siempre había chiflado o cantado, excepto si estuviera leyendo, platicando, o dándole a la botella bien duro. Así fue que tú habías pedido su propia música, ese último día que fuiste a verlo en el funeral.

Después del servicio en el cementerio, te dan a ti, la mayor de los hijos de Papá, la bandera americana que a veces les dan a los veteranos difuntos. La bandera estaba doblada muy bonito en triángulo y la pusieron al lado de Papá en su cajón. El había estado en la marina durante la Segunda Guerra Mundial durante tus primeros años, te acuerdas. Tu hermano Samuelito toma la bandera del cajón, te la trae a ti con una sonrisa cariñosa, tomas la bandera, sobresaltada, no habiéndolo esperado, y apenas dices "Oh! Para mí? Oh. . . Papá!" Sollozas, acurrucando este último obsequio de tu padre, contra el pecho. El mariachi empieza un "Rancho Grande" jubiloso, seguido por el agridulce "Cielito lindo."

En la escuela primaria antigua de Betaville, aquella "Georgian mansion" en mis memorias, todavía se acostumbraba dar homenaje a la bandera. Recuerdo esa bandera allí puesta, cada día. . . No sabía en ese entonces, lo que era racismo, explotación, ni siquiera el patriotismo. Papá dijo que había peleado para defender la bandera, y que se había "naturalizado" como ciudadano durante su servicio militar, "That's when I became a citizen, sabes?" Y su propia familia, ellos de jóvenes, habían empezado a trabajar en los files o campos, así como todavía lo hacen los campesinos de hoy. Tu madre, también, allá andaba en los files, y recordaba "Nos poníamos pañuelos sobre la cabeza, camisas de manga larga, ay Dios qué quemadas nos dábanos, y la espalda, imagínate nomás cómo volvíanos pa' la noche!" Ella y Papá se conocieron cuando ella andaba limpiando casa de algún patron; como mi abuela antes lo hacía, ése era el trabajo que hacía mi'amá cuando conoció a mi padre allá en el Valle Imperial, hace tantos años ya. Esto fue antes de la época en que manejaban los negocitos de mi Nana Petra, y después como he dicho, empezaron a darle al negocio de la agricultura "desde otro ángulo," como contratistas de braceros y de familias campesinas.

Después del funeral, fuimos a Monterrey al wharf. Allí, en uno de los restaurantes favoritos de Papá, platicamos en tonos bajitos y empezamos poco a poco a reírnos, haciendo las paces con nuestras propias memorias, cada uno, de Don Samuel Leyva, el grande y complicado hombre de carne y hueso. "Ah qué Papá, cómo era!" Así estábamos de acuerdo, "He was something else!" Empezamos a compartir allí con cachitos de recuerdos, sus actos de bondad y cariño, a pesar de que él nunca fue para decirte que te quería excepto por los últimos años, mientras todavía hablaba o te murmuraba en respuesta. Notamos el cambio felizmente, porque hasta Esmeralda nos había dicho que a Papá le parecía simpleza andar por ai diciéndole a la gente "I love you." Recordamos también sus muchos ejemplos de generosidad. Hasta cuando tuvieron que empezar de nuevo y sin dinero, Papá y Esmeralda, al regresar de México tantos años atrás, siempre tenían el corazón para recoger a familia o amigos necesitados. "Te acuerdas? Se acuerdan?" "Se acuerdan de la vez que me dio el Ford Torino viejo después que me gradué del College, aquel año que Marisa y yo andábamos tan 'quebradas'?" Una vez, un chicanito trabajador en una gasolinera admiró mucho el Torino viejo, diciéndome "Hey, man, a stick shift Torino! Suave material pa' un 'low-rider', lady!" "Te acuerdas la vez que él y Esmeralda les trajeron mueblitos a mis hijos, porque sabían que no teníamos con qué ponerles una recámara?" "Se acuerdan cómo andaba por ai en el carro, con el perrito francés favorito alli, on his lap?" Era cierto que Papá quería mucho a sus perritos y adoraba a los niños, hablándoles, haciéndoles bromitas. En otra ocasion, después de uno de mis malpartos, él y Esmeralda vinieron al Hospital del Condado a verme. Mamá se quedó en el piso de recepción, "lejos de ellos y para no molestar" dijo ella. Papá dijo muy poco, ni una sola broma; yo en condición grave, y su silencio me decía que estaba preocupadísimo, viéndome febril, quieta y pálida. Me dejó unos centavos, que guardé bajo la almohada y los di a mi madre agradecida. Esta nos estaba alojando, a mí y mis dos criaturas, en esos días. Las dos de nosotras sabíamos lo que era estar encinta, sin marido y comiendo lo que nos daba el Welfare. Memorias y secretos. Buenos algunos, malos otros, pero de todos modos algunas memorias divertidas y todas nuestras.

Vinnie dijo recientemente, "Papá se habría caído de la risa, lo que pasó el año pasado en nuestro Santuario, la Iglesia, digo." Le pregunté de qué se trataba, aunque yo bien sabía que Papá reteconocía los servicios "aleluya" o "del Espíritu Santo" desde su propia juventud. Su familia había vivido al lado de tal Iglesia en Brole, antes que se cambiaran a Betaville. El hacía bromas sobre la gritería y la música que se oían durante los servicios de esa Iglesia vecindaria. Vinnie está contando, "Tom y yo habíamos ido a los championships y concursos de la academia para los perros de la policía, y nos habían gustado, allá en aquel pueblo donde vivimos. Well, a couple of weeks later we were in the middle of a huge revival service, y la Iglesia entera estaba 'rocking', 'Gloria a Dios! Gracias Nuestro Señor! Glory, Gloria, Shalala...! Y así, de veras dándole vuelo, en plena adoración. People just worshipping with the Holy Ghost in them, así con el Espíritu Santo, qué te digo, y de repente Tom y yo vimos this dirty-looking harrapiento, corrió right up the middle aisle, tiró unas bolsitas en frente del altar, right between two of the ministers up there worshipping. Las manos juntas como si rezara, the guy starts to stomp on the bags pisando así haciendo que saliera un polvito blanco, then two dogs, perros de la policía, vienen por el aisle y cogen al guy por las piernas. Entonces, unos policias, algunos en uniforme y otros no, vienen corriendo, luchan con el loco que todavía está estampando las bolsitas de polvo, los policías lo agarran y lo sacan por uno de los exits allá del altar! Yo le dije a Tom, 'Mira, es Sandy, la perra campeona del police academy, allá en frente, agarrándose al skuzzy guy!'" Ya nos tenía risa y risa la Vinnie, y ahogándonos preguntábamos, En la Iglesia, de veras? Y cosas así se nos salían entre risas. Entonces ella añade, "Do you believe it? La mayoría de la gente que estaba en ese servicio, ni cuenta se dio, por estar tan entregados en adoración, el Espíritu Santo en ellos y todo eso, saben? Después, algunos de los que sí habían espiado todo, nos reímos tanto, y Tom y yo más por haberme reconocido a Sandy, al police dog!" Nos pusimos de acuerdo: a Papá le hubiera encantado esta historia. Mamá, pues quedó reteofendida al saber del episodio. "Qué ya ni se respeta a Dios nuestro Señor? Jumf!"

En realidad, Mamá tenía su cuentito o dos sobre los sacerdotes católicos y por ahí. Este ha variado un poquito a través de los años que lo ha contado ella, pero de vez en cuando, lo saca. "Una vez, tu padre y yo sacamos al cura, el suato irlandés compañero de parrandas y director de la Iglesia en frente de nuestra casa en Newdale, para cenar comida mexicana en el restaurante de tu Tía Lita. El cura y tu Papá se pusieron bien borrachos como siempre, así que fui yo quien manejó el carro de regreso a casa, y puse un plato con una tostada enorme en el asiento, entre el cura y yo. Pues los dos bien cuetes, reían y bromeaban y trataban de echarse alguna canción camino a casa, el camino sólo unas dos cuadras de lejos. Cuando llegamos al 'rectory', la casa del cura al lado de la Iglesia, recoge él su sombrero, y a que no sabes qué? La tostada enterita se le cayó del sombrero santo, sobre la cabeza, y el cura quedó todo bañado de chile, frijoles, carne, lechuga. Y los dos compadres parranderos se rieron también, pero ni un tantito como yo, curas católicos apestosos! Y sólo pensar que al año siguiente, fui a ese mismo cura viejo borracho, para rogarle comprensión y consejo cuando empecé a pensar en dejar a tu Papá. Estaba yo ya harta de sus enamoradas! El cura ministro dijo: 'Your husband, Sam, said you'd found a new man, some blonde guy up in Masterton, izit so, me lady? Well, you're nothin' but a lying whore woman, that's what you are!" La llamó puta y todo, y así fue que pronto después, mi madre "recibió el Espíritu Santo" en la iglesia de unas nuevas amistades en un pueblo vecino, y desde entonces, ella "es salvada."

Pero era mi padre quien iba a mis concursos de deletreo y la mayor parte de mis otras funciones escolares. De hecho, fue él quien me llevó a inscribirme mi primerito día de escuela, declarándoles en una ficcioncita suya que yo era de edad, para no perder yo el primer grado del nuevo año escolar. Ningún "kinder" en aquella Betaville school vieja. Papá. Mamá. El me dio la voluntad de buscar metas más allá de los files. Yo anduve embarazada y viviendo yo y mis hijos de la asistencia pública a través de más de un par de años desesperanzados. Yo sabía que había hecho sufrir a mis padres, a los dos, pero he llegado a perdonarlos, como no viví "sin errores" yo misma.

Papá me pasó metas que inspiraban. Mamá toleraba mis ambiciones, en aquel entonces. Ahora, aunque ella apenas razona, nos respeta y la "escuela" que hemos logrado. Lo que ambos nos dieron fueron unas ganas de vivir llenamente, ese afán vital tenaz y el ser persistente que corría en ellos dos.

No la muerte... La pasión, secretos, el cariño, memorias, buenas intenciones, los desafíos, cambios, lo que pueda y lo que no, lo que haré y lo que no: *La vida es mi asunto.* Su/tu hija en tormento su/tu hija hermosa y ahora no lo puedo olvidar y los trozos de periódico y las notas y este testimonio esta autobiografía en ficción este RECORD plática plática plática, y temo perderlos a todos I FEAR, YO TEMO la muerte todavía aquí alrededor yet distant hasta ese mero momento YOU HAD WANTED TO habías querido que they lived life, *querían vivir* BELOVED all our/my beloved y empiezo los "*Cuentos prohibidos*/Las historias tabú," y te propones a entrevistar a estudiantes *campesino/campesina* sobre su familia, padre, madre, hermanos/hermanas, *amigos/amigas...* Sus seres amados... Y cómo y si o no habían cambiado su vida. Y recuerdas algo, algo del Movimiento, something that reminded you te estrujó queriendo un anhelo el creer en ello: *Por vida.* Te dices, escribiendo, "No me importa *lo que piensen* ustedes las chingonas/los chingones *mother/daughterfuckers* allá afuera... Para hoy sólo, sólo puedo con LA VIDA..."

Y hoy, este nuevo dia recuerdas a tu padre y otros seres queridos que se han ido para siempre excepto en el recuerdo, a los miles de tu pueblo de todos colores, que buscaron lo que tú, un lugar seguro, un santuario, una manera de seguir adelante y con ánimo y con amor y las palabras de tu padre aquel día remoto pero como si fuera ayer y te suelta también la carcajada la de tu padre y te levanta te renueva adelante el recuerdo *este nuevo día:*

"Mira este carajo pichón sin una pata, mira nomás cómo brinca y come y vuela más que los demás, ja, ja, qué vivito, qué suave. . . mira, ay va, qué alto va! ja, ja, ja!"

♥

About the Author

Margarita Cota-Cárdenas is the author of *Puppet* (1985, 2000), which also features the character Petra Leyva, and *Marchitas De mayo* (1989). She is Professor Emerita of Spanish at Arizona State University, where she had taught since 1981. She has had many poems and short stories published in anthologies and journals throughout her career.